# The Aphrodite Suicides

Rob Wyllie

# PROLOGUE

It wasn't hard to spot her, even amongst the dense sea of faces emerging from the office block. He'd studied her photo often enough, and not just for business either, because this bird was seriously drop-dead gorgeous. Saddled with a stupid chav name mind you, but he guessed they hadn't employed her for her brains. He watched as she strode across the concrete plaza, tall and confident and *knowing*, her sleek auburn hair flowing over her bare shoulders like a waterfall. Every now and again she gave a little flick of her head, a cascade of hair spinning around her as if in slow motion, just like these fit women in the shampoo adverts. *Knowing.* Christ, what he wouldn't give to have just one night in her bed. He could take her if he wanted, he knew he could, like he'd done in the past with a few of them, but today that wasn't on the cards. The brief from the boss was perfectly straightforward and there was a tidy little fifteen grand earner attached. Today was strictly business. Today was the day she was going to die.

He felt in his pocket for the reassuring caress of cold metal. He liked the Beretta, compact enough to be unobtrusive but deadly accurate at short range. But he wasn't going to be firing it today. The little pistol was simply his persuader if she decided to get awkward.

Now he got a little closer, slipping into the crowd about twenty metres behind her, following the snake of homeward-bound commuters up the stairs and into the entrance of the Tube station. Then through the barriers and onto the down escalator. *District Line, eastbound.* He caught up with her just as she stepped onto the platform, his firm grip on her upper arm causing her to spin round in annoyance. His face was now up close to hers, so that she could hear his whisper. *His people want to speak to you. I'm here to take you to them.*

On this occasion the operation had gone like a dream, her initial surprise quickly evaporating into surly resignation. She'd no idea why they wanted to talk to her, but she'd taken their money so didn't really have a choice in the matter. A ten-minute train ride to his office, a short meeting, and then home. In reality, it wasn't too much of a disruption to her schedule.

Except today she wasn't going on a train. Today she was going under one.

# Chapter 1

As far as Maggie Bainbridge could remember, she'd never met a billionaire before. Although as her colleague Jimmy Stewart pointed out, since the recent split with his missus, Hugo Morgan was now worth only nine hundred and seventy million, which technically downgraded him to mere multi-millionaire status.

Brasenose Investment Trust occupied the top four floors of a stunning glass-fronted office block on Canary Wharf, directly opposite and almost in touching distance of the similarly ostentatious building that housed Addison Redburn, the prestigious international law firm that was Asvina Rani's employer. It was barely nine months since she, the most sought-after and consequently most highly-paid family law solicitor in the capital, had handled Morgan's headline-grabbing divorce. So why were they meeting with him so soon afterwards? Whatever the reason, they wouldn't have to wait long to find out.

A minute or so later she joined them, looking flustered as she apologised for being late. But looking as elegant and beautiful as ever, a fact that wasn't lost on the elderly uniformed commissionaire who was guarding access to the high-speed elevators. He couldn't take his eyes off her.

'Sorry guys, I just couldn't get free of my last client,' she said. 'The poor woman had just found out her husband was leaving her and as you can imagine, she's pretty distraught. But here we are now. All set.'

She gave Jimmy an admiring glance. 'Looking sharp today Mr Stewart. Nice suit.'

He smiled back at her. 'Aye, I thought I'd better make an effort. I wouldn't want to let the firm down in front of such an important client.'

The commissionaire gestured towards the first of the three lifts, eyes still fixed on Asvina.

'This way please, ladies and gents. Floor twenty-three it is. Harriet will meet you up there, get you all sorted.' He kept his finger pressed on the button that held open the doors until they were safely inside. 'Have a good morning.'

Jimmy gave him a thumbs-up as the doors began to close.

'Nice lad. Ex-forces I would say by his bearing.'

Asvina nodded. 'Yes, that wouldn't surprise me. Hugo Morgan was in the army for ten years before he started in the City. He's a big supporter of military charities and suchlike. But I guess you knew all that.'

'So what's this all about anyway?' Maggie asked. 'You didn't give much away on the phone.'

And that much was true, but she had learnt from her friend something of the background of Hugo Morgan, and was quite certain she was not going to like him. How could she like a man who, as a sort of present to himself had decided to dump his wife of twenty-two years on the day he reached his fiftieth birthday?

'I'll let Hugo give you the full details,' Asvina said, 'but let's just say there's to be a new Mrs Morgan.'

Maggie laughed despite herself. 'It's *Hugo* now is it? I hope you're not thinking of trading in your Dav.' She knew there was as much chance of Asvina swapping her lovely husband as there was of the moon going round the sun. And in any case, she earned so much she didn't need a billionaire to look after her.

A discreet ping announced their arrival on the twenty-third floor, the lift opening to an opulent reception area. Behind a curved desk sat a perfectly-groomed young receptionist, the badge on her dress identifying her as Harriet Ibbotson.

'Good morning guys,' she said, smiling a well-trained smile. 'Do you have an appointment?'

She looked and sounded like central casting's posh girl, the voice confident and assured with just a suggestion of upper-class drawl. Maggie couldn't help but admire her expensive flower-print dress, which she had teamed with a matching pink cashmere cardigan. They wouldn't have left much change from a thousand pounds in the type of stores where Miss Ibbotson evidently shopped, and she certainly wasn't paying for it out of her receptionist's salary. Rich daddy she guessed, with a hint of bitterness. It was ever thus, and it was probably mummy or daddy too who had got her this job. But maybe she was being unfair, letting her own working-class prejudices colour her opinion, because Harriet seemed perfectly nice, and efficient too.

'We're here to see Mr Morgan,' Jimmy said, smiling at her. Maggie couldn't help but notice it, the frankly *stupid* reaction whenever he smiled at a woman of any age. They went bloody gaga and she found it *very* annoying.

'He's expecting you,' Harriet said, her gaze fixed on him. 'Please, come this way.' She led them through a set of frosted double doors into a large conference room, dominated by a giant oak boardroom table. Along two walls, floor-to-ceiling glazing afforded breathtaking views across the city.

Hugo Morgan rose to greet them, wearing an amiable expression. 'Welcome to Brasenose Investment Trust. Named it after the old alma mater, I'm sure you guessed that.' He was tall and powerfully-built, with a mop of tousled greying hair, dressed casually in fawn chinos, navy jacket and open-necked white shirt. His face was smooth and tanned, with the vaguely artificial aura that was often the accompaniment to a devotion to Botox. His teeth too, perfectly aligned though they were, had that slightly unnatural dazzle that only top-end dental engineering could deliver. But with or without the work of his cosmetic surgeons, Morgan had a presence about him that Maggie recognised as more than just the effect of his wealth. He would have had this before he got rich, she was sure of that. It was a cliché, but he looked like the sort of man who knew what he wanted and how to get it.

'Take a seat guys, please. How's the family Asvina, all well I take it?'

'Yes, all fine,' she replied. 'And yours?'

He gave a rueful smile. 'Well you know what kids are like. But yes, they're doing great I think, all in all, given the circumstances. You did well for me there, I'm so grateful.'

'I don't know about that,' Asvina said. 'It was the court who gave them the choice and they chose you.'

'And these are your colleagues of course. Maggie Bainbridge, once the most hated woman in Britain, and Captain James Stewart, the Hampstead Hero himself.' He smiled. 'Done my research you see. As you'd expect.'

Maggie gave a wry nod. God, was that damn epithet going to be with her forever?

'Yes, that was me I'm afraid.' And two years on, it still hurt like crazy that it was she who had let Dena Alzahrani walk free. There wouldn't have been any need for a Hampstead Hero if the teenage terrorist had been convicted and locked away for life, like she should have been. And her beautiful niece Daisy would still be alive. It had been her fault, and that was something she was going to have to live with for ever.

'You were badly done by,' he said, 'but I guess justice was done in the end. But what a sensational outcome. Who would have thought it?'

'You served too, didn't you?' Jimmy said. 'Guards wasn't it? In Kosovo. I think we're in the same club.'

Morgan laughed. 'The old George Cross do you mean? Well, you and I both know it's simple self-preservation that drives us so-called heroes. At least it was in my case. I just wanted to get out of the damn Balkans as fast as I could and back to civilisation.'

Jimmy nodded. 'Felt the same about Afghanistan. Nice people, but you never knew who were your friends and who were your enemies. In fact sometimes they were one and the same. Totally mental country when I was there. Still is I think.'

'Yes, but we tried our best, didn't we? Couldn't have done anything more than our duty.'

Harriet had arrived with a tray of hot drinks, which she carefully set down on the table. 'Tea or coffee?' The question was directed at everyone, but Maggie noted that her eyes were fixed on Jimmy. Typical, that was.

'Just leave the tray Harriet,' Morgan said. 'I'll sort it. Tea or coffee Maggie?'

'Coffee please Mr Morgan.'

He smiled. 'Hugo, please.' So that was it then. The first time in her life she had been on first-name terms with a nearly billionaire. Correction, a cold and heartless wife-dumping nearly billionaire. It was important that she wasn't so seduced by his charm that she forgot what sort of man he really was.

'So, I guess you're interested to know why I've called you guys in?' he said. That had to be the understatement of the year. 'Asvina, maybe you can update your team?'

She nodded. 'Certainly. Getting straight to the point, Hugo has decided to remarry and has engaged Addisons to oversee the formal side of the arrangement. I'll be looking after the matter personally of course.'

Maggie smiled to herself. A new Mrs Morgan, no doubt younger and slimmer and sexier than the discarded model. Naturally there would have to be a pre-nuptial agreement given that he would be taking nearly a billion pounds' worth of assets into the marriage. But she was making the assumption that his intended, whoever she was, was no match for him financially, and she realised that need not be correct. And so the question, though a terrible old chestnut, had to be asked.

'That's wonderful Hugo. Who's the lucky lady, may I ask?'

'Her name is Lotti and it's me who is the lucky one I can assure you.'

'Miss Brückner is Swiss and works in a gallery in Knightsbridge,' Asvina said in way of explanation. 'That's how you met her Hugo, isn't it?'

He gave a fond smile. 'That's right. I was looking for some interesting modern art and I found an interesting modern girl instead. Lotti's quite an expert in the subject as it happens. She tells me she studied in Heidelberg and Amsterdam before coming to London.'

*She tells me.* Now Maggie began to understand why she and Jimmy were here. Asvina too had picked up on the nuance.

'This is all my doing Maggie, I take full blame. But marriage is a difficult arena for high net-worth individuals, isn't it? We all want to think it's all about love, passion and romance but you can't ignore the practical side, especially when a relationship hasn't been going very long. So my advice to Hugo, much against his instincts I should say, was that he should perform some due diligence on his intended. Obviously, a very delicate subject. But that's where you two come in.'

Maggie gave her a knowing look. So that was it. They were to dig into the background of the to-be Mrs Hugo Morgan. Looking for secrets and lies and perhaps more besides. Her friend was keen to claim it as her idea, but she doubted very much if *he* was going into the marriage with his eyes closed. No, this was without doubt a Hugo Morgan initiative.

'It goes without saying,' he said, 'that Lotti mustn't discover that she is being...' He tailed off, unable to say the word out loud. *Investigated.* Because that's what was going on here. An investigation, the act itself creating a dark secret that would hang over the marriage, suspended by a thread like that fabled sword she couldn't quite remember the name of. Because if it ever came out, ten or even twenty years down the line, then the relationship was surely finished. *'Didn't you trust me Hugo?'* she would ask, a question to which there could only be one answer.

'Of course,' Maggie said. 'That's understood. Obviously I have a few questions if you don't mind?'

He shrugged. 'Yeah sure. I'll do my best to answer them.'

'And Jimmy, chip in if you think of anything too.'

'Aye, will do.'

Maggie removed a slim notebook and pen from her bag and smiled. 'I know I should use a tablet or something but I'm afraid I like the old-fashioned methods. So, I noticed that Asvina referred to Miss Brückner as your intended. Does that mean you haven't popped the question yet, if you don't mind me putting it that way?'

'No, I haven't asked her yet,' Morgan said, 'but we have talked about it of course and I think we have an understanding. But, well, I suppose it depends on...on this exercise. And when I propose, I want to do it properly, naturally. I'm not sure, but we'll probably take the jet over to Porto Banus and then do it on my yacht.' *As you do*, Maggie thought, but she didn't say it.

'That sounds nice. And what about your children? Have you discussed your plans with them?'

He grimaced. 'Well they've met Lotti of course, and I think they like her. One of them at least. I'm not sure about Rosie. She's at a difficult age.'

'She's eighteen,' Asvina explained, 'and very sweet.'

Morgan smiled. 'Yes, she is.'

'And Lotti,' Jimmy said, furrowing his brow, 'that is, if you don't mind me asking. How old is she?'

Maggie could see Morgan tensing up. It was the question she had been dying to ask him herself, so she was grateful for Jimmy's intervention. The old good-cop bad-cop routine. It seldom failed.

'She's thirty.'

'So just twelve years older than Rosie,' Jimmy said. Christ, thought Maggie, if you're trying to get us blown off the job before we've even started, you're going the right way about it. But thirty? She had expected her to be younger, but not *that* young.

Morgan gave him a sharp look. 'I can do the maths Jimmy.'

'No no, I didn't mean to be insensitive,' Jimmy said, 'but we just need as much background as possible, I'm sure you understand that.' The tone was sympathetic and it seemed to have the desired effect, because a grin began to spread across Morgan's face.

'Yes, I know what everyone will be saying, she's much too young for me, but hell Jimmy, she's so incredibly beautiful, and we've only got one life, haven't we? And believe me if you saw her, you'd feel the same way.'

Fearing how Jimmy might respond, Maggie decided it might be smart to steer the conversation on to less contentious matters.

'So Hugo, I guess we just need to get a few basic facts from you so that we can plan our investigation.' She saw him wince at the word, but really, how else could it be described?

'As much as you know about her, parents, siblings things like that. And of course the name of the gallery where she works. Perhaps it'd be easier if I had a think about it and emailed you a list of questions.' Did it sound as if she was making it up as she was going along? Because that's what she was doing. This was the first time Bainbridge Associates had done this kind of work so she didn't exactly have a proven template to fall back on. But he seemed perfectly relaxed about her suggestion.

'Yeah sure, sounds good. Feel free to ask anything you like.'

'I'd be really interested to know more about your firm Hugo,' Jimmy said. 'I don't know anything about financial services, but it's incredible how well you've done in just, what is it, about eight years?'

'It's nice of you to say so,' Morgan said, with obvious pride. 'It's not rocket science. Brasenose just takes a different approach from its competitors, that's all. It's a simple business model, we scare the shit out of lazy and incompetent management by analysing the hell out of their businesses and exposing their failures. Force them to either perform or get out of the way. That's why they hate us so much.'

Jimmy laughed. 'Sounds simple when you say it like that, but I bet it isn't really.'

'Well it *is*, actually,' Morgan said, 'but listen, why don't you two come and see for yourselves? We're doing one of our quarterly investor updates tomorrow over at the London Hilton on Park Lane. I've heard there's going to be fireworks, it should be fun. Have a word with Harriet on the way out and she'll get you on the attendee list.'

'Nice girl,' Maggie said.

Morgan nodded. 'Yeah, she is. She's an intern, but we'll maybe give her a job at the end of it. But yeah, talk to her and hopefully I'll see you both tomorrow.'

Suddenly a thought came to her. 'I assume Lotti won't be there? Because obviously, we need to stay undercover for the time being.'

He shook his head. 'No no, she'll be at the gallery, I'm pretty sure of that,' he said, getting to his feet. 'Anyway, unless there's anything else?'

So that was it then. Their first-ever due diligence commission, and a whole different ball game from the dry financial investigations they were used to. The truth was, Maggie didn't have the first clue where to start, but somewhere in the back of her mind, a germ of an idea was forming. A crazy idea, it had to be said. Lotti Brückner, thirty years old and in the opinion of the multi-millionaire Hugo Morgan, incredibly beautiful. Jimmy Stewart, thirty-two years old and in the opinion of every woman who had ever set eyes on him, ridiculously attractive. What was it they called it again? A honey-trap, that's what it was. A perfect test of the faithfulness or otherwise of Miss Brückner.

She'd need to double-check, but she was pretty sure there was nothing preventing it in his terms and conditions of employment.

# Chapter 2

They hadn't done a bad job, he had to admit it. Atlee House was still a dump and had been since the day it opened way back in nineteen sixty-three, but at least now it was a nicely-painted dump. The foyer, the first area of the building to be completed, looked and smelt fresh and clean as he dawdled his way towards the staircase. The colour was Silver Sand according to the decorator, as if Detective Inspector Frank Stewart gave a monkey's about that. He would have described it as grey, but it was quite a nice shade of grey and certainly a vast improvement on the previous nicotine-stained brown. And there was even better news to come, because later in the week the knackered old eighties vending machine was finally getting the boot, to be replaced at last by an appliance more suited to the twenty-first century. Although his mate Eleanor Campbell had told him he would need to download an app to use the bloody thing, which filled him with some trepidation. What was so difficult about stuffing a pound coin in a slot? Still, he was sure he would figure it out eventually, and as far as he knew, there would still be Mars Bars. Important, that.

He made his way up the staircase to the first floor and headed to the little meeting room in the corner of the large open-plan office. Since his appointment as acting head of the department, he had briefly considered making it his personal office, but no, that wasn't his style. He had always hated the way the brass shut themselves away in their little private enclaves and he had no desire to become like them, not after nearly twenty years of honourable insubordination. But today he needed a bit of peace and quiet to work on what he hoped would turn into his next case.

The first thing he had to do was come up with a name for it. For some reason, *Operation Dolphin* was spinning round his head and he quite liked the sound of that. There was a certain synergy with his last case, it having been called Operation Shark, and that one had turned out to be a pretty successful investigation. So maybe that was a good omen. Dolphin it would be then, unless he thought of anything better in the meantime.

It had been DC Ronnie French, one of his deadbeat colleagues in deadbeat Department 12B, who had first brought the case to his attention, although it could hardly have been described as a case at that stage. French was quite new to the department and had come with a reputation. Of course everyone in 12B had a back-story, but French's was less complicated than most. He was simply useless.

It was a few days earlier, and Frank had arranged to meet him in the same room where he now sat. The DC had been waiting for him when he got there. Fat and scruffy, French was approaching his fiftieth year and spent all of his waking hours dreaming of his impending early retirement after a long and undistinguished career in the ranks. He had greeted Frank with a perfunctory 'Morning guv,' his face carrying the same sullen expression it had carried for the past thirty years. Frank had known it wasn't personal. He was like that with everybody.

'Morning Frenchie,' he had said, casting him a mildly disapproving glance. It had often occurred to him that he might well end up looking like the DC in a few years' time if he didn't do something about it, although he recognised that dispassionate observers might already mistake them for twins.

'So what have you got for me? Something interesting, that's what you said on the phone.' It would have needed to have been something bloody earth-shattering to get the perma-bored French off his fat arse. That was why Frank had gambled it would be worth a meeting, and he wasn't to be disappointed.

'Yeah guv, quite interesting I think. A suicide that might not be a suicide. A mate of mine down the club brought it to my attention.'

And that was where it had all started. *A suicide that might not be a suicide*. Better known as a murder.

The victim was one Chardonnay Clarke, a pretty young woman of just twenty-three years of age. Correction, not just pretty, but absolutely stunning. She was the niece of a friend of Ronnie French's mate, all members of the Romford snooker club where seemingly he spent most of his leisure time. And whilst her name might have suggested otherwise, she was no stereotypical Essex girl. According to the brief background notes that DC French had thrown together for him, this was a very bright lady, with a string of A levels and a first-class Honours in Philosophy, Politics and Economics from Oxford University. Frank didn't know too much about academia, but he had read somewhere that an Oxford PPE degree was about the most sought-after and prestigious qualification you could get. Not bad for a plumber's daughter from Romford, that was for sure.

After Uni, she had gone to work for one of these international banks down at St Katherine's Dock, although as Ronnie had put it, it wasn't a *real* job, but one of these fake intern things where your rich daddy paid for your place. Except, and this was something that had particularly caught Frank's attention, Chardonnay Clarke didn't have a rich daddy.

It had occurred at around six-thirty in the evening, Tower Hill tube station still packed with returning commuters anxious to get home after a long day in the office. The eye-witness accounts were both hazy and contradictory, which didn't surprise Frank in the slightest. One was adamant that her movement had been chillingly precise and deliberate, that she had waited until the train emerged into the station before stepping off the platform to her death. Another said she had wavered uncertainly before toppling over, as if she was drunk or drugged.

In her handbag they had found her smartphone, still open on her Facebook timeline, where apparently she had been about to tell the world that life had become too painful to bear and so she had decided to end it all. *I'm sorry, I just can't go on,* that's all it said. But for some reason, she never got to press 'Post'.

The police were called of course, but there was no reason to suspect foul play. Interestingly though, or at least interesting to Frank, the post-mortem did find traces of cocaine and heroin in her blood stream. A speedball, that's what they called it on the street, a powerful cocktail of two class A drugs that was as likely to give you a heart attack as give you a thrill. But the Coroner had been unwilling to speculate whether that had contributed to her death, either in the physical or psychological sense.

According to her father, her new job had rather gone to her head and she had started moving in what he called a 'fast set.' *Over-paid bankers, wankers more like, with Ferraris and fancy penthouse pads.* That's how Terry Clarke had described them, but he had been adamant that his daughter was a good girl and certainly wasn't into drugs or anything of that nature. Frank gave a silent laugh at that. The parents were always the last to know.

And that was it, as far as the authorities were concerned. A tragedy for the family, undoubtedly, that's what the Coroner had said at the inquest, but nothing to suggest anything else, especially after the discovery of Chardonnay's virtual suicide note. So the case was closed even before it was opened.

*A suicide that might not be a suicide.* But what was the evidence for that, other than the father's insistence that his girl had everything to live for and so why would she do herself in? Frank hadn't known

Chardonnay, but he had researched the stats, and if her death had been self-inflicted, then it was definitely an outlier. It turned out there was about six thousand suicides in a typical year in the UK and of them, more than three quarters were male. It was a bit of a sweeping statement, but generally speaking women didn't top themselves. That was especially true for young women under the age of twenty-five.

But it wasn't just the statistics that had driven Frank to dive deeper and deeper, getting him to where he was now. Firstly, he bloody hated drugs and what they did to people's lives. For him, it was personal, and as long as he could draw breath he would pursue the scumbags who made their livings from that pernicious trade.

Secondly, it was that photograph of her that French had sent him. Because Chardonnay hadn't just been pretty. She was an off-the-scale beauty, super-model stunning, and in his book, girls like that just wouldn't kill themselves. No way.

And the third thing, and this was the one which really sent him off on what he knew might well turn out to be a wild goose chase, was that he remembered an item that had caught his eye nearly nine months ago in the *Evening Standard*. About a good-looking young lad who had thrown himself in front of a tube train. He could remember at the time looking at the striking photographs of the boy and thinking exactly the same thing as he was now thinking about Chardonnay Clarke. Lads like that didn't just go out and kill themselves.

Which is why he had found himself on a government website, scanning the London suicide data for the past year, because that would tell him if his opinion, rooted in common sense, was backed up by the statistics. It was a surprise to him when he found out that the capital had the lowest rate of any region in the country, at around four per hundred thousand of population. It was less of a surprise that the highest region was Scotland, where the rate was exactly four times higher at sixteen suicides per hundred thousand. Having grown up there, he could understand why. It could be grim up in Pict country.

Searching deeper, he had found the evidence in a particular government chart that supported his hunch. In the last year, just forty-nine people under the age of twenty-five had taken their own lives in London. True, every one told a heartbreaking story, but statistically, it was insignificant. As he had suspected, Chardonnay Clarke was an outlier.

A quick call to the Coroner's office had confirmed what he had hoped. Yes, they did keep data records on each case, confidential data he as a serving police officer could request access to. Containing everything he might need except their identities of course, because this data was, what was it they called it? *Anonymised*, that was it. But that didn't matter at this stage.

He couldn't really explain what he expected to find out from the data. There was just something in the fact that most under twenty-fives didn't do this, so maybe he would discover something that stood out by looking at the few who did. He recalled that there had been a spate of recent incidents where seemingly level-headed youngsters had been encouraged to take their own lives through muddle-headed social media campaigns. Was Chardonnay's case one of them, he wondered, and were there any others like it? Maybe that other guy from a few months ago was one. He'd need to do a bit of digging to find out his name, but that shouldn't be too difficult. That was what he was looking for, patterns and connections. It might lead nowhere, but it was as good a place as any to start.

The only problem was, the data would doubtless come on a spreadsheet, and Frank didn't do spreadsheets. But that didn't matter, because his wee pal Eleanor Campbell did. If there was anything to be found, she would help him find it. And just two days after he had made the request, the spreadsheet had landed in his inbox.

This morning he found the young forensic officer at her adopted desk on the ground floor, and, as was often the case, on her phone. Eleanor's official location was at the main labs over at Maida Vale, but she preferred to be tucked away out of sight and out of mind in Atlee House, a preference that Frank liked to use to his maximum advantage. From her tone, he guessed that she was speaking to her sort-of boyfriend Lloyd, but you didn't need to be a Detective Inspector like him to figure that one out. Because Eleanor was always talking to sort-of Lloyd. A situation that he intended to take full advantage of.

He signalled her to hang up. She responded with her trademark scowl and kept talking.

'Yeah, Lloyd, look, I don't want to talk about this now...No way... look, I've told you a gazillion times before, that's never going to happen...no, I'm not doing that, like never... I've got to go...no, not tonight, not ever I said... Lloyd, no forget it...'

'Problems?' Frank knew he was on safe ground with this, because there always seemed to be problems between Eleanor and her on-off boyfriend.

'He's an idiot.'

'Seems that way,' Frank said, giving a sympathetic half-smile, 'but you know, you really shouldn't be talking to him on police time.' They both knew what that meant. She was expected to trade compliance for him looking the other way.

She heaved a sigh. 'Ok Frank, what do you want?'

He smiled back at her. 'That's my girl. So I've got a wee spreadsheet from the Coroner that I'd like you to help me with. I remembered you told me once about some sort of data matching you could do with this Excel thingy?'

'Yeah, I remember,' she said, without enthusiasm. 'So how many records does it have? Millions I expect.'

'Records?' Frank said. 'If you mean how many lines, forty-nine.'

'Forty-nine?' she replied, with visible relief. 'That's like nothing. Send it to me and I'll take a look.'

'How long do you think it will take to find any patterns?' Frank asked. 'A couple of days I suppose?'

She gave him a scornful look. 'Yeah, more like two minutes, if there's only forty-nine rows. Are you still hiding away in that corner office upstairs?'

'*Working* away, you mean. Aye, I am.'

'Whatever. So, I'll come and see you when I find something.' He noted with some satisfaction that she said *when* not *if*. He wasn't surprised, because if there was one thing he knew about Eleanor Campbell, it was that she didn't lack self-belief.

True to her word, it was barely ten minutes later when she marched into the little meeting room, her laptop under her arm.

'That was quick,' Frank said. 'Find anything?' He knew she would have, otherwise she wouldn't be here.

'Yeah, like it was simples-ville. It took me longer to walk up the stairs than find it.'

'And?'

'And there's two records that might be connected in some way to your girl. Row eight and row twenty-four. Look, I'll show you.'

She placed the laptop on the desk facing Frank and opened the lid.

'They pull together a lot of other data from the credit-checking agencies databases and other places,' Eleanor said. 'Data augmentation they call it. I don't know why, they just do.'

Frank didn't know either, but he suspected it was so the public health authorities could look for patterns too, in their case ones that might help them target their preventative education programs. Things like background and occupation, to see if certain groups were particularly susceptible to giving up on life. He seemed to remember it used to be farmers and dentists who were the worst for some reason. Maybe they still were.

'So things like the cause of death, obviously, but lots of other things like their schools and unis, who they work for, their jobs. Lots of weird stuff like that.'

'And you said you found some matches?' Frank said. 'Yeah, that's right. Twelve on the first pass. That was on method. That's what they call how they done it.'

'So twelve poor sods decided to end it all by stepping in front of trains.'

'Yeah, and like it splits the data between underground and overground for some reason. Underground is the most popular.'

Frank shook his head. 'Bloody hell Eleanor, these are real people, with families, kids, everything. I'm not sure *popular* really describes it.'

'I didn't mean anything by it,' she said, her tone defensive. 'What I mean is more of them jumped in front of a tube train than overground. Eight out of twelve.'

Frank nodded silently to himself. Every now and again the radio travel bulletins would report travel disruption on the Underground because the police were dealing with an incident. It was never spelt out, but everyone knew what it meant.

'So then I was looking for a match on the maximum number of data elements,' Eleanor said. 'I wrote a macro.'

'Sorry?' Frank said.

'A macro. I got it to like search for matches automatically. Gender, occupation, town of birth, things like that.'

He didn't even pretend to understand what she was talking about.

'Aye, well I'll have to take your word for that. But come on, tell me more.'

'Yeah, so although the data is anonymised, it was easy to work out which one was Chardonnay. From her age, town of birth and like obviously the method. You see, here she is here. Row twenty-four.'

Frank nodded. 'So then you just got your wee macro thingy to go and find other lines that were a close match, is that how it works?' Too late, he saw what he had done. *Just*. It didn't take much to offend her, he knew that from bitter experience, and then she could get difficult. Difficult, as in down tools and walk off the job difficult.

'*Just*? Like you think this stuff is easy?' Not more than one minute ago, she herself had said that it was, but Frank knew he wasn't going to get anywhere by reminding her of that.

'No no, of course not,' he said, backtracking. 'A little slip of the tongue, that was all. Of course it's not easy. I couldn't do any of this, no way.'

That seemed to satisfy her. He had found that shameless grovelling often did.

'Yeah, I know you couldn't. So anyway, I ran the macro with the maximum matches setting and that's how it found the other record.'

'Row eight. The other person.'

'Exactly. So there was matches on like four columns. *Method, University, Occupation* and some weird one called *Parental Socio-economic Group.* I've no idea what that is.'

'Right, that's very interesting,' Frank said. 'So does this mean that the other lad killed himself in the same way as Chardonnay? I guess it must do.'

'Correct,' Eleanor said. 'Fatal trauma inflicted by a railway vehicle.'

'And the Uni?'

'Yeah, same. Oxford.'

'And occupation?' Frank said. It was more a statement than a question. 'Do we know who they worked for?'

Eleanor shook her head. 'It says they were interns. I don't know what that is. And no, it doesn't give any info on who they worked for.'

'And then that last one. Socio- whatever. What does that say?'

'I've like no idea what this means either,' she answered, frowning. 'It just says *C2.*'

But Frank knew what it meant. Socio-economic classification C2, *Skilled Manual Workers.* Plumbers and brick-layers and electricians, the solid back-bone of the country. Men and women who were good with their hands. Like Chardonnay's dad Terry. And not exactly the background you expected of students at Oxford, no matter how much they tried to deny their elitism.

He thanked Eleanor for her help, smiling as he escorted her to the door, then closed it behind her. This was very interesting, no doubt about it. Two young working-class kids who had smashed through the class barriers to win places at a prestigious university. Two kids with door-opening qualifications taking the first steps of what was almost certainly destined to be glittering careers. And two young people who had decided that life was no longer worth living. Now he recognised that old familiar feeling in his gut, the one that screamed *something isn't right*.

A suicide that wasn't a suicide. Except now it seemed there might be two of them. Now he'd need to make a proper effort to find out who that other lad in the paper was.

# Chapter 3

The foyer of the Park Lane Hilton was a hubbub of activity, as hundreds of investors milled around, chatting and sipping coffee, waiting for the Brasenose Investment Trust quarterly update to get going. Maggie noted that they'd had to book one of the bigger conference rooms with the capacity to seat a thousand delegates, such was the popularity of the event. Since yesterday's meeting with Hugo Morgan, she'd done some reading up on his firm, enough to discover it was the absolute darling of the small investor community. And why wouldn't it be, given that those who had been in from the start had seen the value of their shares increase ten-fold? Not a bad return in eight years and way above the FTSE gains for the period. It was no wonder that Morgan was revered as a superstar of the industry, and in just a few minutes she would get the opportunity to see him performing for his adoring fans.

Jimmy had been tasked with completing their registration formalities, which was no more difficult than giving their names to one of the girls at the reception desk and in return being issued with a smart lapel badge on which their name was printed. Jimmy being Jimmy, it was no surprise to her when she glanced over to see that he was in conversation with Harriet Ibbotson, he giving every indication of listening intently as she spoke, she gushing with ill-disguised adoration. Looking round, he caught Maggie's eye, raising an arm in greeting before strolling over.

'Nice girl that, like you thought,' he said, handing over her badge. 'Clever too. Got an Economics degree from Cambridge. Wants to make a career in financial services.'

Maggie laughed. 'Did you get her shoe size too?'

'Aye, and her phone number as well. No, only joking about that. But what was interesting, she was saying they don't actually work for their employers.'

She wasn't exactly sure what was interesting about that, but she asked him anyway.

'So?'

'So it's like an agency. She told me their name but I've forgotten already. The company just gives them their requirements and they supply the intern.'

'Fascinating,' she lied. 'But hey, look at the time. We'd better get in and grab a seat before they're all taken. Looks like a sell-out.'

They found seats towards the rear of the auditorium, at least twenty or so rows back from the front. It seemed as if proceedings were to be beamed onto the giant screen which filled the wall behind the speakers' platform, itself flanked on both sides by a towering public address system. It was like a rock concert, with Morgan cast in the role of rock god. She was just about to say as much to Jimmy when a blast of music reverberated around the room.

'Fanfare for the Common Man,' Jimmy shouted above the din. 'Our army band used to do this one all the time. Aaron Copland. Great tune.'

And entirely appropriate, Maggie thought. Investment for the common man could easily have been a Brasenose slogan. In fact, she would mention it to Hugo the next time they spoke.

Suddenly the main lights went out, the music faded and a powerful spotlight strafed the stage. In response, the audience started to clap, beating out a rhythmic swell of anticipation which she guessed was a regular feature of these events. Rock concert? It was more like some weird political rally from the nineteen thirties, or some odd evangelical cult. And then a strident thespian voice boomed out from the PA.

'Ladies and gentlemen, please welcome to the stage Mr --- Hugo--- Morgan!'

As one, the audience rose to its feet, clapping and cheering wildly. Morgan raised a hand in welcome as the spotlight picked him out, staring out into the auditorium and smiling, standing quite still as he waited for the noise to subside. She thought he might bellow 'Hello London' as musical entertainers were given to do, but no, he simply mouthed a thank you and sat down behind the table, flanked by a man and a woman who Maggie assumed were executives of the firm.

'Bloody impressive eh?' Jimmy said. 'Although I was expecting fireworks, didn't he say there would be some?'

She laughed. 'I guess they'll come later. I did wonder what he meant by that.'

The room had now quietened. Morgan rose, cleared his throat and began to speak.

'Well, thank you for that and welcome to our quarter two update. It won't be any surprise to any of you that we've had a great quarter. Because we always have a great quarter, don't we...?' This drew a collective laugh from the audience and a ripple of applause. '...and yes, as Caroline here will no doubt remind me, I have a legal duty to say that the value of your investments can go up as well as down...' He took a sip of water, '...although of course ours never go down', this time stimulating a raucous cheer. Alongside him, the woman, who Maggie took to be the firm's financial director, raised her eyebrows in mock disapproval.

'So, in a few minutes, Caroline will take you through all the numbing detail of the quarter's numbers. I know all you anoraks out there love a nice PowerPoint chart, and she's got hundreds, believe me.' This time an exaggerated groan from the audience. 'But before that I'll just give you the edited highlights. First slide Harriet please.'

He swivelled to face the screen. 'So as you see, we've had another cracking quarter. The share price is up eleven percent to thirty-two pounds sixty, and the value of the fund has now exceeded three billion pounds for the first time.' He turned back towards the audience as a wave of applause swept through the room.

'Thank you, thank you. So as a result I'm delighted to announce a rise in dividend to sixteen pence per share, up from thirteen pence in quarter one.' He took another sip from glass. 'Good news, I'm sure you'll all agree. So let's look at what we've been getting up to on the investment front. Next slide please Harriet.'

He pointed at an aerial image of some sort of industrial site that now filled the screen. 'Some of you may recognise this as Greenway Mining's new cobalt mine in Cumbria. I say new, but they've been digging their bloody great hole for six years now and still not brought a gram of the stuff to the surface. Which is such a shame, because it's a hot product, in huge demand all over the world. But God, their management was crap. I say was, because as you know, we've taken steps to improve that, haven't we?' A collective nodding of heads across the audience with a few random shouts of yes!

But then, out of the blue, a man a couple of rows in front of them got to his feet and began to shout towards the stage. The few members of the audience who recognised who he was nudged their neighbours or exchanged knowing smiles. This was going to be interesting.

'What do you say to the army of small shareholders who have lost their life savings because of you? All these people up there whose retirement plans have been ruined. Do you have anything to say to them? Come on, do you?' So this was the fireworks that Morgan had been anticipating.

'Ah, Mr Gary McGinley of the Chronicle,' he said, in a condescending tone. 'Holding capitalism to account, that's what your rather pompous by-line says if I recall it correctly.' This drew a loud giggle from the crowd. 'A valuable public service no doubt.' More laughter. 'Yes, it's unfortunate that these people made such foolish investment decisions when they would have done so much better if they had trusted us with their savings. Or in fact, had just put their money on a horse at Doncaster races.' This time, loud whoops from the adoring crowd. 'But I expect even you would be forced to agree the unfortunate losses were entirely the fault of the previous management. What do you say to that Mr McGinley?'

There was something about the way he said it that just underscored what Maggie was already feeling in her gut. It was the big ego on display, like a peacock in heat. Despite the superficial charm, she had decided she didn't like this man one bit.

'So are you trying to claim that your report had nothing to do with it?' the journalist said. His tone was unmistakably combative.

Morgan scanned the audience as if to gather strength from his army of supporters.

'On the contrary Mr McGinley, it had everything to do with it. We pride ourselves on being activist investors, and when we discover incompetence and waste, we see it as our duty to expose it. Holding capitalism to account, you might say. You must approve of that, surely?'

'What I want to know is how you found out?' McGinley said. 'That information was company confidential, only known to the company's most senior executives. So how did you find out? Come on, tell us now. I'm sure we'd all like to know.'

Morgan gave him a steely look. 'Activist investors, Mr McGinley, that's our mission statement and we do what it says on the tin. Unlike some, we don't just sit on our backsides and swallow the spin that the fat over-paid management churns out. We make it our business to know what is *really* going on, even when management doesn't.' Around the room, more applause.

'You still haven't answered my question,' McGinley persisted. 'How did you find out?'

Morgan with a nod of the head signalled to one of the muscled security men who had slipped in un-noticed just as the session had got underway and were now flanking the door.

'Thank you Mr McGinley, but I think we have had enough of this unscheduled interruption. Vinny, if you wouldn't mind escorting our guest to the door.'

Vinny the security guy had reached the end of McGinley's row and was beckoning for him to join him in the passageway. 'Would you like to come this way sir, please?' he said in a voice loud enough for everyone in the room to hear. 'Don't want no fuss, does we?', his expression making it plain if there was to be a fuss then he was up for it. For the briefest moment, McGinley seemed as if he might resist, but then evidently thought better of it. He rose to his feet then in a calm voice said,

'If you think you've heard the end of this Morgan, you'd better think again. I'll get to the bottom of this, believe me. I'm not going to let it go.'

'Yes yes no doubt Mr McGinley,' Morgan said, with barely-concealed derision, 'and we'll all look forward to reading about it in your ailing rag. Now if you don't mind...' Another nod to Vinny signalled that for him, the conversation was now over.

'God what was all that about?' Maggie whispered once McGinley had been marched out. 'Was that journalist guy Mr Angry or what?'

'Already on it boss,' Jimmy said, pointing at his phone. 'Just having a wee google to see what comes up. Seems there was some massive screw-up at this Whitehaven mine. Lots of stuff online about it.'

Up on the platform, Morgan had now moved on to discussing the fund's prospects for the coming period, evidently unruffled by the interruption. It was the same super-confident tone, the same relentlessly upbeat message. And the same syrupy air of superiority that was now getting right up Maggie's nose. But as Asvina had often remarked, there was no requirement to like your clients in this line of work. As long as they settled their bills promptly at the end of the month, that was all you needed to concern yourself with.

'And I'm pleased to say you can expect more of the same in quarter two. Growth in the fund value and growth in our share price too, and yes I know Caroline, it is important to note again that the value of your investment can go down as well as up. And on that bombshell, let me hand over to my colleague Ms Short who will go through the detailed numbers. Brace yourselves folks for some weapons-grade tedium.'

He sat down to tumultuous applause, many of the audience on their feet, stomping and cheering. Maggie expected at any moment there would be demands for more, rock-concert style, but eventually the noise subsided and Caroline Short was able to begin her presentation. Morgan had been absolutely right about one thing. This was tedium on an industrial scale, not helped by Short's monotone voice and plodding just-read-the-slide presentation technique. It was all price-earnings ratios and debt indices and multiples of dividend cover and a hundred other technicalities that Maggie didn't even try to understand. But she recognised it for what it was, a carefully choreographed piece of theatre, designed to reassure rather than entertain. Naturally you wanted the charismatic investment genius at the helm, spotting value that others failed to see, picking the right companies and making the audacious calls, buying at the bottom of the cycle and selling at the top. But in the back-office you wanted solid competence and measured calm, giving investors the confidence that the dull but necessary burden of regularity compliance was being met and that as far as could be guaranteed, their money was safe. In its eight years of operation Brasenose Investment Trust had delivered an exemplary performance on that score, and Maggie had little doubt that the dull Ms Caroline Short, doubtless hand-picked by Morgan for her very dullness, would have paid a key role in that. But finally came the words that a thousand numb backsides were literally aching to hear.

'This is my last slide,' she said, giving the audience a bemused look as they applauded her announcement with an enthusiasm born of relief. She kept it mercifully short, Morgan rising to his feet to join in the polite applause that greeted the end of her pitch.

'Thank you Caroline for that tremendously illuminating session. Very interesting to all our friends here, I'm sure.' If he was being ironic then he kept it well hidden. 'So it just leaves me all to thank you for coming today and have a safe onward journey wherever you're heading next.' He raised a hand in acknowledgement then skipped down the steps to shake hands and grab selfies with a group of investors who had congregated at the foot of the platform.

'Popular guy,' Maggie said to Jimmy, who was still buried in his phone.

'What?' he said, distractedly. 'Aye, maybe here but not in West Cumbria. Here, look at this.'

It was an article from the Financial Times, dated around six months earlier. *Greenway Shares Voided after Cut-Price Rescue.*

Maggie gave him a puzzled look. 'Sorry, I don't understand any of that. What does it mean?'

He frowned. 'I've just skimmed it, so I'm not sure I understand it myself, but according to the article there was some giant technical problem with the mine that forced the firm to go into administration. I'm not sure exactly what that involves, I think it's when a company is kind of bust but they try to keep it going. So then Brasenose came along and offered to mount a rescue, but only if the previous company was liquidated - again, I don't exactly know what that means, but in effect all the existing shareholders lose their money. That's what they mean by voided I suppose.'

Maggie nodded. 'Ok, so that was what the McGinley thing was all about?'

'Aye,' Jimmy said, 'I guess so. But I suppose Morgan was right, it wasn't his fault that the mine had problems. That had to be down to the previous guys, surely?'

'Yes, I get that. But McGinley was talking about some report or other. Does it say anything about that?'

Jimmy shook his head. 'No, it doesn't as far as I can see. But see who's coming over. Maybe you can ask him yourself.'

She looked up to see Morgan strolling up the aisle in their direction, beaming a smile and exchanging a few words with some of his investors on the way.

'Hi guys,' he said as he reached them, 'and thanks for coming. What did you think?'

Maggie assumed he was referring to his own performance rather than the journalist's interruption.

'Very impressive Hugo, very impressive.' And that wasn't a little white lie, it *had* been impressive, irrespective of what she thought about him personally. But wasn't it telling that with all his millions, he still needed that affirmation, needed to know that he had done alright? She was about to ask him about the McGinley interruption when he brought up the subject himself.

'Yes, despite that little injection of excitement from our man from the Chronicle. I must apologise for that. Most unsavoury.'

'Did you know he was going to be there?' Maggie asked. She guessed he must have, because attendance at the meeting had been by invitation only.

'Yes, yes Maggie, but we can't be seen to exclude the financial correspondents, even the ones who don't like us. I was expecting him to pull a stunt like that of course.'

'Fireworks,' Jimmy said.

He nodded. 'Exactly. Although I think it turned out to be more of a damp squib, don't you?'

'So what did he mean when he said how did you know?' Maggie said. 'I didn't understand that. What was all that about?'

He looked surprised at her question. 'I refer you to my earlier answer. We're activist investors, it's what we do. As to our exact methods, you will forgive me Maggie if I don't choose to share them with my family law advisors. But let's just say we make sure we do our research.'

Out of the corner of her eye, Maggie saw a woman approaching them. She cut a striking figure, tall and very slim, wearing skinny black jeans, stilettos and a crisp white blouse under a black leather blouson. Her hair was sleek, glossy and expensively cut, and her complexion was smooth and flawless. It was hard to say exactly how old the woman was, but she guessed late forties, maybe just fifty.

'Still talking all that crap Hugo? When you and me both know it's all just a heap of bullshit.' She smiled at Maggie. 'I wouldn't believe a word of it darling. It's all lies, every world of it.'

Morgan's head darted around the room, clearly agitated. 'Where the *hell* is she? Where's Harriet?' Failing to detect the young intern amongst the crowd, he turned to the woman. 'I don't know how the hell you got in here Felicity, but I've got nothing to say to you.'

*Felicity*. So that's who she was. The recently discarded ex-wife. Maggie gave Jimmy a look that said *this might be fun*.

'I'm a shareholder Hugo or had you forgotten? So I was invited. And I've got plenty to say to you, believe me.'

'Not here, for Christ sake,' he said, lowering his voice. 'We don't want to make a scene.'

'Oh no, we wouldn't want that, not if front of your *fan club.*' You could almost cut the venom with a knife as she spat the words at him. Then she turned to Maggie. 'You see, he really is a *shit*. Steer clear of him darling, that's my advice, because he really is a *shit*. Did I say that? He's a *shit*.' It was then that Maggie noticed. The slurring of the words, the eyes just a fraction out of focus, the repetition. Mrs Felicity Morgan had been drinking. And it was clear that making a scene was the reason she had come.

'You see,' she said, raising her voice, 'I *know* darling. Just like that reporter. I know how you do it, but you wouldn't want the world to know all about *that*, would you my love.'

Vinny the security guy had glided onto the scene and was looking at his boss expectantly. Directing a sneer at his ex-wife Morgan said tersely. 'Get her out of here.'

'Sure boss.' He reached over and gripped her upper arm, so tightly that she winced. 'Come on Mrs Morgan, we don't want no trouble, does we?' Pulling her arm free, she directed a withering look at her husband.

'You haven't heard the last of this Hugo. Count on it.' Then summoning as much dignity as she could muster, she swept off.

'Sorry about that,' Morgan said, forcing a smile. 'My ex-wife is finding her new situation rather hard to come to terms with. But no matter.' He seemed anxious to change the subject. 'So, you'll keep me up to date with how our little project is progressing, won't you? And now if you'll forgive me, I want to get round as many of our loyal investors as I can.' And with that he swept off, the fixed smile re-installed for the benefit of his fans.

Jimmy gave her a wry look. 'Christ, that was quite a to-do, wasn't it? First that reporter then the crazy woman.'

She laughed. 'Yeah, mental wasn't it? Massively entertaining.'

'But do you think they're right? Is there something iffy about the way our Hugo goes about his business?'

She shrugged. 'Who knows, it's not something I understand. And I don't really want to either.'

And it was true, it wasn't any of her business and certainly was of no relevance to the job in hand. Which was to find out as much as they could about Miss Lotti Brückner. *Their little project*. Morgan might be reluctant to use the 'i' word, but she wasn't. She had a plan and tomorrow she hoped to meet Miss Brückner for the first time. Yes, tomorrow the investigation would be up and running.

# Chapter 4

Liz Donahue scrolled down her phone book, looking for the number. She was pretty certain she had kept it, but whether it was under 'Chronicle', 'McGinley', 'Gary' or any combination of the three, she couldn't quite remember. Like any good journalist, she had hundreds of names in her book, pretty much everyone she had ever met in the four years she'd been working on her local paper. An invaluable resource until you actually needed to find something. But after some more frantic scrolling, there it was. *'McGinley, Gary, The Chronicle.'* All three tags just for good measure.

Unfortunately, there was no mobile number but she did have an email address and that would do fine for now. This one had been the second suicide connected to the Whitehaven mine debacle. The first, bursting with local interest, had been reported by her *Westmoreland Gazette* in the outraged tones it deserved. William Tompkins, father of four and a pillar of the community, his spirit crushed after losing more than a hundred and fifty grand of his family's money in the Greenway crash, had drunk himself blind on cheap vodka before swallowing four packs of paracetamol. Four days later he had died an agonising death as his liver gave up the ghost. A tragedy, unarguably, and one that her paper was more than happy to lay at the door of Hugo Morgan.

But this one was different, quite different. Which is why Liz had spent nearly twelve hours camped outside the idyllic family home on the fringes of Wastwater. Mrs Belinda Milner had been the CEO of the company, a City darling who commentators said had only landed the job because of its desire to be seen to balance the gender gap in the leadership of publicly-listed companies. With a string of non-executive directorships too, she had been able to dedicate just three days a week to her Greenway duties, which was deemed by many to be totally inadequate. The demise of the company was not going to be the highlight of her CV, that was for sure, but unlike many of her ex-employees she wasn't to be made destitute given the million-plus per annum package she had been on, and in any case this wasn't the first failure she had presided over. No, Belinda Milner was inured to criticism, and this latest career setback would not have caused her to lose a minute's sleep. Let alone go off and kill herself.

But she *had* killed herself, changing into the sleek black designer-label swimsuit in the early hours of a cold November morning before her husband or daughter had wakened, then slipping down to the lakeside and plunging into the icy waters. Swimming out to the centre, she had let the lapping waves envelop her, filling her lungs until she could breathe no more. She left no note behind to explain, leaving her family holding a tawdry secret they were desperate to keep to themselves.

Except that Liz Donahue had already found out the truth. This was going to be a big one, perhaps the biggest story of her life. It had been bitterly cold all day, and there had been no movement in or out of the house all the time she had been there, apart from a van, which had arrived around 3pm. Two men wearing white overalls had got out and started work, without bothering to announce their presence to the occupants of the house. She had detected the sweet smell of acetate thinner as the pair expertly removed the graffiti, the task taking no more than twenty minutes from start to finish.

The slogan had been painted in foot-high letters along the side of Milner's upmarket SUV. *Justice for Greenway.* The incident had occurred too late to make that week's print edition, but she herself had covered it in the online version. There was plenty of locals seeking justice after the Greenway melt-down, but few perceptive enough to see where the real blame lay. Whoever had done this knew the truth.

At around six in the evening and just as she was about to abandon her vigil, came the breakthrough. Milner's daughter, fifteen or sixteen years old and just a week after her mother's funeral, had decided to go for a walk. Liz caught her up just as she left the driveway.

*'Was your mum having an affair April?'* It wasn't her proudest moment but you couldn't let your scruples get in the way of a good story. This one deserved national exposure, but McGinley wasn't going to get it unless he agreed to give her joint credit. She didn't see how he could possibly refuse.

# Chapter 5

Maggie hated the bloody photograph and she hated the bloody profile. In fact she hated everything about the whole damn thing. Especially something the website called 'Your Elevator Pitch.' *A youthful and fun-loving thirty-something, into walks in the countryside, great food and great books.* That described what she would like to be, not what she actually was, but as her friend Asvina had pointed out as they were putting the whole stupid thing together one evening after one too many chardonnays, everyone used great dollops of poetic licence on these dating sites. Besides which, *Burnt-out, bad-tempered forty-something former barrister who recently tried to do herself in,* didn't quite have the same ring to it.

Anyway, thank God it was still sitting there in the 'Draft' folder, the 'Post' button mercifully un-clicked. Right now, she wasn't ready for the wild-west world of online dating, and she doubted if she ever would be. But despite that, she had no doubt that almost unnoticed, something had changed inside her. After the most horrendous two years that anyone could ever have lived through, she was now feeling cautiously positive about the future. Positive enough to think about now meeting someone to share it with. But baby steps, that was the watch-word. She had plenty of time. No need to force the pace.

Her contemplations were interrupted by a sudden jolt as the tube-train driver sharply applied the brakes. She glanced up at the indicator board. *High Street Kensington.* This was her stop. She had calculated it was no more than a five-minute walk to the gallery, but that didn't really matter, since today she was the customer and so she could turn up late if she felt like it. Choosing what to wear had been a surprising challenge, since she really only owned a few smart suits for work, all navy, and then a hotchpotch of casual wear from the high street chains. That definitely wasn't going to create the kind of impression she needed to make. And then she remembered Harriet Ibbotson and the problem was solved. The dress cost nearly seven hundred pounds and the matching tailored jacket much the same, but there was no point in false modesty. She looked amazing in it, even if she said so herself. Which left just the problem of shoes. Four hundred pounds was a ridiculous sum of money to pay, but as she remembered her dad saying rather too often, why spoil the ship for a halfpenny's worth of tar? It wasn't as if she couldn't afford it, not after finally offloading her old family home, but it just didn't seem right in a world riddled with inequality.

But then again, this being a Thursday, she and Jimmy would be as usual meeting his brother Frank in the King's Head after work, and looking amazing would be no obstacle to what she had in mind. For Maggie had finally decided she liked Frank. He didn't have the babe-magnet looks of his brother, thank God - being with someone like that would surely turn you into an insecure wreck -but he was handsome in his own way and above all he was *nice*. And kind and open and honest, everything her late and unlamented husband Phillip never had been.

However, all that would have to wait until later, because she had now reached the front door of The Polperro Gallery. Kensington Church Street was lined wall-to-wall with the places and she wondered how they all could survive with such competition. But looking at the price-tag on a couple of items in their window, perhaps it wasn't so difficult to understand. The gallery felt pleasantly cool, discreetly air-conditioned with a limed-oak floor and walls painted in a subtle off-white silk. Classy, that was the immediate impression, doubtless exactly what the owners intended. Looking around, her eye was drawn by the picture immediately to her left, an arresting landscape of stark greys and khakis which as she got closer revealed itself as a scene from the trenches of World War I. An engraved plaque attached to the bottom edge of the frame read *Ypres September 1917*.

'It's wonderful, isn't it?' The voice was deep and mellifluous, the tone warm and welcoming. 'An undiscovered Paul Nash. We were so lucky to find it, don't you think?'

'I don't know him I'm afraid,' Maggie said. 'I don't really know any artists, to tell the truth. Lowry maybe, but that's about it.'

He held out a hand. 'It's Mrs Slattery, isn't it? I was expecting you. Welcome to the Polperro Gallery. I'm Robert Trelawney. We spoke briefly on the phone.'

'Magdalene, please.'

*Mrs Magdalene Slattery*. That was the name she had decided on. Her own first name, obviously, it would be too difficult to keep up the pretence if she suddenly became an Emma or a Susan. And then the surname of one of her favourite teachers, old Brian Slattery, Chemistry and Biology. A good old solid Yorkshire name for a good old solid Yorkshire girl. And if probed, the story was she had reverted back to her maiden name, but kept the *Mrs*. Perfectly plausible, after the way her fictional husband was supposed to have died.

She guessed Trelawney to be perhaps a couple of years older than her, slim and of medium height, dressed in an expensive-looking light grey suit with crisp white open-necked shirt. His shoes were a highly-polished deep brown leather and like the suit, obviously expensive. Tasteful and classy, just like his gallery. Now she was really glad she had taken the trouble to tidy herself up a bit.

'So when you called, you told me you were interested mainly in twentieth century art? But I wondered, how did you find us?'

She smiled. 'Find you? I've walked past your gallery on many occasions when I've been down this way. Actually, I'm ashamed to say I've just picked a few of you guys more or less at random. In your case, it's just that I liked the name. We used to go on holiday to Cornwall when I was a child.' It sounded perfectly convincing, and after all, why would all of these galleries bother with shop fronts if not to attract window shoppers?

He grinned. 'Well, I was brought up down there, for my sins. Trelawney is Cornish, I'm sure you've worked out. '

'Polperro's a lovely place and a lovely name for a gallery too,' she said. 'And to answer your question yes, I *think* I'm interested in modern art, but I'm really quite new to all of this. It's just that my financial advisors have been nagging me to diversify my asset portfolio or some such gobbledygook. You've got far too much tied up in cash, that's what they're always saying. First off they suggested I look at wine, but really, what can you do with a seventy-year old claret?'

Trelawney laughed. 'Yes, I agree, and it might not even taste nice if one day you decide to drink it. That's the great thing about art, you get the pleasure of being able to look at it every day. Although I'm bound to caution you that there are risks associated with buying a piece or a painting purely for investment purposes. That's why I always advise my clients to buy only artworks they really love.'

Maggie furrowed her brow. 'Is that normal in this business? That sort of advice I mean?'

'More normal than you might think actually,' he said. 'There's still a few unscrupulous dealers around but eventually their bad reputation catches up with them. Most of us are pretty straight. Honest.'

She laughed. 'I believe you. But this one,' pointing to the Nash, 'would you advise me to buy it?'

'Do you like it?'

She gave a sigh. 'Well it's certainly striking, but do I like it? I'm not sure that I do.'

He smiled. 'There's your answer then. But in any case, this probably isn't a picture for a novice collector. I hope you don't mind me calling you that?'

'Not at all. If you assume I know nothing about anything you'll be pretty much right. But when you say this isn't a picture for a novice, what do you mean?'

'Provenance and history. You see, Paul Nash was a very important artist, some would say one of the most important British artists of the early twentieth century. As such, his work has been extensively studied and catalogued. So when a work like this suddenly appears more than seventy years after his death, then there are obviously question marks over its authenticity. That's why we describe it in the catalogue as *attributed* to Paul Nash.'

'So that's a sort-of buyer beware?'

He nodded. 'Exactly. I'm very confident that it is genuine, and a number of experts have concurred with me, but there is always a risk that it could be challenged in the future.'

'After someone has bought it on the assumption it's a genuine Nash?'

'That's it. But a knowledgeable collector will do their due diligence before making up their own mind on that, and of course any doubts will be reflected in the price.'

She gave him an uncertain look. 'I'm not sure if it's the done thing Robert, but am I allowed to ask the obvious question?'

He smiled. 'How much, do you mean? Of course, that's the most important question of all. I can't say for certain, but the record price for a work of his is over two hundred thousand pounds, so I wouldn't be surprised if this goes for a similar sum or even more. We will have it on display here for the next month or so and I would expect we will have no trouble in agreeing a private sale. But if not, then it'll go to auction later in the year.'

'And so would you say that is the sort of sum I should be expecting to spend on an item? Because I've really no idea at all.' And then she realised that she was enjoying her conversation with this lovely man so much that she had almost forgotten why she was here in the first place. 'I mean, is this something you personally can help me with, or are there other people in your firm who deal with this?'

If he found the question odd, he didn't show it. 'Yes, well I'm more of an all-rounder you might say,' he said in an apologetic tone, 'but by coincidence we've got a new member of the team who is very knowledgeable on twentieth century artists, and not just the usual British suspects if I can call them that. She's in today. I'll just pop upstairs and see if she's free.'

And that was how it came to be that less than sixty seconds later, Maggie was shaking hands with the woman who was to be the next Mrs Hugo Morgan.

'I'm Lotti Brückner. Pleased to meet you.'

Involuntarily, Maggie looked her up from top to bottom and it was startlingly obvious that Morgan had not overstated the beauty of this woman in any way. Tall and slim, around five-ten, with a tiny little waist and a full bosom which was displayed to maximum effect by the tight-fitting white tee-shirt, worn above a pair of tailored light grey trousers. Her dark hair was thick and lustrous, swept to one side so that it rested a few inches below her left shoulder. Smart and beautiful, an intoxicating combination which would send most men crazy with desire, that could not be denied. But what struck Maggie most was her complexion, which was ridiculously soft and peachy, like that of a child. Which drove a thought into her mind, and the more she looked at Lotti, the more certain she was. *There's no way this woman is thirty years of age.* But that was stupid of course. Women lied about their age all the time, but as she knew only too well, they generally knocked a few years off, not added them on. Why would you do that? No, she was definitely being stupid. Perhaps Lotti was simply blessed with great genes, a product of her ancestors growing up breathing all that pure mountain air. But still the thought wouldn't go away.

'Pleased to meet you too Lotti,' she said, quite truthfully. 'Robert said you might be able to help me although to be honest, I'm not quite sure what my requirements are.'

Lotti smiled. 'Well, I'm sure we can discover that with some discussions.' Her voice was soft and clear but distinctly accented.

'That would be great,' Maggie said, 'and I hope you don't mind me asking, but do I detect a German lilt?'

She shook her head. 'Nearly. Swiss actually, but I grew up in Zurich so in a German-speaking Canton. It's the biggest one in Switzerland with over a million of us, but still the Germans say we do not speak the language properly. Of course we think the same about them also.'

'Oh dear,' Maggie said. 'I do hope you're not offended.' Not that she cared too much, really. It was just another part of the subterfuge, because if, as she said, she had chosen the gallery at random, how could she know that the pretty sales lady was from Switzerland?

'Not at all,' Lotti said, smiling. 'So maybe I can get you a coffee and then we could sit down and discuss your requirements? And perhaps match them to some of the works that we have for sale here in our gallery.' She turned to her boss. 'Robert, do you wish to sit in on these discussions?'

He shook his head. 'No, I don't think that's necessary Lotti. I'm not sure how much I could add to the party. But I can certainly make the coffee.' He scuttled off, leaving the two of them alone.

'Let's go and sit over here,' Lotti said, pointing to a low glass table in the corner. 'Robert told me about your situation. It must have been rather a difficult time for you.'

It *was* rather difficult, she thought, but only in trying to remember exactly what it was she had said to him yesterday. *Widowed in unusual circumstances and now bringing up my eight-year old son on my own.* That was about the gist of it.

'There's people in far worse situations than me,' she replied. 'At least I've enough money and a lovely home. And my son of course.' All of which was true, thank goodness, making that bit of the story easy to keep up. 'But you heard how my husband died, I suppose?'

'No, Robert didn't mention that.'

'He had a lover. Twenty years younger than him and he had a heart-attack whilst he was screwing the little bitch. Served him right of course, and her too. She had to push him off her then phone for an ambulance.' She didn't have to try too hard to fake the bitterness. It wasn't so much different from what she had suffered in real life.

Lotti shuffled uncomfortably, perhaps feeling that this was a bit too close to home. Good, thought Maggie, because that was the intention. But how far should she push it? No harm in going a bit further, and anyway, she found she was actually enjoying this. Perhaps she should have been an actress instead of a bloody lawyer, she might have been quite good at that.

'It's always the same with these rich and powerful older men, isn't it? They think they can take anything they want, and sod the carnage they leave behind. My David was fifteen years older than me when we married, but then as soon as I hit forty, boom, that was it.' *David.* She'd pulled that name from thin air, and now she'd better remember it. Bound to raise suspicions if you couldn't remember the name of your own husband, whether he was dead or not. 'So when he decided he wanted a younger model, I was dumped. But look, I'm sorry. Over-sharing, I'm always doing that. You're not here to listen to my troubles.'

She wiped a tear from her eye. A *genuine* tear. God, she was getting good at this already. Better start looking out an outfit for the *BAFTAs.*

But if Lotti Brückner was affected by Maggie's performance, she wasn't showing it. 'No, I don't mind at all Magdalene,' she said, giving a little smile. 'But I've been thinking that it may be a good idea for us to start with a little tour of our gallery. We have a big display in the back room and upstairs also. If I can understand the type of paintings you find appealing, then that will help me too.'

Maggie nodded. 'Yes, that sounds perfect. Because as I said, I really have no idea where to start.' And it was true. Acting skills or not, she wouldn't have any problems in playing the part of the naive art collector, since that was exactly what she was.

Robert had returned with the coffee, laying the delicate china mugs carefully on the glass table.

'Looks like you two are all set then,' he said brightly. 'I've got to go out now, but you'll be in good hands with our Miss Brückner I'm sure. But before I go, could I have a word with you Magdalene?' He beckoned her over towards the door, smiling at Lotti, who took the hint and slipped off into the back office.

'Look, I hope you won't find this too forward or presumptuous, but I wondered...would you possibly have dinner with me tomorrow evening? There's a lovely little Italian just round the corner if that's to your taste, and the house red is really very acceptable.'

And before she really knew what she was doing, she had said yes. That was going to make the job a bit more complicated. *Magdalene Slattery, the two-timer.*

# Chapter 6

Frank wasn't entirely sure why the case intrigued him so much, but it did, which was why this morning he had broken with his normal routine to head straight to Paddington Green nick. True, they had better coffee there, and the vending machine offered a wider variety of the teeth-rotting and diabetes-inducing goodies that he loved, but the principle reason for his visit was to meet up with his old mate DI Pete Burnside. He'd given him the briefest of overviews on the phone. *A couple of suicides that might not be suicides. Dig out the files and see what you can find.*

'Good to see you mate,' Pete said as Frank arrived at his desk with latte and Mars Bar in hand. 'How's tricks?'

'Oh, same old same old. Nothing much that looks as if it will turn into anything, other than the one I mentioned to you.'

Burnside laughed. 'Yeah, you must be desperate if you're having to go through the suicides file.'

'Aye, you're not wrong there mate. But the one I looked at came to me from Ronnie French. You remember him?'

'He's that fat lazy DC from your manor?'

'That's the one. You're right, he's always been an idle turd, but I have to admit he's always had a good nose for the dark side. Well anyway, it was him that sniffed this one out. This girl walked in front of a train, but there might be a drugs angle and you know how much I hate that stuff and the low-lives that peddle them.'

Burnside nodded. 'Yeah, you and me both. So, you didn't exactly give me much to go on but I went through the records on our crime system here and funnily enough, there was another case that seemed to match your one. A young bloke who decided to step off a railway platform just as a train was coming in. I remember it, it was about nine months ago and the transport muppets called us into have a look, but that's just routine.'

'Aye, that's the one I read about,' Frank said, taking a slurp of his coffee. 'Any others?'

'Give us a chance mate, we've only been at it a day. But no, I don't think so.'

'Only joking pal,' Frank said. 'So tell me about the one you did dig up.'

Burnside spun his monitor round to face Frank. 'We've been busy mate, and all for you. I hope you're bloody grateful.'

Frank gave a wry smile. 'That depends on what you've got. But it might be worth a pint, you never know. Anyway, what am I looking at?'

'We've got the post-mortem pictures. The mortuary tries to tidy them up best as they can but you don't really want to look at them for too long. But of course we've managed to get a few snaps from his social media too.'

'That's brilliant Pete, it really is,' Frank said. 'So, do we know who he is? I suppose you worked that out by now.'

'Meet Luke Brown. Twenty-four years of age, lived in Clapham, mixed-race, born and raised in Leicester, graduated from Oxford two years ago, working as an intern at some insurance company over at Canary Wharf.'

Frank stared at the screen, struggling to take in what he was seeing.

'Pete, mate, I'm no judge of this kind of thing, and I know he's a young guy and all that, but is it just me, or is our Luke a bloody good-looking boy? I mean, my brother Jimmy's irresistible to women, but this lad would give him a run for his money that's for sure. What do you think?'

Burnside gave him a contemptuous look. 'Why are you asking me, you cheeky bastard? As it happens, I did think the same, but as you say, everybody's good-looking at that age.'

'*I* wasn't,' Frank said. 'Not like that anyway. But come on mate, there's something going on here. No idea what, but something.'

'If you say so. And I kinda agree, it is a bit odd how close the two cases are. But who knows, it's probably just coincidence.' His friend smiled. 'Anyway, you know that pint you were on about? So if you make it two, then maybe I'll let you know the *really* interesting stuff we found out.'

'Two pints? Aye well, I suppose I could just about run to that. Alright, what have you got?'

'So the first thing that I thought was a bit odd was this guy had written a suicide note that turned up on social media after he did it.'

'Christ,' Frank said, 'that's exactly the same as my girl'.

'Yeah, so obviously that meant the Coroner chalked it down as a suicide.'

'Aye, took the easy way out you mean.'

'A bit harsh Frank,' Burnside said. 'There wasn't any evidence that it could have been anything else. Although the post-mortems did find evidence of some drug use, it was no more than recreational amounts. But before you say anything else, we didn't just leave it there.'

'Tell me more,' Frank said, interested.

'Well believe it or not mate, even the Met are using interns these days. It's cheap labour isn't it? Anyroads, Yvonne Sharp's the girl we've got. Sharp lady. See what I did there? Sharp by name and sharp by nature.'

Frank gave him a mock-contemptuous look. 'You make that one up yourself mate?'

Burnside ignored the jibe. 'To be honest, we were a bit stuck for something for her to do, so I gave her a morning on your case and she did really well. First of all she spoke to the insurance company that Luke Brown was assigned to. Alexia they're called. German or Dutch-owned I think, and apparently big in marine insurance. Yvonne also got the name of the intern agency that employed him. Some outfit called The Oxbridge Agency. You know, as in Oxford and Cambridge universities.'

'Yeah, got that.'

'Well I thought I'd better spell it out, you being a northern hick and all that. But anyway, here's the thing. Yvonne herself had an interview with them, just last year. As I said, she's a clever girl. Did Law at Cambridge and that's where she came across them. Apparently they market themselves pretty heavily on their campuses. Oxford and Cambridge I mean. So as I said, she had an interview, but didn't much like the culture. She got the impression they were very elitist and upper class and she didn't think she would fit in, even if her parents could afford their fee, which they couldn't. So she came direct to us instead.'

'What, they *charge* to give these kids a crap non-job?'

Burnside nodded. 'Apparently that's quite common.'

'And yet our two were working-class kids. Remarkable, isn't it?'

'I suppose it is,' Burnside said, sounding unconvinced. 'But there was something else that our Yvonne found out. Something pretty interesting in my opinion.'

'What?'

'Just two days before he died, Luke Brown was asked to leave.'

'You mean he was sacked?'

'I suppose you could describe it that way, but I expect these kids aren't on an employment contract as such, so the firms can dispense with them anytime they want. Yvonne talked to a girl in their HR team who was pretty tight-lipped as you might imagine. What was it she said? It was an internal matter and it simply coincided with a budget review. And that was as much as she could get out of her. Said the matter was now closed as far as the firm was concerned.'

Frank pursed his lips. 'So what do you think mate? Caught thieving? Or maybe looking at some inappropriate stuff on his laptop?'

'Yeah, it could be that, I don't know. As I said, their HR lot weren't too keen to say much, but Yvonne got the impression that there was something that wasn't quite right. I suppose if you really needed to find out we could send a couple of uniforms round. Say that we're re-looking at the death of Luke, and we've got some questions.'

'Which is the truth in fact. Aye, maybe that's an option but let me think about it first. But that agency outfit. The Oxbridge Agency. Find out anything about them?'

Burnside laughed. 'Frank Stewart, you are a right bloody dinosaur aren't you? They're not a secret society as far as I can tell, so you'll probably find their address on this new thing we've got now called google.'

'Cheeky swine,' Frank said. 'I just thought maybe your wonder-kid Yvonne might have wheedled out something, that was all. But no worries, I can look into that myself, no bother.'

Burnside gave him an enquiring look. 'So have I earned my pints then?'

'Aye, and some. You've done a cracking job mate, you really have. I'm actually down the Old King's Head after work tonight if you can be arsed to make the trip into town.'

'Yeah, I'd forgot it was Thursday. That's your regular night with your brother and that very lovely boss of his, isn't it? But I'm afraid it'll have to be some other time, I've got a call with the kids tonight and I don't want to miss it.'

Frank nodded. He forgotten about Pete's horrible situation, his former wife now re-married and living in Australia with his two kids, their relationship just another casualty of the job, with its late nights and broken promises and all the stresses it brought with it. He really felt for him.

'Aye, sure mate. Some other time, eh? Well, I'll be getting back over to my gaff and I'll see you soon. Cheers Pete.'

*That very lovely boss of his.* Pete was right, Maggie Bainbridge *was* lovely, in every conceivable way. Lovely to look at and with the sweetest nature of any woman he had ever met, despite everything she had been through. And God, hadn't she been through some shitty times. It was cringingly old-fashioned he knew, but sometimes he just wanted to wrap his arms around her and tell her he would make everything better. But of course, he hadn't said a thing in the nearly two years he had known her. Too scared, but too scared of what? Of rejection, of dying with embarrassment, of the gentle mocking he would have to suffer from his brother? Well, whatever it was, surely now was the time to shake of his pathetic self-doubt and just bloody do it. What's the worst that could happen? So she might say no, but wasn't that what he was expecting anyway?

Perhaps the truth was he was scared that she might say yes, and then he would find himself racing down the same path that Pete Burnside had followed. Everything starting off so perfect and sunny and optimistic until the job crushed every good thing out of their lives. But bugger this pessimism, tonight he was going to grab this thing by the throat for once. Tonight, he was going to ask Maggie Bainbridge to have dinner with him. He'd seen a nice little Italian just round the corner from the Old King's Head and that looked as good a place as any. *Maggie, will you have dinner with me?* How hard could that be?

Now, as he battled through the stop-go traffic of the North Circular back to Atlee House, he could turn his attention to what he had learned in the last hour. Old Pete had done a great job for him, and that wee nugget about Luke Brown, the fact that he seemed to have been sacked for some reason, made it doubly interesting. Although, when he thought about it, it could have given him a motive to take his own life, which rather put the kibosh on his murder theory. But he would figure out where that fitted in at a later date. No, the more he thought about it, the more convinced he was right. Two near-identical deaths. Two kids from the same modest background. Two kids blessed by the fates with brains and good looks. Two kids that surely had no reason to kill themselves. What did it all mean?

But right now, there was a more pressing priority. That name, *Operation Dolphin*. It just wasn't going to cut it. It wasn't just the fact that the causes of death were the same. It wasn't even that the victims were all listed as working for that Oxbridge Agency outfit. No, it was their bloody photographs. Because Luke Brown and Chardonnay Clarke shared one characteristic that he just knew was going to turn out to be ten times more important than all the others combined. They were ridiculously, arrestingly, sensationally good-looking kids, and so the case, for that is what it undoubtedly had become, demanded a more appropriate moniker.

And then, with an uncharacteristic flash of inspiration, it came to him. Surely there was only one that would suffice. *Sorted.* Operation *Aphrodite* was now up and running.

# Chapter 7

'Aphrodite? Well I suppose it's better than the usual rubbish names you come up with. Some sort of Greek goddess, wasn't she?'

They were in the Old King's Head in Shoreditch for their semi-regular Thursday meet-up, and Jimmy had just fought his way back from the crowded bar after the always-regular buying of the first round. Frank believed there was a sort of natural hierarchy in families which demanded that wee brothers always bought big brothers the first drink, and so far Jimmy had never challenged the convention.

'Aye, she was,' Frank said. 'Goddess of love and beauty and everything in between.'

Jimmy grinned as he placed the drinks on the table. 'You must have looked that up I suppose.'

'Nah,' Frank lied. 'If I was on *Mastermind*, Greek mythology would be my specialist subject.' He raised his glass and downed a generous measure. 'Ah, that's better. Cheers mate. Where's Maggie by the way?'

'She should be here in five or ten minutes,' Jimmy said, at first failing to detect the hint of anxiety in his brother's voice. 'She was just meeting Asvina for a quick coffee. Looks like something's cropped up on the case we're working on. Which is a dead interesting one, by the way. Have you ever met a billionaire Frank?'

'Not as I recall. So who're we talking about?'

'The guy's name is Hugo Morgan. He runs something called an Investment Trust. I don't really understand them to be honest but that's how he made his money. And it turns out he's an ex-army bloke like myself.'

'Never heard of him.'

'Don't you read the papers mate? The divorce of the century they called it. His ex-wife walked away with more than thirty million in cash.'

'What, actual cash?' Frank said, laughing. 'She must have needed a lot of suitcases. But aye, now that you mention it, I do remember. So that was him was it?'

'Yeah, the same guy. Reached his fiftieth and decided he wanted someone younger and sexier.'

'We could all do with some of that mate,' Frank said. But that wasn't quite true. In fact it wasn't true at all. There was only one woman that he wanted and right now he was hoping against hope that her meeting with her friend wouldn't last so long that she would decide to give the pub a miss. He stole an anxious glance towards the door and this time Jimmy did notice.

'Don't worry mate, she'll be here.'

'What're you talking about?' he said, avoiding his brother's gaze.

Jimmy gave a wry smile. 'Don't come it with me bruv, I've seen the way you look at her. What I don't understand is why don't you just get off your fat arse and ask her out?'

'Nah, couldn't do that.' Which was exactly what he intended to do later that same evening. If he could find the courage from somewhere that was.

Jimmy shrugged. 'Well, it's your loss pal. But if you take my advice, you better move fast because she's not going to be on the market for ever.'

'She's not a bloody second-hand car you know.'

'Just a figure of speech,' Jimmy said, his tone apologetic. 'You know what I mean. But talk of the devil, here she is in person.'

He leapt to his feet and waved an arm. 'Over here Maggie', bellowing to make himself heard above the background din. She spun round, giving a smile of recognition then began to squeeze her way through the throng of early-evening drinkers.

'Hi Jimmy, Hi Frank. I see you've already got me a drink, that's brilliant.'

Jimmy laughed. 'Aye, took a risk that you might just want one. Anyway, that call from Asvina. That was all a bit mysterious. What was it all about?'

'Nothing really,' she said, grimacing. 'Nothing other than she's heard on the legal jungle drums that Morgan's ex-wife might be looking to contest her settlement.'

'What, can she do that?' Jimmy asked, surprised. 'I thought these things were full and final.'

'Well, that's where it gets interesting. Because apparently that journalist guy McGinley has been in touch with her and has suggested that Morgan might not have been exactly accurate with his financial disclosures. Anyway, Asvina's looking into it, to see if there's anything she can do to nip it in the bud. Before Morgan gets to hear about it and throws his toys out of the pram.'

Jimmy nodded. 'So do you think maybe the wife's found out about his relationship with the new girlfriend and decided to try and throw a spanner in the works?'

'Yeah, Asvina thinks it's a possibility. It seems that the ex-Mrs Morgan is still off-the-scale bitter about the whole thing.'

Frank gave a look of mock disgust. 'Hey guys, I thought we're meeting up for a wee social drink. If you're going to talk shop all night, at least clue me in, eh?'

Maggie laughed. 'Yes you're right Frank. Sorry. So come on, tell us what you're working on. Although I know everything in your dodgy department is probably top secret.'

'Far from it,' he said. 'This one's a wee bit sad actually, what I'm working on. I was just saying to my brother before you came in. Look at this.'

He passed his phone over to them, pointing to the photograph. 'That's a wee girl called Chardonnay Clarke. Just twenty-three. Swipe left and the other one's Luke Brown.'

'God, they're good-looking, aren't they?' Maggie said, examining the pictures. 'Oh what it is to be young.'

'Hence Aphrodite,' Jimmy said, nodding. 'I get it now.'

'Aye, they're were both very good-looking and now they're both very dead.'

'Murdered?' Maggie said. 'How awful.'

'Aye it is awful,' Frank said. 'Except the inquests said suicide, not murder.'

'Chardonnay looks a little bit like Lotti, don't you think Jimmy?' Maggie said, screwing up her eyes. 'She's pretty enough to be a member of your Aphrodite club, that's for sure.'

'And this Lotti is?' Frank enquired.

Maggie smiled. 'Hugo Morgan's new girlfriend. I should have said, that's what we're doing. Checking her out before he proposes to her.'

*Important work.* That's what he was about to say, but just in the nick of time he managed to check himself. Mocking the line of work of the woman you were about to ask to dinner, however gently, probably wasn't the smartest move, even he could see that.

'Aye, well marriage is for life isn't it, so it's as well to be sure I suppose.' He said it without thinking then immediately regretted it. Out of the frying pan into the fire. It wasn't meant to be directed at Jimmy of course but that's how it came out. Why couldn't he just keep his big mouth shut? It was something he often asked himself. He looked at his brother, and knew he was thinking about Flora.

'Look I'm sorry mate, I didn't mean anything by it.' He took a crumpled twenty-pound note from his pocket. 'Same again folks?'

Jimmy gave him an encouraging smile. 'I'll go. Still on the Doom Bar?' And then he gave a wink. 'Looks busy up there mate, this might take a while.'

And now Frank knew what he meant. It was now or never. Tomorrow was Friday, the start of the weekend and for many if not most people, the best part of the week. But not for him. For him, the weekend was an interminable desert of loneliness, of cold takeaway curries and warm beer and too many whiskies and boring football on the television. But he had more than enough of that and now, as he approached his forty-third birthday, it was time to finally do something about it. Yes, it was now or never. And here he was with Maggie Bainbridge. Alone with her at last.

# Chapter 8

It would have been better if they could have gone into the grounds of the house itself, but with an eight-foot wall surrounding the place, a pair of massive cast-iron gates guarding the entrance to his driveway and that damn dog, that would have to wait for another time. Besides which, the message would be just as clear to Morgan whether it was daubed on the outside wall or on the walls of the house itself. It was three o'clock in the morning, so the chances of them being observed were slight, but just to be sure they checked one more time before removing the aerosols from the back-pack. The wall was clearly illuminated by the bright LED streetlight, making it a straightforward task. A minute later it was done, the message spelt out in foot-high silver-grey letters.

*Justice for Greenway*

# Chapter 9

She had only ever seen Miss Harriet Ibbotson in a work setting, so had no idea what that lady might wear to a first date. Something stunning, no doubt, but classy too, alluring but not too in-your-face. Not an easy look to pull off, especially for a forty-two-year-old who hadn't been on a first date for more than nine years. Maggie remembered the previous occasion as if it was yesterday. Of course she had hardly known her to-be husband at that point, but looking back, she could see his choice of restaurant, a long-since-bust and ferociously over-priced fake bistro, should have been a warning sign. The place had been briefly popular with the gossip-pages set, a place to see and be seen. The fact that it served food was purely incidental. In short, Phillip Brooks' kind of place.

So this evening she had played it safe. A little navy dress, a little shorter than she would have worn to work, but not too short. A glittery throw, but not too glittery, not Xmas-party glittery. And heels, a little higher than everyday, but not such that she would fall over with every step. She wondered what Miss Ibbotson would make of it. She was of course about twenty years younger than Maggie, and in her opinion, rather more attractive, so would probably look sensational no matter what she threw on. But putting comparisons aside, all in all she was quietly pleased with the effect.

The restaurant was exactly as Robert Trelawney had described it, dark and cosy and unprepossessing, decorated in a quaintly old-fashioned style with lit candles on every table in raffia-wrapped Chianti bottles, and crisp white linen tablecloths. There was only around a dozen tables but every place was taken, even at this early hour. He was already there, waiting in the tiny reception area.

'Hi Magdalene, I'm so glad you could make it,' he said, shooting her a smile. 'Sorry if it's a little early, but unless you're in at seven then you won't get a table. But the food is wonderful, I'm sure you'll just love it.'

She looked at him and chuckled to herself, imagining he had faced the same dilemma as her over what to wear. She didn't see him as a jeans-and T-shirt sort of a guy, and this evening he, like her, had evidently decided to play it safe. Dark navy corduroy trousers with a light-grey woollen sports jacket over a light-blue shirt, formally cut but worn without a tie. What her dad might have called smart-casual, but with a touch of class. She liked it very much.

A young waiter led them through to their table which was already provisioned, with breadsticks in paper packets, a tiny bowl of mixed olives and a bottle of sparkling mineral water. He pulled back Maggie's chair and waited deferentially until she was seated before handing each of them a leather-bound menu. This wasn't one of these places with the chalked special boards, where you had to make a special trip half way across the room then try to memorise it all before an impatient waitress came to take your order. All their dishes were on the menu, and from the faded print she guessed it hadn't changed for many years, and was probably all the better for that.

'They've got a very nice wine list here Magdalene,' Robert said, 'but I'd recommend you try the house first, because they pride themselves on always picking excellent ones. Especially the red.'

*Magdalene*. God, she'd better remember. Remember she wasn't Maggie Bainbridge, hopeless ex-barrister and once the Most Hated Woman in Britain, but Mrs Magdalene Slattery, rich Hampstead widow and embryonic collector of modern art. She'd better remember, because the question was bound to come up on a first date, and she'd need to be ready with the answers. *Tell me all about yourself.* She'd worked up a story, she just hoped it would be convincing.

She giggled. 'I like the sound of *first* Robert. It sounds as if we're in for a good night. Yes, the house will be great, and red's my favourite. Although I like white too. And rosé, if I'm being honest. And champagne.'

The wine arrived, and then there was small-talk whilst they perused the menu and settled on their choices, but it was easy small-talk, light and natural, not at all stilted as it so often can be.

'Are you bothering with a starter?' he asked. 'Perhaps go straight to mains?'

She wasn't really focussed on the food at all and the question took her slightly by surprise.

'What? No.. no, mains are good for me.' Now she had a moment to think about it, she was actually starving and wouldn't have minded starting with one of the delicious-looking cannelloni dishes she had seen served to an adjacent table. Out of the blue, a hint of suspicion crept into her mind. Was he having second thoughts and trying to get this over with as possible? No, surely that wasn't the case, he seemed perfectly relaxed. And then another thought struck her, causing her to give an involuntary giggle. Maybe he was careful with money. The house wine, served informally by the carafe, was nice, she couldn't deny the fact, but it was also less than half the price of the cheapest bottle on the list.

'You know, I felt awful afterwards,' Robert said, shooting her a curious look. 'After I asked you out I mean. It was just so *forward*, and believe me, that's not like me at all. I just don't know what came over me. In fact, I almost got Lotti to call you and cancel it.'

'I'm glad you didn't,' Maggie said, quite truthfully. 'Then I wouldn't have got to sample this lovely house red. I'm not a wine expert, but it does taste deliciously warm and fruity.'

'Yes, with a good nose too and a hint of blackberry, don't you think?' He held his glass up to his nose, swilled it around and sniffed, his face taking on a serious expression for a second or two. And then he laughed. 'Actually, that's all bollocks. I don't know the first thing about wine really. I either like it or I don't, simple as that.'

'Snap,' she said, amused. 'And here was me imagining you would be a real wine buff. It sort of goes with the art dealer image somehow.'

He shrugged. 'Well, yes, and some of us do collect wine that's true. But as I said before, with collectable wine, you can't tell whether you like it or not until you drink it, and then you don't have it any more. No, I'll stick to paintings, thank you very much.'

And then, as the waiter was clearing away the plates and smoothing down the tablecloths in preparation for the arrival of their mains, he asked it. *Tell me all there is to know about Mrs Magdalene Slattery.*

It wasn't difficult to sketch out a childhood story for Magdalene Hardwick. That last bit, the maiden name, she had almost forgotten about but managed somehow to pull it out of thin air. Brought up in Yorkshire of course, because there was no disguising her accent, and then onto the University of Manchester to study -what? It couldn't be law, obviously, because then there would be questions as to why she hadn't become a lawyer. *English*, that would be better. An MA in English, and then a move to London and a succession of dead-end jobs in publishing. She just hoped he didn't ask for details.

'I hadn't really done anything with my life,' she heard herself saying, 'and then I met...' Christ, had she mentioned her fictional husband's name to him before, she couldn't remember. '...*David*.' Now she remembered. It was Lotti that she had talked to about him, not Robert. And at least for this next part it wouldn't be difficult to merge the real and the fictional.

'Looking back, I don't think I ever really loved him. A terrible thing to say I know, but it was just... well, my biological clock was well and truly ticking and I wanted a baby and I thought it would be a nice comfortable life. It was all right at first, but he was much older than me, and he turned out not to be very nice.'

'But he did give you a son,' Robert said in a kindly tone, 'who I know you love very much.'

She could feel herself reddening. 'I do. Very much. Ollie's everything to me.' It was true. He was more than everything, more than could ever be put into words, and somehow she felt she was betraying her love for her son by dragging him into this silly subterfuge, but she had no choice. Magdalene Slattery's son had to be Ollie, he could never be a Jack or a Kieran or any other name.

At least with that out of the way, it would be his turn. Initially, just after he had asked her out, she had entertained a vague suspicion that he might be married. It was just something about the way he looked, she couldn't exactly put a finger on it. But if he was, he wouldn't have brought her here, to this lovely little place where he was obviously a regular. No, Robert Trelawney wasn't married.

'So Robert,' she said, toying with her glass, 'what about you? Any dark secrets to reveal?'

'Afraid not,' he said, grinning. 'Bit of a posh boy upbringing, I must confess. My family's been farming in Cornwall for centuries, own half of Bodmin Moor. But I was the third son. My oldest brother inherited the estate a couple of years ago when father died and is making rather a good fist of running the place I think. In the old days of course I would have been marked out for the church, but we're a bit more enlightened nowadays. They still packed me off to a succession of ghastly boarding schools though. The English upper classes have always liked to subcontract the bringing up of their children.'

Maggie nodded. 'But you seem relatively unscathed by the experience, if I'm any judge.'

'What? Yes, it was all I knew, and I was good at sport you see, so that made a difference with fitting in and all that. Played cricket and rugger. Too much of both probably.'

'Did you go to Uni?'

'Afraid not. Flunked my A levels big time. Father wasn't exactly pleased. He wanted me to be a doctor or a vet or something respectable like that.'

She smiled. 'So what *did* you do then?'

'Bummed around, I guess that's how you would describe it. Took a bit of a gap year that somehow seemed to last until I was about thirty.

Australia, Far East, the US. It was fun whilst it lasted, but eventually you have to grow up, don't you?'

With no little envy, she contrasted that with how she had spent her twenties. The training contract at Addisons, and then the move to Drake Chambers where she slogged for years in the hope of making silk. The long hours sweating over tedious low-rent briefs whilst the toxic class snobbery and misogyny of the profession created a glass ceiling that no working class girl could ever hope to break through. That's how she portrayed it, but deep down, she knew that wasn't wholly true. The fact was, she hadn't been much of a barrister, although, briefly she had been the most famous one in the country. But one thing was certain. All work and no play had made Maggie a dull girl, she could see that now.

'So how did you get into the art world then?' she asked. 'It's quite a jump isn't it?'

'Friend of a friend of father's I'm afraid,' he said, the tone apologetic. 'I'd just got back from schlepping around India and was a bit hard up, and he was looking for someone to help him out on the sales front, so with nothing else on the cards, I thought I might as well give it a try. That was ten years ago, and I've been here ever since. Found something tolerably interesting that I also was quite good at. Learned the ropes under his tutelage and then bought the place off him a while back. That's when I renamed it the Polperro.'

So far, so interesting, but he hadn't yet mentioned anything about the subject she was most interested in. Relationships, and in particular was there an ex or even several ex Mrs Robert Trelawneys. Seemingly, he had read her mind, as his face broke into a grin.

'But I guess what you really want to know is how a guy as good-looking as me gets to forty-five years of age unmarried. I sometimes ask myself the same thing.'

She laughed. 'It must be because you're too modest. Seriously, it never entered my mind.' At least that was one advantage of pretending to be someone else. It wasn't really you who was lying.

'I know it sounds like a cliché, but I just haven't met the right woman yet.' He was right, it did sound like a cliché. All it needed was for him to add 'until now' and they would be square bang in Mills & Boon territory. But he didn't, causing her to experience a slight but perceptible *frisson* of disappointment.

'I didn't meet the right man either, but it didn't stop me marrying him. Big mistake.'

'But we mustn't look back, don't you think?' he said. 'Nothing you can do about the past.' Smiling, he raised his glass. 'Here's to bright futures. For both of us.'

'Bright futures.' That was something she never thought she would hear herself say, but somehow, it felt right. For eight years, she had lived a kind of half-life, married to a man she knew she didn't love, but clinging on out of fear. Until a teenage terrorist took the matter out of her hands. *Bright futures*. After all she had been through, it was no less than she deserved, but whether or not it involved Robert Trelawney, she could not say. *Yet*.

But then suddenly she remembered that, technically speaking, this was supposed to be work.

'I was very impressed with Lotti. She's a really lovely girl and she seems very knowledgeable.'

'Yes, she is. I was very lucky to secure her services.' He gave her a conspiratorial look. 'Especially since I don't have to pay her.'

'Excuse me?' She hated that phrase, but like so many other imported from the outposts of the English-speaking world, annoyingly she found herself saying it all the time. And she couldn't hide her surprise. 'You don't pay her?'

'Well no, not exactly.' Was it her imagination, or was he sounding embarrassed? 'She earns commission of course, on any sales. You see, I was looking for an intern. Someone at the start of their career, looking for a foot in the door.'

*Interns*. She knew all about them. Nowadays, it was the only way to get a start in a legal career, treated like a slave for twelve hours a day and expected to like it.

'Isn't she a bit old to be an intern?' *Damn*, that was a mistake. How would Magdalene Slattery have any idea how old a woman she had barely met was? 'I mean, she seems so incredibly experienced from the little time that I have spent with her.'

If he noticed the slip, he didn't mention it. 'No you're right. It's her family you see. Been in the trade for generations. A friend of a friend recommended her to me. One of the skiing set. The St Moritz crowd. Her family runs a little gallery out there.'

Yes, she could imagine the type. Back at Drakes Chambers, the partners spoke of little else during the winter, of the upmarket chalet that they took for three weeks each year straddling the February half-term, of the *perfect* powder and the *simply divine* chalet-maid who cooked for them. Each year she had been invited, but the invitation was decidedly half-hearted, and she was glad because she wouldn't have wanted to spend any of her precious holiday allowance with a single one of them. And she couldn't have afforded it anyway, not unless she asked Phillip to pay, which she would never have done. Which got her wondering about Robert.

'Do you ski then?' she asked.

'Did once,' he said, 'but the old dodgy knee put paid to that. Rugger injury of course.' It sounded convincing, but there was just something in the tone that caused her to doubt it. It wouldn't be cheap to be a member of the St Moritz set. But whatever, the state of his finances wasn't really any of her business.

'But coming back to Lotti,' he continued. 'I do feel a bit guilty of course, but she was very keen to work in London to broaden her experience so the arrangement suits as both.'

'She's very beautiful, isn't she?' Maggie said, grinning. 'I guess that must have helped with her application.'

He shrugged. 'She is beautiful, but I agreed to take her on before I had even met her.'

'So you must have been pleased when you did get to meet her in the flesh so to speak.'

'Well of course. In our business although it *is* quite important to know about art of course, it's mainly about relationships, forming a bond with the client.'

And she wouldn't have any problem in that department, would she, thought Maggie. Especially bonding with billionaires with an interest in modern art.

After that, she relaxed into the evening, aided by the wine and the amiable company. It all felt so natural, stirring feelings she hadn't felt for a very long time. They decided against dessert, electing instead to share the cheese platter. And then all too soon for her, the lovely evening wound to a close. Or maybe not.

She watched as he took a credit card from his wallet and signalled the waiter to bring the bill.

'Perhaps skip coffee? We can have it at my place if you like, it's just around the corner.'

'Yes, that would be lovely,' she said, unsure of what she was agreeing to and not caring either. And at least he hadn't suggested they split the tab.

\*\*\*

*Personal protection was more his thing, so this wasn't his normal line of work. Not that he was too bothered about that. If that's what the boss wanted him to do, then that was fine by him, and besides, three hundred and fifty quid cash in hand was not to be sniffed at. Keep your eye on him for a couple of days, see what he's up to, that was the instruction. So that's what he did, hanging around that poxy gallery of his, watching all the comings and goings, then following him round the corner to his fancy flat in Bedford Gardens at the end of the working day. Last night, Trelawney hadn't gone out at all and so he had called it a day around nine. But this evening it was different. Tonight, he'd closed up the gallery at 6pm prompt and then walked home at pace, in fact he'd broke into a jog at one point. Big night in prospect by the look of things. And then half an hour later out he comes, all dressed up with somewhere to go. Round another couple of corners until he arrived at an Italian place. Fazolli's. For a date, with a fit-looking bird he hadn't seen before. Absolute gold-dust.*

*They didn't have a table for one, so they said, but he was good at persuasion and a few words in the ear of the poncey head waiter soon put that right. A quiet spot tucked up against the wall, barely illuminated. About three of four tables back from theirs, his seat facing the woman. Smart looking, forty-ish but when he got a better look at her, a bit mumsy for his tastes. It wasn't hard to sneak a couple of pictures and then he could relax a bit and enjoy his lasagne. Made sure he was done before them so he could settle down outside and wait for them to leave.*

*Ten minutes later he sees them leaving, all giggles and kisses. It was pretty obvious that the evening was only going to end one way, and fair play to the boy, he wouldn't have minded himself. But he followed them the couple of blocks back to his place to make sure, then hung about outside for about an hour just for insurance. In case she had second thoughts. But she didn't. Great. Tomorrow morning he'd be back outside at six-thirty prompt and snap her coming out wearing the same clothes she wore last night. As he said, absolute gold-dust. The boss was going to be pleased, no doubt about it.*

# Chapter 10

Frank had never been to Oxford before, as far as he could recall. He'd seen it on telly plenty of times of course, mainly down to *Morse* and its multiple successors, but never had any reason to visit until now. It made a change from the capital though and he was very much looking forward to it, especially given the news that he'd got from Ronnie French last night.

He was just about to ask Yvonne if she'd ever been to the town when he remembered, causing him to change tack.

'Did you enjoy your time at Oxford then? Quite a place to be a student I imagine, with all that history and the like.'

They were on the M40, the mid-morning traffic light on the northbound carriageway. Across the central reservation the London-bound businessmen and women weren't so lucky, a lorry breakdown in the Stokenchurch cutting causing a tailback that already stretched for six miles.

'Glad we're not going that way,' she said. 'Yeah, I enjoyed my time at uni sir. But actually I was at Cambridge, the other place. The light blues.'

He glanced at her, mystified.

'Sorry, the colour our sports teams wear. As opposed to the dark blue, which is Oxford. Before I went I thought everyone would be terribly posh and everything but they weren't all like that.' Aye, just most of them, he thought.

'So this Sophie woman we're meeting,' Frank said. 'You can just tell what she's going to be like don't you, with a name like that. *She'll* be posh, and tall and skinny too. And good looking, a bit like the Duchess of Cambridge. They always are.'

Yvonne laughed. 'Tut- tut sir, that's awful. Haven't you been on the unconscious bias course?'

'Unconscious bias? Believe me, my bias is never unconscious. But no, I haven't been on the course 'cos I don't need it. I'm never wrong on these things.'

'If you say so sir. But honestly, you should go on it. It's really good. It makes you think.'

'Aye, well we'll see who's right soon enough. Mark my words, I won't be far wrong.'

And he wasn't far wrong, because Sophie Fitzwilliam did turn out to be very much as he expected, tall and slim and very attractive and effortlessly posh. Except, unlike the Duchess, she was distinctly and unarguably black. He saw Yvonne smirk at him as Ms Fitzwilliam came to collect them from the reception area. It had been Pete Burnside's suggestion that the young intern should accompany him on the visit and he was happy enough to acquiesce. In truth, he suspected they were struggling to find anything for her to do and a wee trip up to Oxford would fill one of the days of her four-week assignment. But he was glad of the company, and she was sweet and funny and, he had decided before they had even left London, way too smart to be a copper.

They were led through to a plush meeting room, with a polished solid oak floor, the walls a light violet pastel. Dotted around the room hung a series of framed photographs, posed shots of self-assured looking youngsters that Frank assumed to be some of the agency's past clients, if that's how they should be described.

'Welcome to The Oxbridge Agency Inspector. I do hope we can be of assistance to you.' Her tone was smooth and measured but Frank couldn't help notice the wary look.

'Aye, I hope so too. By the way, this is Yvonne Sharp. She's with us for a few weeks on an internship. Trying to decide whether to be a cop or a robber. I mean lawyer.'

'Well, I know which I would choose Yvonne,' Fitzwilliam said pleasantly. 'But I think I'll let you make up your own mind on that.'

'Aye, that's probably a good idea,' Frank said. 'But anyway, I mentioned on the phone the reason we're here.'

'You did. Very sad and completely devastating for the agency as you can imagine. But I'm not sure I understand why the police have to be involved after all this time.'

*After all this time.* It had only been a few months since Chardonnay Clark had died. He could just about understand her desire to put it all behind her, but surely that was a bit premature. But soon she would find out that this investigation was not going away any time soon.

'Her parents are really shattered as you can imagine. Nice people. Don't you think you've let them down?'

Her expression hardened. 'I really feel for them of course, but I can assure you we bear no responsibility for what happened to either of these young people. However, be in no doubt that the welfare of our interns is and always had been our greatest concern.' It sounded exactly like the corporate speak it was.

Frank smiled. 'Aye, well that's good to hear. But anyway, let me give you a bit of background. I work for Department 12B, a wee backwater of the Met. They shove us tiddly cases that might turn into bigger cases. You know, where there are suspicions but no real evidence, stuff like that. And you've got to admit when two kids who are working for the same intern agency decide to commit suicide within a few months of one another, some people might see that as suspicious.'

Fitzwilliam shook her head. 'Of course, it was a terrible tragedy and a traumatic period for us, but we looked carefully at all our processes and procedures and it was quite clear that we were not to blame in any way. Care and concern for our people is at the heart of our HR operation, and I can assure you that if we had known that these young people were at risk in any way then naturally we would have stepped in.'

And that of course was the heart of the whole affair, because neither of these youngsters had given the slightest hint that they had been intending to take their own lives. Except for the after-the-fact virtual suicide notes, which in a blinding flash of clarity, Frank recognised for what they were. Almost certainly fake. Must be. Perhaps, or even probably, this agency had nothing to do with any of it, but he needed to know more before he could be sure.

'So maybe you can tell me how the agency works. How you select your interns, that kind of thing. And how you make your money.'

She seemed to relax, happy to be able to leave the uncomfortable subject matter behind.

'Our business thrives because there is great competition for entry-level places with the top-end organisations. I set up the business to service this demand.'

'Aye, and I see you've got some amazing customers. HBB Bank, Superfare Supermarkets, Alexia Life. Big names.'

She smiled. 'Yes, they are indeed big names, amongst the biggest. But you misunderstand our business model Inspector. These organisations are not our customers. They are our suppliers. They supply the intern opportunities that our young people crave. No, our customers are our young graduates, or to be more accurate, their parents.'

Yvonne gave him a knowing look. 'You see sir, it's all about money. All these rich mummies and daddies paying a fortune to buy their precious little darlings onto the first rung of the ladder.'

Frank raised an eyebrow. 'Is Yvonne right Miss Fitzwilliam. Is that how it works?'

She smiled. 'It's *Mrs*. And yes, that's how it works, and why should I deny it, I'm proud of our business. We simply satisfy a demand like any other.'

'And how much are we talking, money-wise?' Frank asked. 'To get on this ladder?'

Yvonne leapt in before she could answer. 'They charge about twenty-five grand sir. Now you can see why I didn't get a place.'

He grimaced. 'Bloody hell, that's steep. And how much do you pay the organisations - sorry, your suppliers - to take one of your interns?'

Fitzwilliam gave him a cold look. 'That's company confidential.'

'But not as much as twenty-five grand I assume.'

'It's a win-win for all parties,' she said smoothly. 'No-one complains about our fees. As I said, we are simply satisfying a demand that exists. If we didn't do it, someone else would.'

Which was no doubt true, he could see that. If you were the sort of parent who had paid a few hundred grand to send your kid to private schools for ten years or more, and then stumped up thousands more to get them through university, another twenty-five grand was probably neither here nor there. And as for The Oxbridge Agency, even if they had to slip their supplier organisations ten grand to take one of their interns, there was still a very tidy profit being made. Nice work if you could get it. But the thing was, the two kids who had died had been in a completely different boat. *Socio-economic class C3.* They didn't have parents who could afford twenty-five thousand quid.

'Aye, I don't doubt there's a big demand,' Frank said, 'but what about the two kids we're interested in? They weren't from well-off backgrounds, were they?'

Fitzwilliam smiled. 'No they weren't, and that's why they came in on our scholarship programme.'

Frank looked puzzled. 'So what's that all about?'

'Look, we recognise the privileged position that most of our interns are in. It's a simple fact of life and we can't change it. But what we can do is give a helping hand to talented young people from less favoured backgrounds. So each year, we fund a small handful of scholarship places, selected solely on merit. Naturally, they don't have to pay the fee and we also provide them with a nominal salary whilst they are on deployment.'

Frank raised an eyebrow. 'So that's a lot different from your normal business model. Must cost you a bit of money.'

Her reply sounded rehearsed. 'We like to give something back. It's a fundamental part of our corporate ethos. Luke Brown was the perfect case in point. A boy from a very deprived background. It was our privilege and pleasure to help him.'

'Tell me about him,' Frank said, smiling. 'And without the corporate bull if you don't mind. No offence.'

She gave him a hard look but made no reference to his barb. 'He was brought up in care from the age of eleven. His father abandoned the family and his mother had a breakdown and drunk herself to death. With nothing but absolute determination to better himself, Luke overcame all obstacles to win a place at Oxford. Of all our scholarship beneficiaries, he is possibly the one I'm proudest of. But then we are proud of everyone who has benefited from the scheme. You can find everything about it on our website, and we also have a glossy brochure I can let you have.'

'Aye that would be great,' he said.

'Actually sir, I've got it here,' Yvonne said, showing him her phone. *'All about the Oxbridge Scholarship.* Is this it Mrs Fitzwilliam?'

'Yes that's it,' she said, her tone betraying suspicion.

Frank took the phone from her. The slick website was stuffed with more corporate speak about levelling playing fields and rewarding exceptional talent and providing opportunities for everyone, regardless of background. All very dull and worthy and no doubt excellent for the agency's image. But that wasn't what caught his eye.

'Pardon me for asking, but is it a model agency you're running here?'

She gave him a sharp look. 'What do you mean?'

'Well it's just all these guys and girls. I'm no expert, but they're all bloody good-looking aren't they? What's that all about?'

She smiled. 'You may not like it Inspector, but it is one of life's truisms that attractive people generally do better in life. We all have to use the talents we are given, and one's looks are no different. And so yes, it is a factor when we decide to whom we award our scholarships. We are looking for young people who will make an immediate impression.' Was he imagining it, or did her look say *and so you'd have no chance of getting one pal?* Probably. And it almost certainly explained why they hadn't taken on Yvonne Sharp. She was a lovely girl, but there was no getting away from the fact that she was of plain appearance. Their loss, the Met's gain as far as he was concerned.

'Aye, but the thing is Miss Fitzwilliam...'

'It's Mrs..'

'Aye, sorry I forgot, but the thing is, the two young people in question, Chardonnay and Luke, they haven't ended up doing better in life, have they? Why do you think that was?'

He could see her expression harden. 'I hope you are not implying it had anything to do with the agency. Because that would be a very serious accusation.'

'I'm not accusing you or the agency of anything. But so far your agency is the only connection we have between them, so it's my job to look into it.' *Whether you like it or not, Mrs. la-di-dah Fitzwilliam.*

Out of the blue Yvonne said, 'Would it be ok if I asked a question sir? Sorry if it's one you were going to ask yourself.'

He nodded. 'No, go ahead.' He noticed Fitzwilliam glancing at her watch. 'And don't worry, we'll not be taking up much more of your time. On you go Yvonne.'

'Thank you sir. My question is, how you decide which intern goes where? So for example, how did Chardonnay end up at HBB Bank and how did Luke go to Alexia Life?'

Fitzwilliam's eyes narrowed. 'That's an interesting question. So we find out the sectors that our young people are interested in and see if we can find a match with our suppliers. I can only assume Chardonnay must have been attracted to HBB because she was interested in a career in banking or finance. Similarly with Luke Brown too. But of course, I personally am not involved in arranging assignments. We have a team who are responsible for that. Our account managers.'

'Aye, that makes sense,' Frank said. 'And once they're assigned, I presume you get some feedback on how they're doing?'

She nodded. 'Yes, of course. Our account managers will speak with the organisations once a month, to find out how they are progressing. And they speak with the interns too of course.'

'And there weren't any concerns raised about any of these two kids?' Frank asked. 'Nothing that might give any hint about what they were planning to do to themselves?'

She spat out the reply. 'No of course not.'

'But Luke Brown was sacked wasn't he? Just two days before supposedly taking his own life. What did you do when you found out about that?'

She hesitated before answering. 'Well the truth is I didn't do anything about it because it was not something that was brought to my personal attention at the time, and there was no reason why it should have been. As I said, the day to day supervision of the intern cohort is in the hands of the account management team.' The tone was confident, but there was just something in her voice that gave it away. Frank knew she was lying.

'But after he died, you would have looked into it then, surely?'

'Yes, I did ask some questions, of course. But there was no big drama as far as I could see. Occasionally these assignments don't work out, and this was just one of these occasions. I think in fact it coincided with some organisational reviews in the business and they did not have an ongoing need for him.' She fidgeted with her necklace, her discomfort plain to see. Frank smiled to himself. So his hunch had been right. There was something going on here. Time to apply the screw. By letting her stew for a week or so.

He glanced at Yvonne and winked. 'Aye well, we'll leave that for now.' Getting to his feet, he continued, 'So you've been very helpful Mrs Fitzwilliam, very helpful. There's quite a bit more we need to go through with you but that will have to wait until the next time. I'll give you a call in advance, just to let you know the stuff we'll want to see. Probably a full list of all your scholarship kids over the last five years, a list of all your supplier organisations with contact details, interview records, stuff like that.'

Fitzwilliam looked as if she was about to protest, but evidently thought better of it. 'Well, if it's really necessary Inspector?'

He smiled back at her. 'Oh aye. It really is necessary Mrs Fitzwilliam. Anyway, we'll give it a good think through and let you know. But thanks for all your help. We'll love you and leave you now.'

Twenty minutes later they were back on the M40 heading south, Yvonne still flushed with excitement after her first face-to-face interview, Frank finally relaxed after battling through the nightmare Oxford traffic.

'So how's the decision going?' Frank asked, grinning. 'Cop or robber?'

'No contest sir. Cop of course. I loved that today.'

'Good stuff. So what did you make of it all?'

'She was lying sir. No doubt about it.'

'Aye, I got that feeling too.'

She gave him a serious look. 'It was more than a feeling for me sir. You see, when I had my interview with them, they made it very plain that you didn't get any choice as to where you were assigned. You had to agree to be totally flexible and go anywhere they told you. That was something they stressed very much.'

'So all that stuff about consulting with the kids...'

'...was a lie sir. Definitely.'

So that was it, no doubts at all. Sophie Fitzwilliam was lying. Which naturally got him wondering why she would do that.

# Chapter 11

They'd never really had a cross word in the year or so they had worked together. Until today, the relationship had been easy and relaxed, like a comfortable pair of old slippers. Or like she imagined a good marriage would be, although she had never experienced that herself during her eight miserable years with Phillip. Today however was different. Jimmy Stewart wasn't happy and he wasn't taking any trouble to hide his feelings, pacing around their little Fleet Street office wearing a thunderous expression.

'Absolutely no way Maggie, absolutely no way. That's not what ah signed up for and I'm no' doing it.' She just loved the way his Glasgow accent broadened when he was agitated. It made her laugh, which was probably not the ideal way to handle the somewhat delicate matter.

'I know it's a lot to ask,' she said, trying her best to be serious, 'but I couldn't think of any other way to get you in there. Unless you can come up with a better idea yourself of course.' She knew he wouldn't be able to, but there was no harm in asking.

'Well no, but I don't see why I need to be *in* there at all,' he said, his voice betraying defeat. 'Can't you handle this yourself?'

She shook her head. 'It's hard enough for me to pretend to be interested in modern art. You've no idea how many hours I've had to spend on line trying to get at least a semblance of knowledge. And we did agree that we need to find out how faithful Miss Brückner is or is likely to be, didn't we? As a key part of our investigation.'

'Aye, we did but...'

'Yes, so unless she is gay, which I think is unlikely, I don't think there's much I can do to help in that department. Not that she would be likely to fancy an old woman like me.'

'She fancies an old man like Morgan.'

'Oh yeah, like what first attracted you to the multi-millionaire Hugo Morgan?'

He gave a wry smile. 'Aye, point taken. But what about that guy you're seeing? The gallery owner. If she's so beautiful, it's odds-on he's tried it on with her in the past. Couldn't you just ask him?'

She looked at him, open-mouthed. 'You mean Robert?' She didn't expect it to come out the way it did, a hint of familiarity that suggested Robert Trelawney was already part of her life. Correction, her *fake* life. 'I don't see how I could do that without blowing my cover.'

'Well maybe *I* could. You know, get a bit matey with him, a bit of laddish banter. We could even compare notes about you. Or here's a better one. Maybe I could threaten to beat the crap out of him for making a pass at my girl. Aye, that would be better.' Too late, he realised what he'd done.

She laughed. 'Excellent, excellent, so you *will* come with me to the gallery. Now obviously you can't use your own name. We don't want anybody googling Jimmy Stewart and your bloody Hampstead Hero story popping up all over the place. James we can use, that's fine, but you need to come up with a new surname.'

'McDuff.'

'What?'

'McDuff. It just came to me. He was my old RSM. Ally McDuff. He was from Forres in the Highlands. A great lad.'

'Fine, James McDuff it is. So the back story is you've recently left the army and haven't quite worked out what to do next.'

'So far, so true.'

'We met quite by chance in a bar, resulting in fireworks. Lust at first sight, at least on my part. Now I can't keep my hands off you.'

'And yet you agreed to go out with Mr gallery guy. How's that supposed to fit in?'

'All part of the narrative. The wronged widow going a bit crazy, grabbing everything that's out there, and bugger the consequences.'

He shook his head. 'Bloody hell Maggie, you've got this all worked out haven't you?'

She laughed. 'Not all my own work I'm afraid. I nicked it from the plot of a trashy novel I've been reading. It's every older woman's fantasy, according to these books anyway. The hunky young stud insatiably satisfying her every desire, twenty-four by seven. Sheer animal passion.' To her surprise, his face began to redden. 'But it's not mine, honestly. Not my fantasy, I mean. And anyway, in the book, the heroine chooses love and money over lust, and you - I mean the young hunk -gets dumped. Sorry mate.'

Now he was laughing too. 'Well that's a relief. No, I didn't mean that the way it sounded, honestly, you're looking very lovely at the moment and it would be an honour to play your toy-boy.'

The compliment took her by surprise. 'Harriet Ibbotson, Hugo Morgan's intern. She's the one to thank. And spending eight hundred pounds on an outfit and two hundred pounds on my hair.' She was thrilled that he had noticed. It had been money well spent.

Jimmy smiled. 'Aye, but just remember, you owe me big time. Silent and broody, is that what you want?'

'Silent and shifty actually. I want your eyes all over Lotti when I'm not looking and I want her to notice. Think you can do that?'

'Suppose so,' he said, uncertainly. They decided to take a black cab, on the twin grounds that Morgan was generous with the expenses and more importantly, she didn't want to walk any further than was strictly necessary in these heels. Now she just had to remember her homework. First there was Andre Dehrain, the French painter she found on Google. He had, this apparently a well-known fact amongst art lovers, painted Big Ben and other London riverside scenes, in what she took to be an impressionistic style, although she didn't actually know what that meant. She genuinely loved some of his portrait work too, particularly one he'd done in 1923, *Portrait de Madame Francis Carco*. An astonishingly attractive young woman, perfectly captured by the artist, her brooding sexuality bursting from the canvas. There was Paul Nash of course, and that picture she had seen in her earlier visit. Then LS Lowry, perhaps the most famous of the British artists. She knew that it was rare for any of his original works to come on the market and when they did, they fetched an eye-watering price, but that didn't matter. Hopefully their little project would be concluded before any money had to change hands. But then again, it would be Hugo Morgan's money she would be spending if it went that far, and since the purchases would be those recommended by his fiancé-to-be, he would hardly be in a position to complain.

Lotti was waiting at the door when they arrived, dressed in similar style as before in grey tailored trousers and a white tee. And, Maggie noted with envy, a pair of glittery ballet flats. Today her hair was tied up and she was wearing more make-up than before, a subtle salmon-pink foundation and heavy mascara ringing her eyes. Still very attractive, but at first glance she looked older. Maggie couldn't help wondering if that was by design. But then she looked closer at her eyes. Revealing, she was convinced, the crystal clarity and sparkle of youth. Just like Chardonnay Clarke and Luke Brown.

If she was surprised to see this woman who'd had dinner with her boss accompanied by a man, she didn't show it. 'It is very lovely to see you again,' she said. 'I am very much looking forward to it. We are able to use Robert's office today, he's at Christies with another client. There's a Matisse as the star lot and it of course has attracted much international interest. Our client hopes he will be successful but it will be very difficult I think.' Through all of this, she hadn't looked at Jimmy once. A good sign perhaps, but suddenly it opened up a possibility that Maggie hadn't previously considered. What if Miss Brückner was not actually attracted to men? It was a possibility, however unlikely, that couldn't be ruled out, and *that* was something Hugo Morgan would definitely want to know about.

She led them upstairs and along a passageway to the back of the building where Robert Trelawney had his office. Like the rest of his gallery, the room was simply but tastefully decorated, one wall lined with limed oak bookshelves holding neatly arranged volumes that Maggie took to be works of reference. There was no desk, but in one corner was a large circular table in matching limed oak, surrounded by half a dozen chairs. On top of the desk lay a number of auction catalogues, page clips inserted to bookmark particular points of interest.

'I've been doing some preparation, just to see what's on the market at the moment that might be of interest. We have two or three works ourselves that might be good for you. Please, take a seat.'

Maggie smiled as she sat down. 'That sounds great Lotti. But can I introduce you to my friend James. He's interested in twentieth century art too. Aren't you darling? So I thought I would bring him along, I hope you don't mind.'

He gave a half-smile and mumbled something inaudible in their direction. Lotti returned a polite smile but nothing more. This was something Maggie hadn't seen before, a woman who seemed totally immune to the charms of Jimmy Stewart. She was either super-professional or maybe she really was besottedly in love with Hugo Morgan to the exclusion of all others. If that truly was the case, this investigation would be over before it had even started.

'We didn't really discuss budget, did we Maggie?' Lotti was saying as she thumbed through one of the catalogues, 'but I've assumed around a hundred and fifty to two hundred thousand would be a reasonable sum to get you started. We can assemble a very nice portfolio for that. And quite by chance there are some exceptional works on the market at the moment.'

'Two hundred sounds great,' Maggie said, smiling. 'What do you think James?'

'Aye, sound,' he said. 'It's your money, although if it was me I'd buy a Ferrari.' She saw him sneak a glance at Lotti and shoot her a crooked smile. And for a split second the young girl held his gaze, a flicker of reaction in her eyes, then with a definite movement, looked away.

'Don't worry darling James,' Maggie said, squeezing his arm and kissing his cheek. 'You shall have your Ferrari.'

'Sound,' he said again.

Lotti wore the faintest smile as she waited patiently for this little love scene to conclude, before continuing. 'So the French were very prominent in the art of the period so I have a number of examples of their work. Also the later Flemish school was very popular.'

Maggie nodded. 'I came across Andre Dehrain in my googling. I like his work very much.'

'I agree, a fine artist, and popular too. Although he was a controversial figure in France. I do not know if that concerns you?'

'What do you mean?'

'You see, he was regarded as a collaborator during the war and afterwards his works were devalued as a result because many collectors shunned his paintings. Although that is not so much of an issue today. But you may also wish to consider Piet Mondrian. He was Dutch, and very much the pioneer of the abstract style in twentieth century art. His works do come on the market occasionally and are very sought after. There is also Carles Casagemas, a Catalan and a great friend of Pablo Picasso. There is a very pretty landscape of his going under the hammer in a few days' time which we may be able to secure for you. To be honest, he was not the greatest of artists but because of his friendship with Picasso and his extraordinary life story, he is prized by many collectors.'

'Extraordinary? How do you mean?'

'He fell crazily in love with a beautiful model, but then suffered terrible depression because he was unable to consummate the relationship. *Impotenz*. The German word, it is almost the same.'

Jimmy chuckled. 'Could'nae get it up eh? That's awful for a chap, so it is.' He gave Lotti a look that so clearly signalled *but that wouldn't be a problem for me*. Maggie chuckled to herself. It was nice to see him embracing the role, even although she doubted his exaggerated Glaswegian would be understood.

Lotti seemed unable to decide if he was trying to be funny or not. 'Yes, I suppose it is. For him, it was obviously important, because he then committed suicide in a crazy fashion.'

'This is fascinating,' Maggie said, truthfully, 'please, tell me more.'

Lotti nodded. 'So he invited the model, who was called Germaine Gargallo, and a few friends to dinner at the Hippodrome Cafe in Paris, where he proposed to her. When she turned him down, he drew a pistol and tried to shoot her but missed. He then turned the gun on himself and put a bullet through his head. As a result, he died of course. He was just twenty-one years of age at the time.'

'Good lord, that's awful,' Maggie said. 'Just twenty-one?'

'Yes,' Lotti said, 'and he was quite remarkably beautiful too. Picasso painted many portraits of him, including one of him lying in his coffin, which is perhaps the most famous of them. Of course, I don't think we could afford *that* work even if it ever came up for sale. Right now it is in the Musée Picasso in Paris and I doubt if they plan to sell it.'

To her surprise, Maggie found herself being absorbed into this world, transported by the infectious enthusiasm of Lotti Brückner. Which made her revise her opinion of the young woman, because although she might look as if she should still be wearing school uniform, she obviously knew what she was talking about.

'What I find interesting Lotti is how you came to learn so much about this subject,' Maggie said. 'Because I guess it's a huge field.' And then it was revealed.

'It's my family business Magdalene. My great-grandfather started a gallery almost one hundred years ago and now it is run by my mum and dad. *Gallerei Brückner*.'

'In Zurich?'

'Yes, we have a small one there, but our main gallery is in St Moritz. The town gets many rich visitors and they are often very interested in art. So it has been a very nice business for us through the years.'

'St Moritz sounds like a place,' Jimmy said. 'So how come you ended up in smelly old London?'

She smiled. 'Perhaps one day I will take over the family business, but I wanted to have more experiences in my life before then. And of course London is a very big market in the art world.' To Maggie, it all sounded so terribly plausible, which made it all the more likely that it was true. So far there was nothing about Lotti Brückner that might cause any concern to Hugo Morgan. Except, curiously, she still hadn't mentioned him at all. A fact that Jimmy had obviously noticed.

'Aye, and you'll probably meet someone, a lovely-looking girl like you. In fact I expect you've already got a boyfriend.' Once more he shot her the crooked smile, and once more, she studiously ignored it.

'Yes, there is someone,' she said, demurely. 'He's very nice. But I'm sure you're not interested in my rather dull private life. Come, let's have a look at some of the paintings I have bookmarked for you.' The message was polite but clear. *Subject closed*. Maggie decided it would be prudent to park that line of enquiry for a while. Instead she said,

'It must be lovely to come from a nice family like yours Lotti. My mum and dad divorced in 1991 and it affected me rather badly. It was a year I'll never forget. I was just twelve years old.'

She seemed uncertain how to react. 'Yes...yes, I am very lucky. I know that.'

Maggie smiled to herself before quickly changed the subject. *So it looked like her assumption might be correct after all.*

'Sorry, sorry, too much information again. Yes, let's look at what you've found for me.'

Then for the next hour she was immersed in the fascinating world of twentieth-century European art, guided by a young woman whose expertise seemed unchallengeable. Lotti had put together a shortlist of around twenty paintings, some rather affordable, some with auction estimates running well into six figures. When all of this was over, Maggie could imagine her real self buying one or two of the more modestly-priced items to decorate the walls of her little Hampstead study. She chuckled inwardly when she thought of what her Ollie's reaction would be to that. *Ugh*, his go-to word of disapproval. To him, just eight years old, the only pictures that should be stuck on a wall were of cars, the faster and more exotic the better.

At the end of the hour, they had narrowed the selection down to five or six items that which they would definitely try to acquire. Her favourite on the list was a work by Casagemas, the subject a Spanish townscape which she thought was painted rather in the style of Lowry. To her surprise, Lotti agreed with her.

'Yes, I think they do have much similarity. Neither was what you would call a great technical artist...'

'You mean they couldn't really draw,' Jimmy said.

'Perhaps you could say that,' Lotti said, smiling, 'but of course Carles Casagemas was very young and was still learning. And they were both very good at capturing the atmosphere of a scene and bringing it to life. That is a very important talent that many more technically gifted artists do not possess.'

She closed her notebook and stood up. 'So, good progress I think Magdalene? And I must ask, have you been to an art auction before?'

'Never.'

'Well I think you will find it very interesting. The little Casagemas is under the hammer at Sotheby's next Tuesday and you really must come along. The guide is only eighteen thousand pounds which I think is an amazing opportunity for you. Especially since you like the painting so much.'

Maggie nodded. 'Yes, I'll look forward to that, it's very exciting. And I must say, you have been *so* helpful, I really do feel I'm in good hands.' And it was true. Lotti Brückner had an authority about her that could not be easily faked. As far as that part of her back-story was concerned, Hugo Morgan had nothing to be worried about.

But there was something he should be *very* worried about. 1991 was a big year, the year of the traumatic fake divorce of the non-existent Magdalene Slattery's non-existent parents. And also, if Lotti Brückner was really thirty years old, the year of her birth. And yet she had said nothing. No reaction. Nil. Suspicious, because in Maggie's experience, whenever your birth year was mentioned in conversation, you just couldn't help yourself. You would smile modestly and say *that was the year I was born*. Everyone did it, as if it was a programmed reaction. Lotti hadn't. So she had *definitely* lied to Morgan about her age.

Then to her surprise, she noticed Jimmy take out a cheap ballpoint from an inner pocket of his jacket and reach across for one of the catalogues. She wasn't wearing her reading glasses, but by squinting hard she could just about make out what he had scribbled in a corner of the cover, before, with a knowing smile, he slid it across the table to Lotti.

*James McDuff 07461 095712*

# Chapter 12

It was an incongruous setting for a meeting with a billionaire, but the fact that she could have given him an update on the Lotti investigation in a five-minute phone call was neither here nor there. He was the customer, and if he wanted a face-to-face meeting in a fast-food restaurant, then so be it. It was early for lunch, just quarter to twelve, and the place was only half-full when she arrived. Hugo Morgan was already there, seated in a quiet corner opposite a young girl in school uniform who could only be his youngest daughter Jasmine. Two tables away, Maggie recognised Vinny the security guy who had been at the Brasenose Trust quarterly update, dressed casually in an ill-fitting track suit and Chelsea FC beanie hat, clearly trying but failing to merge into the background. She shouldn't have been surprised. A rich and prominent financier needed to be very careful when he ventured out in public, especially with the events of the last couple of days. First the graffiti on the wall of his Kensington mansion, then the threatening letters in the post, the crude messages formed from words snipped from newspapers, like something from a nineteen-forties movie. *Actions have Consequences. Justice for Greenway.* As she approached him, she noticed he had one in front of him now, studying it closely as if that would yield a clue to its origin.

'Hello Hugo,' she said, glancing at the sheet as she took the seat opposite him. 'I've heard.'

He smiled. 'Yes, pathetic isn't it? I mean, Justice for Greenway, what a joke. They should have been sending all this stuff to bloody Belinda Milner. It was her that screwed these shareholders, not me.'

Maggie looked at him, momentarily dumbstruck. Bloody Belinda Milner, dismissed so callously by this man, had killed herself leaving a husband and teenage daughter. But the fact didn't seem to concern him in the least.

'Yeah, she was totally useless,' he continued. 'Anyway, this is my youngest daughter Jasmine. We call her Yazz.'

She gave Maggie a shy smile. 'Hi.'

'Hi Yazz, nice to meet you,' Maggie said. 'Gosh, is that a double cheeseburger? I haven't had one of these for ages, but you've helped me make up my mind. That's what I'm going to have too.'

'We don't do this too often,' Morgan said apologetically, 'but we've been at the dentist this morning getting measured up for a brace so we decided a little treat was called for. Although as you can see we've opted for water rather than anything teeth-rotting. And Yazz is as thin as a pencil so it won't do her any harm, will it darling?'

'No dad,' she said through a mouthful of fries.

This was a side of Hugo Morgan Maggie hadn't seen before. He was much more relaxed in the company of his youngest, shorn of the thrusting action-man demeanour that was his normal accompaniment, and the girl was perfectly delightful and clearly adored by her father. But then she remembered the discarded Felicity Morgan, shut out from these precious family moments simply for getting too old. Yes, maybe her initial impression was right after all. It was best not to get taken in by all this happy families stuff. And it was a bit strange that he was here for an update on the Lotti matter in the company of one of his kids. But then she learned Morgan's tame gorilla wasn't just there to protect his boss. He was the baby-sitter too.

'Yazz, go and sit with Vinny, will you darling?'

'Can I get a coke please?'

He smiled. 'Yes, well I'm sure if you ask him nicely he might get you one.' Obediently, she picked up her burger carton and slid off to Vinny's table.

'What a lovely girl' Maggie said. 'You must be very proud of her.'

'I am of course. She's lovely. Both of them are. I'm very lucky. Are you eating by the way? If you are I'll get Vinny to sort it.'

She tapped her phone. 'I've got the app. My son Ollie loves them. I know I shouldn't indulge him, but as you say, an occasional treat doesn't do any harm.' She gave a guilty shrug which he acknowledged with a wry smile.

'Anyway, how have you got on? With Lotti.'

'Yes, well I've made contact. Twice in fact, and undercover of course. I'm now Mrs Magdalene Slattery, a rich Hampstead widow. It's all going pretty well I think.'

He looked at her sharply. 'Especially with Robert Trelawney?'

She blushed. 'How did you know about that?'

'Lotti's told me all about her new client. About you.'

Now she was beginning to realise what she had known from the start, that accepting Robert's invite had been a mistake, adding an unnecessary complication to affairs. But it probably wasn't going to be a smart move to admit that right now.

'I thought it might help me with the investigation, find out what he knows about her. After all, he would have presumably checked her credentials before taking her on.' Said out loud, it sounded perfectly plausible. 'I do feel a little bad about deceiving him, but it's part of the job I'm afraid.'

Her explanation seemed to have convinced him. He shrugged then said, 'Yeah, I guess so. So, what about Lotti?'

Maggie smiled, happy to leave the little awkwardness behind. 'Yes, well, so far, so good I think. She certainly is very knowledgeable about her subject, I've no doubt about that. And so far she has been very discreet about her private life. She has told me she is with someone - that's you of course- but that is all she's revealed. As I say, very discreet and professional.'

She wondered if Lotti had mentioned Jimmy to her fiancé. No particular reason why she should perhaps, but given that she had told Morgan about the Trelawney date, she might be expected to mention that her new client Magdalene Slattery seemed to already have a boyfriend. That would be the type of tittle-tattle that a couple might find amusing. But he didn't bring it up.

'Well that's all very reassuring,' Morgan said. 'So what happens next?'

Maggie had anticipated the question and was able to answer it half-truthfully. 'Well Lotti has arranged for me to go to Sotheby's to look at a Casagemas...'

He gave her an amused look. 'A what...?'

'He's a Catalan artist,' she said, laughing. 'And no, I'd never heard of him either. But maybe you should look him up Hugo, because I think you may end up owning one of his paintings soon. But yes, Lotti and I are going to the auction together and it will give me the chance to get to know her better.'

The other thing that would happen next, and which in actual fact was happening at that very moment, was a deep dive into Lotti Brückner's back-story. The family history, the galleries in Switzerland, that should be relatively easy to verify, as would be her academic record. If she really was a graduate of Germany's prestigious Heidelberg University, then there would be records, and naturally the year of her graduation, if she had earned a degree at the institution, would give a pretty reliable clue to her real age. Neither she nor Jimmy spoke German, but Elsa, the super-smart Czech girl who administered their shared Fleet Street office did, and she would run through a burning ring of fire for her adored Jimmy Stewart. Maggie had left them scouring the internet for contact phone numbers and she wouldn't be the least surprised if they had progress to report when she got back. But she wasn't planning to share any of this with Hugo Morgan right now.

'Yes, so I think a couple of more meetings and I should have all the information I need. But it all looks perfectly ok at the moment.' Except for that thing about her age. They needed to get to the bottom of that and she intended to keep that doubt to herself until she had some evidence that either confirmed or demolished her suspicions.

Morgan nodded. 'Well that's great Maggie, I'm relieved. But actually, that's not the only reason I wanted to meet with you.'

She couldn't hide her surprise. 'Excuse me?'

He slid the cut-and-paste letter across the table. 'These guys. I want you to find out who's doing this. Find out who's behind it all.' Now she understood why he wanted to meet in person. This wasn't something you could do over the phone.

'Hugo, this isn't really our line of work...'

'Why not?' he said. 'You're investigators, aren't you?'

'Yes, but... isn't this a matter for the police?'

'I've tried them and they don't want to know. *No crime has been committed sir. Just some cranks sir, ignore them and they'll go away.* That's all they had to say. Bloody useless. So come on. Will you do it, or do I need to find someone else?'

She was acutely aware of what happened the last time she'd given an impulsive answer to an unexpected question. But this time she had a Plan B. So in for a penny, in for a pound. That was another of her dad's favourites. But she tried her best to sound reluctant.

'Ok Hugo, we'll take a look for you. But please understand, I'm not promising anything, and obviously if anything serious happens, you'll have to get the police involved.' That was the stock answer, but she already knew a policeman who might well be interested in Hugo Morgan and his little Justice for Greenway problem. *Plan B*. What was it he said his department did? *Cases that weren't really cases but might become cases*, something like that. The only problem was, she wasn't sure if Frank was still speaking to her. How could she have known he was going to ask her then, of all times? First he went bright red, then he clammed up, then with barely a word to either of them, he'd made some stupid excuse before rushing out of the bar. What a fool she had been, blurting it out without thinking. *I'm sorry, I've got a date with another guy.* No wonder he'd reacted the way he did, and now God knows when or even if they would get another chance.

Morgan nodded. 'Yeah understood. But I'd like to avoid that if at all possible. It's not great for business. It spooks the investors and we've got a lot of money to spend on that damn mine if we've any hope of turning it around.'

'Well obviously we'll try,' she said. 'But really Hugo, this isn't something we've done before.' That was true, and what was also true was that she didn't have the faintest clue where to start. But she realised she was already intrigued by the case, and she was pretty sure that if she and Jimmy brainstormed it for half an hour or so, some plan of action, however half-baked, would probably emerge. Somewhere to start at least, which was all they needed.

'Expenses are no object of course,' he was saying, 'because I expect you'll have to go up there and dig around a bit. Quite a nice part of the country.'

She smiled. 'Yes, I love the Lakes. We went there a lot when I was a child.'

Yazz and Vinny the security guy had appeared alongside them with her order, which they had collected from the counter. This time it was Yazz who was wearing the Chelsea beanie hat, pulled down so that it almost covered her eyes. 'Double cheeseburger with large fries and a large Diet Coke,' he announced in a comically formal tone. 'And a large regular Coke for the little lady.'

Yazz gave her father a fond smile. 'Is that all right daddy? Vinny said you wouldn't mind, not this once.'

He laughed. 'Sure darling, but you'll have to brush your teeth twice as much tonight before bed. And don't forget to give Vinny his hat back. It's his most treasured possession.'

'He's fond of her, isn't he?' Maggie said after they had gone back to their table.

'Yeah, versatile guy. He'll do anything for us. He's officially my driver, but he can handle himself, so, yeah, he comes in very useful.'

She'd witnessed his usefulness first hand at the Brasenose event when that journalist was intent in causing trouble. Officially, he might be his driver but she had little doubt where his real value to Morgan lay. The menacing hard-man, the skills honed on match days in the quiet streets around Stamford Bridge. After a few pints at the Red Lion, there would be a bit of a rumpus with the away supporters, then onto the match itself, a few more beers at the ground warming them up for the monkey chants and profanities they enjoyed hurling at their opponent's black players. Yes, a handy guy to have around when there was trouble, no doubt.

But then a thought came to her. That journalist from the Chronicle, whatever his name was. If anyone knew who was behind this Justice for Greenway stuff, it would be him. It shouldn't be too hard to track him down and she knew he would definitely agree to speak to them as soon as she mentioned she was working for Hugo Morgan. Brilliant. Now she had a plan and couldn't wait to get started.

'Hugo, if you don't mind, I'm just going to take my lunch with me and head back to the office. You've just doubled our case load so we don't have time to hang about. And Jimmy's been doing some more work on Lotti's background. I'm keen to find out how he's got on.'

He gave a broad smile as he stood up, extending a hand. 'Yeah, by all means Maggie. I'm paying you by the hour so I don't want you swanning around on lunch dates on my tab. So off you go then. Quicker you get started the better, and let me know as soon as you find out anything interesting.'

That wasn't going to take long.

***

She got back to the office to find Jimmy and Elsa half way through their own takeaway meal, his desk littered with half a tree's worth of so-called eco packaging, which caused just as much litter and landfill as the old polystyrene items. She was sitting on the edge of his desk, leaning over, quite deliberately in Maggie's opinion, so that he could get a view of her neat cleavage, on full display in the deep v-neck of her lambswool sweater, and as usual, they were sharing some private joke. *Minx*. That was the word that always came to mind when she thought of Elsa. Pretty and smart, and no more than twenty-five years old, lust for life radiating from every pore. And a lust for Jimmy Stewart too, although as far as she was aware, a lust unconsummated. He didn't speak about his private life much, although she was pretty sure he wasn't seeing anyone at the moment. What she did know was that he had been hit pretty hard when his relationship with that Swedish country singer had fallen apart. From time to time she caught him looking at her Facebook and Instagram posts. Astrid Sorensen, a real princess and bursting with raw sexuality. Nashville's new biggest thing. The woman who had ruined his marriage, leaving him wallowing in regret.

'Hi guys, I see you're having fun,' Maggie said brightly. 'You know, I was just thinking. We've not really looked at Lotti's social media, have we?'

'There isn't any,' Jimmy said. 'Not that we can find.'

Elsa nodded. 'Yes, that was first place we looked. But nothing.'

'Nothing at all?'

'She's on email and WhatsApp but that's all,' Jimmy said. 'We thought maybe it was because of Hugo.'

'We Google search and found she was on Instagram until few months ago,' Elsa said, 'but her account is deleted now so no information. So we think Hugo says no to social media. That can be only explanation.'

Maggie smiled. 'Well we can easily find out if that's true. I'll ask him. But don't worry about that right now. Have you found anything else?'

'Yeah lots,' Jimmy said. 'Elsa's a wee genius, she should have been an actress.'

She already is, thought Maggie, a wry smile crossing her lips.

'*Zu erste*,' he said. 'That means firstly in German. Elsa's been teaching me. Zu erste, we called the gallery in Zurich.'

'Yes, I call gallery and ask for Lotti. The girl says Abwarten bitte...'

'That means please wait in German,' Jimmy said, raising a hand in apology when he saw the sharp look from Maggie.

'A moment later, another voice who is Frau Brückner. Lotti's mother I think. I say I am Elsa Berger and I was at Heidelberg with Lotti. It is my thirtieth birthday and I want her to come to party but I can't find her because she is not on Facebook...'

'Which is true,' Jimmy said, 'although of course you know that.'

'And she says Heidelberg? Of course, very nice, then tells me Lotti is now working in London.'

Maggie gave a deep sigh. 'Well, that's all very...' Disappointing, that was the word she was searching for. But why should it be? They had been engaged to check out the background of Lotti Brückner, and if she turned out to be exactly who and what she said she was, then that had to be considered a success.

'...satisfactory isn't it?'

'And there's more,' Jimmy said. 'I hope you won't be too disappointed.

'What do you mean?'

He gave Elsa a nod, indicating she should continue.

'So I phone registrar office of Heidelberg University and ask for help. I am HR in big company and Miss L Brückner wants job. Can you confirm she holds degree I ask? She says it is online and I must email for one-time user-code and password. I email and user-code and password comes.'

Maggie laughed. 'I like the way you're telling the story Elsa but I'm desperate to know the ending.'

'But for you, it may not be happy ending,' Elsa said. 'Because to cut long story shorter, we found out that Fraulein L Brückner is graduate of Heidelberg University, with first class honours in Fine Arts with English Language.'

Jimmy gave Maggie a look of disappointment. 'In twenty-eleven. Making her by my calculation, thirty or thirty-one years of age.'

So that was it then. It seemed that in all regards Lotti Brückner was who she said she was. A quick update for the benefit of Hugo Morgan and that investigation could be closed down. At least she would now be able to enjoy the auction, and when she was there she would be sure to ask Lotti the secret of her youthful looks. Then that could be Mrs Magdalene Slattery's final appearance before she mysteriously vanished off the face of the earth. But would she disappear, that was the dilemma? Because after the success of their first date, the lovely dinner which led to coffee at his sleek townhouse and much more besides, Robert Trelawney had asked to see her again.

And she had said yes.

*** 

*They knew of course where he parked the Bentley, in a so-called secure underground garage just off Strafford Street, no more than five minutes walk from his office. So-called secure, because it had only cost fifty quid to persuade the fat Greek guy they'd laughably put in charge of security to look away for as long as they needed. Morgan's Continental GT W12, to give it its full name, had been ordered with all the extras, the 21-inch diamond-cut alloys alone adding three grand to the price, the in-your-face St James Red paint-job another four. Nearly a quarter a million just for a motor-car. It was obscene, especially considering what he'd had done to all these poor bastards up in Cumbria. Now they were looking forward to see his face after what they had planned for his precious wheels. And they would get to see it too, because that was part of the deal with the fat Greek. Make sure you point a CCTV camera in that direction and don't bloody miss it when he turns up.*

Naturally it needed to be done with care, because concentred sulphuric acid was nasty stuff. Firstly they donned gloves, eye-protectors and masks, checking each other to make sure they were properly protected and no flesh was exposed. Then moving slowly and deliberately, they removed the heavy one litre glass bottle from the back-pack and carefully unscrewed the top, making sure to hold it at arm's length. It was only half-full because they didn't want any spills, but that was plenty enough for what they had planned. Starting with the bonnet, they poured a generous measure onto the surface just below the windscreen, allowing gravity to spread the pool of caustic liquid forward and sideways across the gleaming paintwork. Not that it would be gleaming for very long, not once the acid got to work. Already black patches were beginning to appear, the atmosphere turning toxic as fumes rose from the blistering layer of acetate lacquer. Then on the roof, the spread made easy by the sleek fastback styling. That was twenty grand's worth of damage already, not that the money side of it would worry Hugo Morgan. That wasn't the point. It was all about the message. Actions had consequences. If he didn't know that before, he would now. And just in case there was any doubt who was responsible, they had come prepared with a neatly-printed calling card, which they slipped under a windscreen wiper.

*Justice for Greenway*

It was a nice touch to add the pictures of the two daughters to the card. Then he would know that this was just a little aperitif before the serious action started. When people started to die.

# Chapter 13

It had been a while since Frank had been to a snooker hall, at least fifteen years by a quick calculation. That was back in Glasgow, a seedy little dump just off Ballater Street, which formed the northern boundary of the original Gorbals before the whole area was raised to the ground in the sixties. To be replaced by the disturbing fantasies of the celebrated French Modernist Le Corbusier, a nutter if ever there was one. Naturally no-one mourned the passing of the old tenement slums, but it had taken over a hundred years for the area to become an uninhabitable dump, a feat the French architect had achieved in less than twenty. At the time Frank was just beginning his career, posted to Cumberland Street nick. There, Thursday night snooker was a ritual, attended by anyone whose shift allowed it, and plenty more who turned up for a game and a couple of pints when they should have been pounding the beat. He'd been back to the area a couple of times since, and now the Corbusier experiment had been swept away, to be replaced by something more in keeping with the present aspirations of his home city. Neat low-rise social and private housing, unobtrusive commercial development interspersed with dots of green space. It looked so much better, but it was still the same low-lifes who lived there, which is why his old cop shop had been treated to a multi-million pound upgrade, the new building looking more like a mid-market hotel in its subtle pastel blue and grey paint job, with CCTV everywhere and equipped with three times the holding cell capacity of its predecessor. On the corner where Cumberland Street met Jane Place, a statue of a figure stood mounted on a four-metre high stone column, one of a handful that had been erected around the area in the forlorn hope that easy access to *object d'art* would encourage the locals to take a pride in their neighbourhood. This one, for no obvious reason, depicted and was titled *Girl with a Rucksack*. Wags speculated she was there in homage to the area's thriving drugs trade, and that the rucksack must be full of speed, the drug of choice amongst the locals.

The old snooker hall had been swept away too, but the leisure needs of the community were now met by the bingo emporium that had replaced it, the dole money disappearing into the gaudy slot machines, recently equipped with contactless technology to make it easier to take money from people who didn't have it in the first place. So much for progress.

The Romford Snooker Centre was also quite a new development, a faceless tin shed erected on a retail park on the outskirts of the Essex town. Nondescript on the outside, it was perfectly presentable if somewhat bland on the inside. There was a bar with a choice of just two beers, a fizzy bitter and a fizzy lager, and a tiny cafe that served an unappetizing range of over-priced microwaved fast food. But the snooker facilities themselves were top-notch, sixteen tables equipped with ironed-smooth baize and laid out to allow plenty of elbow room for the players.

Back in the day, Frank had been quite good at the game, and he was pleased to discover that he still had it. Ronnie French on the other hand didn't have it, and self-evidently never had, despite his protestations. Unless of course he was setting up Frank for a sting, which he doubted. Frenchie wasn't bright enough to pull a stunt like that.

'Bit rusty Frank my old son,' he was saying as Frank prepared to pot an easy black to win the match. 'Don't get the chance to play much nowadays, what with work and all that.'

Frank shot him a wry smile as he bulleted the ball into the pocket with a confident stroke. 'I'm your guv'nor Frenchie, remember? But I'll try and remember not to overwork you in future. Come on, let me buy you a pint to cheer you up.'

They wandered over to the bar and grabbed a vacant table.

'When's Terry Clarke coming?' Frank asked. 'Shall I get one in for him?'

'Should be here in a few minutes guv. He's a lager man, so yeah, get one in for him.'

That first meeting with the victim's family. You never got used to it, no matter how long you were in the job, and if you did, then you were probably in the wrong line of work. He'd done a few suicides too, and if anything they were worse. With a murder, at least there was someone to blame, somewhere to direct the bitterness and anger. With a suicide, there was the same crushing loss but the only person to blame was yourself. Surely you could have done more to prevent it happening? How could you not have known their state of mind? So in a funny way, maybe the fact that Chardonnay Clarke's death was looking less and less like a suicide might bring some comfort to the family. He hoped so at least.

Clarke appeared just as Frank was swiping his card across the contactless terminal proffered by the teenage barman. Expertly, he picked up the three pints and shuffled back to the table, setting them down without spilling a drop.

'This is Terry guv,' French said, needlessly. 'Terry Clarke. Chardonnay's dad.'

'Pleased to meet you Terry,' Frank said, extending a hand, 'and I'm really sorry for your loss. It must have been awful for you and your family. I'm Frank Stewart. I'm a DI with the Met. Same crew as your mate Frenchie here. Department 12B.'

'You're a Jock, ain't you?' Clarke said. 'We had one of them back in the old Upton Park days. Frankie McAvennie, remember him? Scored a shed load of goals. He was a bit of a lad mind you.'

Frank nodded. 'Aye, I remember him. Blonde streaks. Went to the Celtic for a spell, didn't he? On the front pages nearly as often as he was on the back.'

Clarke gave a half-smile. 'Yeah, you're right there. But a great player, and a Hammer through and through. Still comes to watch us at the new place from time to time. Gets a big welcome.'

But they both knew they weren't there to talk about the football. His voice barely audible, Clarke said,

'So is it a murder enquiry now Frank? 'Cos I know my Chardonnay would never have killed herself. Never in a thousand years.' His eyes, dull and bloodshot after weeks of grief, began to fill up.

'Look Terry, I'm sure Ronnie's told you what we do in our department. We just dig around in things where there's grounds for suspicion. And when I heard the circumstances surrounding your daughter's death, well of course we had to investigate. The way it works is if we dig up enough stuff, you know, solid evidence, then it gets handed over to the murder squad. But no, we're not there yet.' He could see Terry Clarke's shoulders droop with disappointment, but there was no point in raising false hopes.

'But he's the best Terry,' French chipped in, unexpectedly. 'Once the guv'nor gets his teeth into something, he never lets go.'

Frank gave him a surprised look. 'Well cheers for that mate, I didn't know you cared. Look Terry, we think we might have something here and I'll get to the bottom of it if I can. But I need your help, and most of all, I need you to be really honest with me about your daughter. Is that ok?'

'Sure Frank, sure.' That's what he said, but Frank wasn't convinced he meant it.

'She was a special girl, your Chardonnay, wasn't she?' Frank said. 'Brains, beauty, brilliant qualifications. You and your wife must have been... must be very proud of her.'

Clarke smiled weakly. 'Yeah, we was. She got her looks from my Sharon. She was a beauty too. Still is, though this thing has broken her. Totally broken her. Chardonnay was our only child, see?'

That was what made these encounters so impossibly difficult, because there was just nothing you could say that provided any relief for their suffering. All you had was the old platitudes, but you were expected to trot them out nonetheless. So he did.

'I know Terry, I really feel for you and Sharon.' That much at least was true. 'So, can you tell me something about this job she had at the bank?'

'HBB.'

'Aye, that's it.'

'Yeah, she was really loving it. She was always great with numbers my girl was, and they had her in the corporate finance area. Took to it like a duck to water. And she was making a packet too. Way more than I do on the tools and that's a fact.'

Frank gave him a puzzled look. 'Hang on Terry, what do you mean she was making a packet? She was just an intern, wasn't she? They don't get paid, at least not so far as I'm aware.'

'Well, I don't know all about that,' Clarke said stiffly, 'but I know what she told me. Seventy-five grand she was pulling down, without a word of a lie.'

'Are you really sure about that?' Frank said, unable to hide his surprise. 'She wouldn't be exaggerating or making it up?'

'My girl wasn't a liar,' Clarke said, the tone now combative.

'But didn't you think that was a lot of money for a young person with no experience?'

'She was special, my girl,' he replied sharply. 'They must have thought she was worth it. Look, I don't like where you're going with this.'

That was always the danger when dealing with the families. Lose their trust or piss them off and they just clammed up. Frank sensed that Terry Clarke would have to be handled with kid gloves if he was going to keep him onside. He gave an apologetic smile.

'No, sorry Terry, it's just my normal clumsy way with words. It's the Glasgow upbringing. You can take the boy out of Glasgow but you can't take... well, you know the saying I expect. Come on, let's have another beer. Frenchie, your shout I think.'

They filled the few minutes it took French to sort the drinks with more football talk. The subject was some guy called Christian Dailly, another West Ham Scot who Frank didn't remember but pretended he did.

'Class he was,' Terry was saying, 'always had time on the ball. But a bit of a nancy. Didn't like the rough and tumble.'

'Aye, that's right,' Frank said, not sure what he was agreeing with. 'Look, to get back to Chardonnay. I think Ronnie told me that she was socialising quite a lot with some folks from HBB. A fast set, that's how you described it. What can you tell me about that?'

'They was always out on the town. Bars, nightclubs, fancy restaurants and all. And I'm sure they was doing drugs too. Though she says she wasn't.' To Frank, it sounded like the bog-standard lifestyle of any reasonably well-off twenty-something, and while he wasn't going to share this observation with her father, recreational drug use had long been a fact of life amongst that age group. But as he'd often remarked, the parents were usually the last to know.

'And did you meet any of these pals Terry? What were they like?'

'She was seeing a guy. From the office.' It was dropped into the conversation as if it was the most natural thing in the world. And it was something that Ronnie French had omitted from his case briefing, probably because he didn't know.

'Posh guy, Jeremy something or other,' Terry continued. 'Me and Sharon met him the once. He was a lot older than her, but he wasn't married or nothing. It was all straight up, regular like.'

'And he was one of this fast set?'

'Yeah, there was eight or ten of them. All loaded, swanky types the lot of them. But that Jeremy was all right. Sharon liked him the one time they met.'

Frank nodded. 'And was it serious, would you say? The relationship I mean.'

Terry forced a smile. 'I don't know, you'd need to ask my Sharon about that.' He raised a hand, the index and middle fingers intertwined. 'They were like that, Chardonnay and her mum. Shared everything they did. Two peas in a pod.'

'She sounds nice, your Sharon,' Frank said truthfully. He wondered if the relationship would survive the terrible blow it had suffered, having seen plenty that had crumbled in similar circumstances. Terry Clarke was a decent guy, he'd already made up his mind about that, and now his solid marriage was all he had to cling on to.

'Yeah, she was really supporting Chardonnay when she was having her problems.'

Frank gave a double-take, not sure that he had heard him properly.

'What was that Terry? What problems?'

'We don't know what it was, honest we don't. But she was in a right state them last two or three weeks before she died. Totally depressed she was. Although she never would have done herself in, not my Chardonnay. I know she wouldn't.'

And to Frank it sounded exactly what it was. Hope, not belief.

***

Of course, this had all been so totally typical Ronnie French, the very definition of the lazy half-arsed corner-cutter, Frank could see that now. Frenchie didn't have a clue about the fancy boyfriend and he wouldn't have even bothered to ask Terry Clarke what state of mind his daughter had been in the days before her death. A mate says *my girl wouldn't have killed herself* and that was good enough for him. Tomorrow when they were back in the office, he was going to wring his bloody neck.

But maybe something could be salvaged from the mess. He would go and talk to the boyfriend anyway, and it was definitely worth paying Mrs Sophie Fitzwilliam another visit. On second thoughts, that would be a nice wee job for that fat lazy so-and-so French. Get him off his backside and send him up the M40 to see what he could make of it. Find out if someone really had been paying Chardonnay Clarke seventy-five grand per annum. And if so, why? That was a question that wanted answering and Ronnie French was just the man to ask it. As long as he hadn't forgotten by the time he got there.

# Chapter 14

As Maggie had predicted, it hadn't been too difficult to arrange an audience with Gary McGinley of the *Chronicle*. Jimmy had found his email, not exactly a challenge since it was printed under his by-line at the top of his weekly column, and shot off a quick two-liner that explained they were lawyers working for Hugo Morgan and wanted to talk about the Greenway Mining affair. No more than a minute after it hit his inbox, McGinley was on the phone, ranting and raving about powerful individuals interfering with the freedom of the press, and if they thought they could now buy his silence, then they had another thing coming.

'Wait a minute,' she heard Jimmy saying, trying to stem the torrent of invective, 'we don't know anything about any injunction. That's got nothing to do with us, I can assure you. Really.'

So, a bloody press injunction. Something that Morgan had conveniently omitted to mention to them. She guessed it was something to do with the Greenway Mining report, whatever that was, and also that he hadn't used Addison Redburn, Asvina's firm to get it, otherwise she would have told them about it.

Eventually Jimmy managed to calm him down, and just two hours later they were meeting with him in their favourite Starbucks on Fleet Street, somewhat apt Maggie thought, although the national papers hadn't carried that famous address for more than twenty years now.

'We witnessed that little scene at the Park Lane Hilton,' Maggie said, as they queued to order their drinks, 'and I was looking forward to reading what it was all about. But now I'm beginning to understand why I haven't seen anything.'

He nodded. 'Yeah, money and power. Once they have it, it's so easily abused.'

'So what's this all about?' Jimmy said. 'This injunction thing.'

'Same old story,' McGinley said. 'Trying to shut up the press.'

Maggie smiled to herself. They liked to have it both ways, these journalists. All high and mighty when they printed the latest dubiously-obtained gossip about celebrities and royalty, banging on about the public having the right to know, but they weren't so happy when the establishment fought back.

They found a table in the corner where they could just about make themselves heard above the babble of the lunchtime customers.

'So what is that they - and I guess you mean Hugo Morgan - are trying to shut up?' Maggie asked.

'Dirty tricks,' McGinley replied, taking a sip from his latte. 'We were all ready to expose how Morgan goes about his work when we had this slapped on us. But our legal guys are fighting it, and it's all going to come out sooner or later, mark my words.'

Maggie smiled inwardly. The only people to benefit from these kind of cases were the lawyers, scampering back and forth to the court at seven hundred pounds an hour plus expenses. She almost wished that she hadn't given up the profession. Not that she had had any choice. After the Alzahrani case, it had given up on her.

'So can you tell us? How does he go about his work?'

McGinley gave her a dismissive look. 'What, so you can go scuttling back to him with all my secrets? You must think I was born yesterday.'

'But he must already know what you were going to print,' Jimmy said, smiling, 'otherwise he wouldn't have been able to get this injunction thing, would he? So they can hardly be secrets.'

'That's where you're wrong mate,' McGinley said. 'He thinks he knows, but he doesn't.'

Maggie was already beginning to tire of this guy's air of smug superiority.

'Well, actually Gary, you must think I was born yesterday too, because I'm a lawyer, and there's no way a judge will grant an injunction without good reason.'

McGinley leaned back in his chair, the smugness outwardly undiminished. But Maggie caught Jimmy's eye and saw that he was thinking the same thing as her. If he's so sure of himself, what's he doing here? He must want something.

'Anyway, I assume you two are here to offer some sort of a deal. Come on, let's hear it. I'm a busy man.'

Maggie gave an inward grimace. So this was why he had turned up. Maybe this was going to prove more difficult than she expected.

'Believe me Gary, what we wanted to talk to you about has got nothing to do with this injunction. I told you, we didn't know anything about it until you called us back.'

'So what do you want then?' he said, drumming his fingers impatiently on the table.

'Have you heard of Justice for Greenway?' Maggie said.

'No, what's that?' The surly expression melted, to be replaced by a mixture of surprise and interest.

'We don't really know,' Maggie said, 'but Morgan's been the target of some fairly serious vandalism and harassment carried out in their name. First someone sprayed graffiti all over the wall of his house and then they trashed his Bentley the other day. Oh, and there's these.'

She took a couple of the poison pen letters from her handbag and placed them on the table side by side.

'As you can see, these are some pretty nasty threats. That's why he's asked us to find out who's behind it. We wondered if you might have any ideas?'

He gave her a sarcastic look. 'Are you joking? He screwed nearly two thousand people when he pulled that Phoenix from the ashes stunt up in Cumbria. And then there's Belinda Milner's family. So, yeah, I've got plenty of ideas.'

'What do you mean, Belinda Milner's family?' Jimmy said.

'I thought you were supposed to be investigators. Milner, the boss lady. You know she drowned herself in the lake, just fifty yards from her back door. But what you might not know is that just before then, Morgan had sacked her and screwed her out of her three million bonus.'

'So you think her husband or someone might be involved in this?' Jimmy said. 'That's what we really could do with knowing. Or is there someone else?'

'You really don't get the newspaper business, do you mate?' McGinley said. 'This looks like a story. So if I did have any ideas, why would I tell you?'

Maggie could feel her hackles rising.

'Well I assume *you* do get the newspaper business, Gary, because you've been in it long enough. So you'll get it that if Hugo takes this Justice for Greenway thing to the Telegraph or another paper, then your little story's going to be just white noise in the background. After your publisher's spent all that money on these fancy lawyers. And they don't come cheap, you know that. I wonder what they would think about that. I don't think they would be too happy.'

That idea had just come to her out of the blue, but now that she thought about it, she rather liked it. So too, it seemed, did Jimmy.

'Aye, the Times, they'd love this too. That's a brilliant idea. In fact, I don't know why we're wasting our time with this guy. Come on Maggie, we can get a coffee back at the office.' He stood up as if to leave. 'It was nice to meet you Gary.'

McGinley's face melted into a grim expression. Maggie guessed his mind was racing through the implications of his rival getting their hands on this juicy story, and not liking the outcome one little bit.

' Well, look... maybe we can work something out here.'

Maggie smiled sweetly. 'I'm sure we can Gary.'

'Aye, no bother,' Jimmy said, 'and maybe you can start with the whole Greenway thing. What did you mean when you said it was a Phoenix from the ashes stunt?'

McGinley was silent for a moment, evidently weighing up whether he should reveal what he knew. Then finally he said,

'Morgan knew only too well that if the problems with the mine went public, the company was as good as bust and he could then pick it up for a song. The company knew that too, which is why only three insiders got to know the shit they were in.'

Maggie gave him a puzzled look. 'What shit was this?'

'You mean you don't know? That they'd spent five years and four hundred million quid digging this bloody great hole on the edge of the Lake District and then, two years behind schedule, when they finally start bringing the ore to the surface, they find that instead of naught point five percent cobalt, it's just a tenth of that?'

'Whoa, now that is *serious* shit,' Jimmy said.

'Exactly,' McGinley replied. 'That's why they tried so badly to hush it up. Piet Stellenburg's the Chief Geological Officer and it was him that did the original surveys. So at first, he's the only guy that knows naught point *naught* five is a disaster.'

'So he's in deep trouble then,' Maggie said, 'not to put too fine a point on it.'

'Yeah, too right,' McGinley said. 'So for a week or so he decides to sit on it. Tells nobody. Meanwhile Belinda Milner is all over the business media telling anyone who'll listen what a fabulous success the project has become. She was a good-looking woman, and everywhere you looked there's a picture of her with the hard hat and the hi-viz jacket holding a great lump of rock over her head. She used to run a bloody high street retail chain before she got the Greenway gig so of course she's no idea what she's got in her hand. But the City buys into the hype, the shares shoot up eighty percent, and now the local paper is running stories of ordinary miners who're now sitting on a hundred grand's worth of the B shares.'

'B shares? What are they?' Maggie said.

McGinley smiled. 'I'll come back to them later if you don't mind. Anyway, Stellenburg's getting more and more spooked and eventually decides to come clean. So he tells Belinda.'

'Who decides to continue the cover up?' Jimmy asked.

'Exactly. Slightly influenced by the mega-bonus she's looking at based on the rise of the share price. A three million quid bonanza is in touching distance, and she only has to get through a few months to the end of their financial year for it to pay out.'

'But didn't you say three people knew?' Maggie said. 'Who was the other one?'

'A guy called Mark De Bruin. Another South African. He was in charge of operations. A very experienced mining guy. Somehow Milner and Stellenburg managed to keep it to themselves for a month or so more, but eventually he smelt a rat and took a look at the lab results himself.'

'And he said nothing after he found out?' Maggie said.

'Nope. He was on a big bonus too you see.'

She shook her head. 'And nobody else knew? I mean that's impossible surely?'

McGinley shrugged. 'Well I think a few people on the ground might have sussed out that the cobalt yield was lower than expected, but nobody really grasped the significance. I talked to one of the lab technicians for example, and he said anybody who raised concerns was just told by De Bruin or Stellenburg that it was early days and they'd be ramping up the yield soon enough.'

'But then somehow Hugo Morgan found out the truth,' Jimmy said, 'and that's when it all went pear-shaped.'

Maggie gave McGinley a knowing look. 'And you think you knew who told him. Your big story. Until Morgan's lawyers shut you down.'

He shrugged. 'Yeah, for now. But we'll soon get that overturned.'

'Well in that case, you might as well tell us,' Maggie said, smiling. 'If Hugo Morgan already knows, and it's all going to come out anyway.'

But it seemed McGinley wasn't quite ready to play ball. 'You're supposed to be investigators. Figure it out for yourself. A quiz question with just three possible answers so it shouldn't be that hard.'

Maggie saw Jimmy's expression harden. Sometimes that didn't end well, but when he spoke, his voice was calm although the tone was menacing.

'Listen pal, we don't really have time to play your stupid wee games. Either tell us or just bugger off.'

McGinley held up his hands and gave a condescending smile. 'Yeah yeah, it's just us scribblers. The desire to hang on to our secrets. It's engrained in us. So let me just say you need to think about winners and losers.'

'What do you mean by that?' Maggie said, annoyed.

He shrugged. 'Three people knew. Two lost out big-time, leaving just one winner. Figure that out and maybe you'll have your answer.' Draining his cup, he got up to leave, the arrogance reinstated.

'Well, it was nice to meet you both and thanks for the tip-off on the Justice for Greenway story. That'll make a nice sidebar to my Morgan feature. But look, I feel bad about this. So here's a little tip for you. The other suicide, the guy who lost a hundred and fifty grand overnight. Maybe his family's not feeling too happy about things either. So why don't you give a girl called Liz Donahue a call. She's a reporter on some crap little paper up there and she'll know who he is no doubt. *Au Revoir*.'

***

Back in the office, Maggie was able to agree with Jimmy that all things considered, the meeting had been a success. True, Gary McGinley was an arse, but that was probably to be expected given his profession, and he was no worse than a lot of lawyers she knew. The fact was, they'd come away with some solid leads in their quest to find out who was behind Justice for Greenway and that represented progress. Winners and losers, that's what McGinley had said. Belinda Milner, the CEO-for-hire who'd lost her job, her reputation and her three-million-pound bonus. And then had taken her own life. Then there was Stellenburg, the geologist guy who had cocked up the original surveys and had slinked off back to South Africa, his reputation in tatters. As far as losers were concerned, there were none bigger than that pair,

The winner? That had to be operations boss Mark De Bruin, who, it turned out, had now been hired by Morgan to run the reborn company, on a lucrative earnings package that the Financial Times in a highly-critical article described as 'insensitive, given the losses sustained by the original shareholders.' Was he Morgan's mole, spilling the secret that let the financier make his move? It seemed possible, and they'd know soon enough, once McGinley's paper got the injunction overturned. Assuming he was right of course.

But then what of the one hundred and fifty grand guy, who had bet his family's future on the success of the mine only to lose everything as a result of Morgan's financial re-engineering, 'B' shareholders getting nothing once the banks and the revenue had grabbed their share? Miss Liz Donahue of the Westmoreland Gazette would help them with that line of enquiry.

So that was it. Progress, and lots of it, perfectly timed for when she had to report back to their client tomorrow. A couple of leads identified in the *Justice* matter, and excellent news on the Lotti front. He would surely be very satisfied with all of that, and she very much liked satisfied clients.

With that sorted, she could turn her thoughts to the other matter which had been causing her concern. What to wear for her date tonight with Robert Trelawney.

# Chapter 15

It was Jimmy who had been given the job of speaking to Liz Donahue of the Westmoreland Gazette. They could have simply given her a call, but after a brief discussion of the pros and cons, they had decided instead on a face to face meeting. Actually, there wasn't too many cons. The journey from Euston up to Oxenholme took less than three hours, and the three hundred quid that would allow them to travel first-class wouldn't make much of a dent in the generous budget Hugo Morgan had agreed for the investigation. All in all, it would be quite a nice day out.

More contentious however was the debate around which of them should go. He hadn't really reflected before on the fact that whenever there was some sweet-talking of a woman to be done, Maggie automatically assumed that he would achieve a superior result to her. But the more he thought about it, the more uncomfortable it made him feel. Fair enough, he could see it made sense in the Lotti Brückner investigation, where there was an obvious need to test her faithfulness, but here, he was just talking to a bloody local newspaper reporter. It wouldn't matter what he looked like, he could even be an overweight grey-haired forty-something like his brother Frank. That made him chuckle to himself. This time, after some half-hearted resistance he had given in, but next time... the next time his bloody boss wanted him for a spot of honey-trapping, he was going to say something. Well, maybe.

The Westmoreland Times operated behind a dingy shop-front tucked away down a back street in the pretty market town of Kendal. The windows looked as if they hadn't been cleaned in decades, making it hard to tell if the photographs of Old Kendal in the window were genuine sepia or just looked that way through the layers of grime.

Pushing open the door caused a bell to sound a discreet heralding of his presence. In the tiny office, a woman sat behind an ancient desk hammering away on her computer keyboard.

'Just a mo,' she said without looking up, 'don't want to lose my train of thought. I've been buggering about with this piece all morning. It's an absolute bitch.'

A few moments later, she gave an audible sigh of relief. 'Thank God that's done.' She peered at him good-naturedly over rimless spectacles. 'You're Jimmy Stewart I'm guessing?'

She looked about forty, short and slightly rotund but pretty, with bright intelligent eyes and a pleasant ruddy complexion. Her hair, dyed a vibrant purple, was cropped short and she wore a shapeless cable-knit cardigan over a pair of denim dungarees. And a pair of men's brogues. It was important not to judge by appearances, he knew that, but there was every indication that Maggie Bainbridge's little scheme had already gone rather pear-shaped. That was all to the good as far as he was concerned.

He shot her a smile. 'Hello, that's right and you must be Liz. As I explained on the phone, we got your name from Gary McGinley of the Chronicle. I was hoping you might be able to answer some questions about Greenway Mining and a few related things.'

'And you're definitely not with the Chronicle?' Right away, he detected the suspicion in her voice. 'Because if you are, you can sod off back to London on the next train. Particularly if you're a friend of that arse McGinley.'

Jimmy laughed. 'So you think that too? Aye, I've only met him once but he's an arse right enough. So what did he do to upset you?'

'I sent him a lead for a story. A Greenway Mining story as it happens, and a bloody big one too. But he just blanked me. He got some spotty kid from his office to call me to say that what I had wasn't relevant to his line of enquiry. Not so much as a thank you either. *Arse.*'

'Aye, well as I told you I'm a private investigator, not a reporter. With Bainbridge Associates. You won't have heard of us, we're pretty small. But we're acting for Hugo Morgan.' He gave her an ironic look. 'Who I guess you *will* have heard of.'

She nodded. 'Oh yeah Hugo Morgan, I know all about him. He's pretty famous around these parts. Not that he would dare show his face within a hundred miles of the Lakes.' She scuttled off in the direction of the small kitchen that was tucked away in the corner of the office, still talking. 'Of course, it's not really him they should be blaming but we like things nice and simple up here. Coffee or tea?'

'Coffee please. White no sugar.'

She stood hands on hips waiting for the kettle to boil. 'Yeah, in some ways Morgan is a saviour, but don't try telling that to the locals.'

'They blame him for losing their investments I suppose. I can understand that.'

She pointed to a rackety plastic chair opposite her desk. 'Take a seat Jimmy. I'll bring the drinks over.' She tip-toed across the office with the over-filled mugs, placing them down on a pair of stained beer-mats. 'Watch, it's bloody hot. Yeah, see the reality is that Morgan actually saved the mine and about eighty percent of the jobs but it was the way he went about it that pissed everybody off.'

'By somehow managing to expose the cover up, I suppose that's what you mean? By the way, did you know McGinley thinks he knows how Morgan found out about the fact the geology had all gone tits-up? The Chronicle was going to run the story a couple of days ago until Morgan took out an injunction.'

She laughed. 'You mean the De Bruin story? You know, McGinley really is an idiot if he thinks that's what happened.'

He gave her a puzzled look. 'I'm not sure I understand.'

'Mark De Bruin was one of just three people who knew the truth about that cobalt seam, and now he's sitting pretty as CEO of Morgan's new operation. So in McGinley's simple world, it must have been him who spilled the beans.'

'Aye, winners and losers, that's what McGinley said we should look at,' Jimmy said. 'And Marc De Bruin was the big winner I guess.'

Donahue snorted. 'Except I happen to know that's complete rubbish.'

He looked surprised. 'How come?'

'Because I've done my homework, and a company connected to Brasenose Trust was taking a position in Greenway shares long before De Bruin figured out what was happening.'

'Taking a position?' Jimmy said. 'What does that mean?'

'I think it's also called short selling,' she said, 'or shorting, or buying futures, or some crap like that. Actually, I don't really know what it means. All I know is that it allows an investor to make money if the price of a share falls.' She beamed him a smile. 'It's all double-Dutch to me.'

He grinned. 'Me too. But I thought that sort of thing was illegal. Insider trading isn't it?'

'Well it would have been if Morgan had actually carried out any trading. But he didn't.'

Jimmy looked mystified. 'Sorry, I'm lost here, you'll need to help me out.'

'Well, Hugo obviously was on to something, some inside information as you say, that he knew would cause the shares to drop in value. But then when he found out just how big that something was, he quickly changed his plans. Realised he'd never pull off the short selling operation without being detected.'

Jimmy smiled. 'Aye, I get it now. So he decides to spill the beans on the fact that the ore that's being extracted is way down on cobalt content, causing the share price to crash and the banks to panic.'

'Exactly,' Donahue said, 'and when the banks decided to pull the plug, he waltzed in and picked it up from the administrators for a song. His offer was way below asset value, but since it was the only deal in town they had little option but to go along with it. The banks got about a quarter of their money back and felt themselves lucky not to have lost everything, and Morgan paid off a couple of the big institutional shareholders because he knew he would need their support going forward, but the small shareholders got nothing.'

'Those would be the 'B' shares?' Jimmy said.

'Oh, you've heard of them? Yeah, what a rip-off that was. You handed over your cash for a bit of paper that could only be redeemed by the company itself, on some never-never date in the future. But the thing was, that was the work of Belinda Milner and her fancy City advisors. Nothing to do with Morgan at all. He just spotted they weren't worth the paper they were printed on, and that's what caused the real stink up here. There was a ton of local investors, ordinary folks who'd bet all their savings on the big sure-fire deal.'

'Belinda Milner? She was the boss wasn't she? The woman who drowned herself.'

'Yeah, she was,' Donahue said, her tone non-committal. Jimmy stayed silent for a few seconds, but it was clear that the reporter wasn't planning to elaborate, so he decided to park that line of enquiry for now. Instead he said,

'Actually, I wanted to ask you about something connected to the local investors and the B shares and all that. A story I think you wrote for your wee paper. About one of the miners who lost a hundred and fifty grand I think it was. And then killed himself.'

'Not so much of the wee paper if you don't mind.' She screwed up her face in mock hurt. 'You must be talking about the Tompkins family. William Tompkins was one of the foreman at the mine and he got really taken in by the great big fairytale Belinda Milner and her mates were spinning. So not only did he invest all his savings in the project, he persuaded his extended family to do the same. Brothers, sisters, cousins, even his mum and dad, they all chipped in to buy shares. And of course they lost the lot. Everything.'

'And so he killed himself. Another tragedy.'

She nodded. 'A terrible death too. He swallowed about a hundred paracetamol tablets.'

Jimmy wondered how that would feel like, to see your dreams of a comfortable future snatched from you by events outside your control. You were likely to be seriously pissed off, and in your anger, it would probably never occur to you that by and large you were the architect of your own misfortune. But if you had also been responsible for the same fate befalling your entire family, then that would be a wholly different kettle of fish. He could imagine the shame would be unbearable, and for William Tompkins it had been so unbearable that he had taken his own life.

But placing all your eggs in one basket was as dumb an investment strategy as he could think of, and yet hundreds of the locals had fallen into that trap, plunging their money into what they surely must have understood to be a high-risk venture. And now that it had all fallen apart, it was only natural that they would look for someone to blame, and that someone was Hugo Morgan and his avaricious investment trust. As he understood it, Morgan had been under no obligation to pay them anything, but a small gesture would have won him a ton of goodwill in the area and he wondered if he would live to rue that decision one day. *Actions have consequences.* And the people behind Justice for Greenway, whoever they were, seemed to be intent on an escalating campaign.

'I'm guessing these Tompkins aren't very happy. Do you think they might try to get revenge? Because someone's running a harassment campaign against Morgan, Justice for Greenway is what it's called. Fairly low-level stuff at the moment but there have been some more serious threats.'

'Justice for Greenway you say? Well that's interesting, because there's been a few incidents up here under that banner. A couple directed at Milner and a couple at Marc De Bruin. It does cross my mind that the Tompkins lot might be behind it, but to be honest, there's a thousand people up here who might have done it. And these Tompkins, let's just say they're not the brightest sandwiches in the picnic. But having said that, they're pretty pissed off with the whole situation, that's for sure, so perhaps it is them. I really couldn't say.'

'Maybe I should go and see one of these guys,' Jimmy said. 'They live locally I assume?'

She grinned. 'Yeah, Whitehaven. But I wouldn't go alone if I was you, not if you're planning to mention you're working for Morgan. They're pretty handy with their fists, that's what I've heard.'

'Thanks for that Liz. Forewarned is forearmed, eh?' He didn't like to tell her that he'd done plenty of door-knocking out in Helmand where the residents were often pretty handy with the improvised explosive devices and the AK-47s. Compared to that, dealing with the Tompkins would be child's play. That was the theory anyway. It remained to be seen how it worked out in practice. But the more he thought about it, the less likely it seemed that this family would be behind a sophisticated London-based harassment campaign. Nonetheless it was a line of enquiry that would need to be followed up.

'I assume you have an address? Not that it should be too hard to track him down I guess.'

She chuckled. 'I thought you were supposed to be the investigator? Yeah, of course I have it, one of the sons. And I'll give it to you if I can tag along when you go visiting. There should be another story in that.'

He laughed. 'Ok, it's a deal Liz, I'll look forward to that. Now, do you mind if I ask you about the story you were going to give to our mate Gary McGinley. The Greenway one.'

Her eyes narrowed. 'Look Jimmy, this could be the biggest thing that's ever happened to me in my career. I need to know I can trust you.'

'Of course, I get that, totally.' And in that moment, it became clear what he should do. He had only just met Liz Donahue, but already he knew she was good and honest, a quality that experience had taught him was not always in ready supply in this world. Besides which, she was immersed in the life of the community up here and if anyone could help them work out who was behind the harassment of Hugo Morgan, it was her. He gave her one of his special smiles.

'And I'd be exactly the same if I was in your position Liz, believe me. So, see what you think about this. Tell me, when's your paper planning on running your big story?'

She dropped her voice to a whisper, as if worried they would be overheard. 'In about a week I hope, but I've not even told Jonathan my editor the details yet. There's just one more fact I have to verify and then it'll be ready to go. All I've said to him is it's huge and he'll probably have to get it checked out with the owners in Swindon and then it'll probably have to go through legal.'

'Woah, it *must* be huge.'

'It is. Bigger than any story I've ever done in my life.' He saw her face flush as if overwhelmed by the anticipation of what it would mean to her.

He nodded. 'Aye, well I respect that you would want to protect it, absolutely. All I ask is if it had any bearing on the Justice for Greenway thing, then you'll tell me everything you know afterwards.' He knew it was a lot to ask given how little he was able to offer in return. But then again, they were working for Hugo Morgan. Out of the blue, the thought came to him.

'And maybe, and I'm not promising anything, we could get you an interview with the man himself. Give him the chance to put his point of view direct to the community. I'm guessing you'd welcome that opportunity?'

Her eyes widened. 'You could do that?'

He nodded. 'I think so. To be honest, he feels a bit hard done to, I mean not that I feel sorry for him or anything. But he is adamant it was the previous management who screwed up and I think he'd like to put the record straight. As he sees it of course.'

'That would be amazing, definitely.'

Jimmy suddenly had a thought. 'Just one thing though Liz. This article. It doesn't concern Morgan in any way does it? Because if it does, he might not be so willing to cooperate.'

He could tell by the way she looked at him that he had struck a nerve.

'Yeah, it concerns Morgan all right. Big time. You see, I think I know how he found out about the problem with the cobalt yield, and it wasn't because Marc De Bruin told him, no matter what McGinley might think.'

'Bloody hell,' he said, 'so come on now, are you going to tell me who it was?' He knew she wouldn't, but there was no harm in asking. She was silent for a moment, Jimmy guessing she was deciding how much she should reveal. Finally she said,

'Look, I've got an idea. Why don't we see if we can meet with Tompkins tomorrow morning, ask him what he knows? You could stay at my place tonight, it's just round the corner. Ruthie was making a big veggie lasagne and baking some bread, so I'm sure there'll be more than enough to go round.'

'Ruthie?'

'My wife. She's lovely, and she's a very good judge of people. You'll like her.'

Jimmy laughed. 'So I'll be under scrutiny, will I?'

'Put it that way if you like. But I'm sure she'll like you too, and if she does... well, maybe I'll tell you more. So what do you say Mr Detective? Deal?'

He hesitated for a moment. 'I was actually planning to head back tonight but...well, I suppose it wouldn't do any harm to talk to the Tompkins lot whilst I'm up here. Yeah, Liz, let's do it.'

She smiled warmly. 'That's great Jimmy. I'll message Ruthie and tell her to expect one more for dinner.'

'Fantastic,' he said. 'So maybe I'll just catch the bus down to the lake and have a wee wander round, and then pick up a bottle of wine or two. Oh aye, and a tooth brush and a razor.'

On the bus, he took out his phone and, suppressing a laugh, composed a careful WhatsApp to his boss.

*Hi Maggie, going well up here in the lovely Lakes. Staying the night with Liz! Just popping down to Boots for some overnight supplies, if you know what I mean :-) x*

***

All in all, it had been a cracking evening. As Liz had intimated, her wife Ruthie was sweet and lovely, and to his surprise, much younger than her spouse, not far off his own age in fact - and very pretty. Disconcertingly pretty in fact, so much so that he had barely been able to take his eyes off her the whole night, which had every prospect of being a bit awkward. But far from being offended, Liz had seemed amused and even flattered by his obvious attentions and it was clear too that Ruthie was deeply besotted by her wife. As the wine flowed, so did the laughter, which was the accompaniment to what he half-remembered as sparkling conversation. With him doing most of the talking. Maybe not so good.

Breakfast had been set for 8am, and he awoke to the enticing smells of bacon and sausages frying on the griddle pan, Ruthie's semi-militant veganism seemingly no obstacle to rustling up a hearty start to the day for their guest. A long hot shower went some way to blasting away his emerging hangover, and there was a distinct spring in his step as he made his way downstairs. Liz was already at the little kitchen table, munching on a slice of toast which he guessed had been made from the leftovers of the delicious home-baked ciabatta from the previous evening.

'Morning Jimmy,' she said, a wicked smile on her face. 'Sweet dreams?'

'Out like a light.'

Ruthie called over from the hob. 'Glad to hear it. Two eggs or three? And do you prefer them runny like Liz?'

'You know what, I know it's greedy but I could deal with three no bother. And yes, soft please.'

'On their way. I must say Jimmy, you were on good form last night. All these stories from your army days. Fascinating.'

He gave an embarrassed smile. 'Oh God, did I really talk that much? I'm sorry. I'll blame the wine and the great company.'

'Sounds like you were a real action man,' Liz said, laughing, 'which might come in useful when we meet the Tompkins bunch this morning.'

And so it had proved. They arrived on Wayne Tompkins' Whitehaven doorstep after a pleasant ninety-minute drive through beautiful Lakeland countryside. Outside stood a battered white van which evidently his father had used for the handyman business he started up after losing his job in the mine. *W Tompkins & Sons. Building works, gardens cleared. No job too small.* Liz had mentioned that his brother had lost his job too. No savings, no job and few prospects. Added to the death of their father, it was no surprise they felt sore about the whole thing.

Tompkins had answered the door himself, and when Liz asked him straight out if he or any of his extended family were behind the Justice for Greenway stuff, he let out a string of invective, and for a moment it looked as if things might get violent. That was, until he took another look at Jimmy, and decided that he was likely to come off second best in any altercation with the six-foot-two fourteen-stone ex-soldier. After that, he calmed down and it soon became clear that his overriding emotion regarding the Greenway affair was sadness, not anger. Although he stopped short of inviting them in.

'My family's lost all their savings because of them people. They trusted my dad and they lost everything. Bastards, all of them.'

'Who do you mean?' Jimmy asked.

'Milner, Morgan, all of them. Bloody vultures.'

'It didn't work out well for Belinda Milner though, did it?'

He shrugged. 'Well, yeah that was a tragedy for her kid and her bloke. We didn't want that to happen. But she was a right cow, and no mistake.'

'We? Who's we?'

'My family. But we didn't do nothing, honest we didn't.' That caused Liz and Jimmy to smile at one another. Guilt was written all over this guy's face.

'Someone graffiti'd her house, just a day or two before she died,' Liz said. 'Justice for Greenway in foot-high letters.'

Jimmy nodded. 'And a few days later, someone daubed the same message on Morgan's garden wall down in London. A wee bit of a coincidence, don't you think?'

'Nowt to do with us,' he said defensively, 'although I can't says that I'm not glad.'

They were disturbed by the deafening sound of a rorty car exhaust, Jimmy glancing round to catch sight of a lowered Fiesta pulling up sharply behind the Tompkins van. The elderly car had been treated to a plainly expensive paint-job, a glimmering sea of purples and vermilions reflecting the morning sun in their eyes.

'That's my brother Karl.'

'Nice wheels,' Jimmy said.

'Yeah he's into his motors,' Tompkins said, his pride obvious. 'That's his business in fact, does them up for all the lads around here. Nice little earner it is.'

I bet it is, Jimmy thought, the ownership of a crassly-customised hot hatch as much a class identifier in these parts as a tattoo. Karl Tompkins was around thirty, a couple of years younger than his brother, stocky but broad and almost as muscle-packed as Jimmy, his hair cropped short and wearing a black sleeveless top that displayed tattoo-infested biceps. So far, so stereotypical.

'What's this?' he said, ignoring them and addressing his brother.

'She's from the Gazette. He's some sort of private eye. They want to know about Justice for Greenway. I told them we didn't know nothing.'

'So who says we do?' The brother's tone was distinctly aggressive and it was instructive he had directed the comment at Liz, because Jimmy knew a bully when he saw one. But there was something else he recognised. A regimental tattoo.

'Royal Engineers eh? Served alongside a lot of you boys out in Helmand. Great bunch of lads.'

Karl seemed momentarily nonplussed. 'What? Yeah, they was. You was there too then?'

'Aye, too right,' Jimmy said. 'Bomb squad. Mental it was.' He didn't mention that he had been an officer. In his experience, squaddies either developed a lifelong respect for authority or they went completely the other way. He had only encountered Karl Tompkins for two seconds but he had no doubt which side of the fence this guy would sit on.

'Yeah these fecken' IEDs were everywhere. Took a lot of our mates they did. But you lads were fecken' brave, and make no mistake. I wouldn't have done it.'

'Just doing my job, same as everyone,' Jimmy said. 'How long were you in?'

'He was in eight years,' his brother interjected, 'Made sergeant. Bloody proud we was, the whole family. Especially my dad.'

'Then you got a job in the mine when you came out,' Liz said. 'A really good job, so it must have been gutting for you, everything that happened last year. You know, the Morgan stuff and all that.'

Karl looked at her suspiciously. 'Yeah, he's a bastard all right. Treated everyone round here like shit. But what's that got to do with you?'

'We're working for him,' Jimmy said. 'Someone calling themselves Justice for Greenway has been harassing him. So naturally we thought it would be good to start up here, given this is where the mine is.'

'Nowt to do with us.'

'Aye that's what your brother told us,' Liz said, shooting him a sardonic smile. 'But I expect the CCTV at Oxenholme would have caught any of you Tompkins catching a London train any time over the last few weeks. I know the station manager really well, I'm sure he'd be happy to let me take a look at the footage.'

'You'd better watch what you're saying,' Wayne sneered. 'And you can look at all the pictures you like, you won't find nothing.'

And that's where they left it. Discussing the matter on the way back to Kendal, they agreed it was pretty much one hundred percent certain that one of the Tompkins brothers had been behind the harassment of Belinda Milner. As for the Morgan stuff, that seemed a bit less likely, although a former sergeant in the Engineers would certainly have the logistical and technical expertise to pull of such a campaign. So they didn't rule out that he or his brother or even someone else in the family could have driven to London with a van-load of aerosol cans. Jimmy didn't know if it was a possibility, but maybe he could persuade his brother Frank to get an APNR search done on one or two cameras on the M6, and of course Liz could talk to her mate at the station, but he didn't hold out much hope for either of these leads.

An hour into the journey, they were dawdling down the eastern edge of Thirlmere with the brooding majesty of Helvellyn rising just ahead of them, and it was impossible to talk of anything but the stark beauty of the national park. But then soon she was telling him of her difficult upbringing in Newcastle, how her family had shut her out when in her late teens she had came out, and how finding Ruthie at a time she had all but given up hope of love had saved her. And in that moment Jimmy knew he had found a friend for life, his initial warm feeling for this woman reinforced by every subsequent minute he had spent in her company. Not only that, he was pretty sure she felt the same way about him. Which meant it was probably a good time to return to the subject of her big story. The story that she hoped would make her name, the story that would reveal how Hugo Morgan found out about the problems at the mine. So he asked her if he'd passed the Ruthie test, and she said yes he had, and then he asked if she would now tell him, or at least give him a clue. And she said she would. *Pillow talk*. Pillow talk, that's all she was prepared to give away and he didn't push it. If he wanted to know more, he would have to figure it out for himself. As they approached the outskirts of Kendal, he reflected once again that Liz Donahue was one of life's good people and it was a privilege to know her.

Words that he would find himself repeating to Ruthie when he attended the funeral.

# Chapter 16

Frank had decided to take the tube out to Tower Hill, the nearest station to the HBB offices which were located a couple of streets behind St Katherine's Dock. He could have got one of his deadbeat DCs to drive him, and that would have been a lot quicker and a lot more convenient, but he wanted take a look at the location of Chardonnay's death before he met with Jeremy Hart. It wasn't that he was looking for anything specific, he just wanted to take in the scene and remind himself that she had been a real living person and not just the name on the cover of the case folder. Alighting on the east-bound platform, he made his way along to the end against the flow of the handful of passengers who had disembarked, to the point where departing trains sped off into the darkness. Directly opposite was the spot where Chardonnay had been pushed to her death, the act expertly timed to coincide with a train emerging at over thirty miles an hour on the west-bound line. That evening back in October the station would have been packed with home-bound commuters, and he wondered if anyone would have noticed a beautiful young woman being forced against her will to the end of the platform. Because surely that was what must have happened. Anywhere else, the train would have been slowing and the victim might well have survived. Too much of a chance to take if you wanted a clean kill.

A few metres along the deserted platform, a Transport for London official emerged from a small glass fronted cubicle and began to approach him, a mildly suspicious expression on her face. Frank shot her a smile, fumbling in an inside pocket for his warrant card.

'Hi, I'm Detective Inspector Stewart with the Met. I just wondered, do you have any idea how long they keep your CCTV footage?'

She shrugged. 'Don't know mate. You'd need to ask security. What's this all about?'

'Nothing really, just wondered. Here, do you remember an incident a few months back, when a young woman fell in front of a train? On the other platform, just over there.'

'Nah, wasn't here mate. I was at Bank then. But we get quite a lot of them. It's nothing special.'

*Nothing special.* A life so easily dismissed by this ignorant woman. But Chardonnay Clarke *was* something special, someone very special indeed and he wasn't going to rest until he'd found out what happened to her.

Hart was mid to late thirties, short, overweight and balding, his unprepossessing appearance redeemed in part by an immaculate navy Italian suit and dazzling white shirt. The card he handed Frank read *Jeremy R C Hart, Chief Financial Officer*. Two middle names, when most people had to make do with one, if they were lucky. And as certain an indicator of class as an old school tie. *Posh guy, Jeremy something or other*. That was how Terry Clarke had described him and his assessment was accurate, if only to judge by his accent. He was also pretty young to be occupying such an elevated position in a big international bank, and Frank speculated how much of his career success was down to his ability as opposed to his obviously privileged upbringing. Not what you know but who you know.

HBB's office was open plan and garishly decorated in bright primary colours, looking more like a primary school than a temple of high finance. Hart led him through a maze of desks occupied almost exclusively by twenty-somethings, each with eyes glued to their laptop screens, to an area separated from the rest of the office by a floor-to-ceiling perspex screen. A label stuck to the outside read *Silent Space 1*.

'We come here when we need a bit of peace and quiet,' Hart explained. 'Which is quite a lot of the time, because it's generally pretty manic around here. Our main offices are over at Canary Wharf, this is just a bit of overspill capacity we're renting at the moment. We're still trying to work out what the takeover means for us in terms of headcount.'

'Aye, I think I read something about that. You've been bought by a German bank, haven't you?'

'Yes, that's right. CommerzialBank Stuttgart.' He didn't sound as if it was a development he much welcomed. Frank was no expert, but takeovers generally had an impact on jobs, or headcount as Hart described it, and like in war, it was the vanquished that lost out. He wondered if this guy's own position might be at risk.

The only seating provided was a pair of oblong foam blocks arranged facing one another about a metre apart. With no other option on offer, he perched himself uncomfortably on the corner of one.

'You know why I'm here Jeremy,' he said. 'Chardonnay Clarke.'

Hart stared at his shoes and gave a deep sigh. 'I know. I still haven't come to terms with what happened. I don't think I ever will.'

'You were close, I think?' Frank said, trying his best to sound empathetic.

'Close?' he said, his indignation obvious. 'I loved her. I'd never met anyone like her before. She was special. Very special.'

And way out of your league too pal, was Frank's immediate reaction, but he didn't say it. Not in so many words at least.

'I'm sorry to have to ask this question, but do you think she felt the same way about you?'

He gave Frank a dismissive look. 'Yes, I know what you're thinking, the same as everyone else did. Why would a girl like that fall for someone like me? Well, the fact is we were soul mates and we were blessed to have found each other. We thought the same way about everything. We loved the same books, the same films, the same music. Everything. It was if we had known each other for the whole of our lives. We talked about our future together. It was that serious.'

'What, do you mean marriage? But she was only what, twenty-three, twenty-four?'

'What's that got to do with it? You might find this hard to understand Inspector, but our ages were irrelevant. We were in love.'

'And yet she took her own life.' Frank left the obvious question hanging in the air, unasked. *Why?*

'I know. Something changed towards the end,' he said, his voice betraying the pain he was so plainly feeling. 'I don't know what. And I was too tied up in the Brasenose thing to notice.'

Frank felt his pulse start to rise as his *something's-not-right* instinct kicked in. Terry Clarke had been adamant. *My girl would never have done herself in.* But here was her lover with seemingly no doubts that it could have been anything other than suicide. Which meant he must have known a reason why she had been driven to commit that terrible final act. And *the Brasenose thing*. What was that all about? He had to ask.

'Brasenose? That's an Oxford college, isn't it?'

'Well yes it is, but this is actually Brasenose Investment Trust. It's a financial firm run by a guy called Hugo Morgan. I don't expect you'll have heard of him.'

But Frank had heard of him, but in what context? It was something that Maggie and Jimmy were working on, he was pretty sure of that. And then he remembered. The billionaire who had dumped his wife as a fiftieth birthday present to himself.

'Well funnily enough Jeremy I have. My brother's actually met him a couple of times I think.'

'Really?' Hart seemed mildly interested. 'Is he in finance too?'

Frank laughed. 'You wouldn't think that if you met him. No, he works around the legal profession, investigating divorces and such like. But sorry, I interrupted you. Carry on, please.'

'So, you know about the Stuttgart take-over. It was an agreed deal, but that actually can be rather complicated when the target, us in this case, is publicly quoted. Most of our stock was in the hands of just a handful of big institutions and so we had to sound out what sort of offer they might be willing to accept in the event of a take-over. As you can imagine, it's a very delicate operation.'

Frank had no idea what he was talking about so had no opinion whether it was a delicate operation or not. But he nodded along anyway.

'Aye, sure, sure, get that.'

'The last thing you want is an institution at the last minute holding out for a better offer, that could blow the whole deal apart of course. So we'd been working on it for several months, sounding out our investors and eventually settled on a price of around eight pounds fifty pence a share. That was the price that everyone was happy with. Our stockholders were getting a fair return on their investment and it was a price that Stuttgart were willing to pay. So win-win.'

Frank nodded. 'I'm sensing there's a *but*.'

Hart gave a rueful smile. 'Yeah, a big but. So, just three weeks before Stuttgart are due to go public with the offer, our registrar draws to my attention that there's been an unusual volume of trades in the preceding two or three weeks. Someone has been quietly building up a position in our stock to the extent that this entity now controls nearly eleven percent.'

'And that's this Brasenose outfit?'

'Well no, not exactly. The company behind it was called Jasmine Holdings, registered in Guernsey. We'd no idea who the owners were at that stage.'

Frank smiled. 'You'll need to forgive me, high finance isn't my thing. But I guess that spelt trouble in some way?'

He nodded. 'You could say that all right. It put the bank, and me in particular, in deep shit. With that sort of volume of trades, we were legally obliged to inform the FCA - that's the regulator - and then they started asking awkward questions about whether there had been a leak and if there was a connection between any of the bank's officers and this Jasmine outfit.'

'Aye, I think I understand how serious that would have been,' Frank said, 'because it would have been insider trading, am I right?'

'Exactly,' Hart said, 'and not a great career move for a CFO like me, to be caught up in something like that. Naturally my CEO Simon Parkside and all the Stuttgart guys are going mental, accusing everybody in this room, me included, of leaking the deal. It was horribly stressful and I didn't sleep for nearly two weeks.'

Frank gave a sympathetic smile. 'Aye, it must have been hard for everyone, I can see that. So how did it all play out?'

'Like a complete nightmare, that's how it played out, if you must know. So not long afterwards, Hugo Morgan goes public and reveals that his Brasenose Trust is the hundred percent owner of the Jasmine shell company. He named it after his youngest daughter apparently. Next he's all over the financial press slagging off the deal, a deal that somehow he knows all the details of. He was giving it his usual activist investor shtick, about how we were ripping off the small shareholders and how he intended to ride to their rescue. Anyway, the long and short of it was that unless the offer was upped to ten pounds a share, he wouldn't sell.'

Frank looked puzzled. 'Sorry, but I thought you said he only had bought eleven percent. Would that have been enough to stop the deal going through?'

Hart shook his head. 'Well in theory no, but Morgan knows that as soon as he publicly questions the value of a deal, it doesn't take long for some of the other big institutional shareholders to start questioning their judgement too. And that's exactly what happened here. Herd instincts I think they call it. Next thing you know, everybody is saying that maybe eight pounds fifty is too cheap after all.'

'But what about the Germans?' Frank said. 'Wasn't there a risk that they would just walk away?'

Hart gave a rueful smile. 'That's the genius of Morgan. He's got an amazing instinct for the true value of a company. He bet that CommerzialBank would bitch to high heavens but go through with it in the end, and that's exactly how it played out. And we were left looking like idiots for trying to sell the bank on the cheap.'

'And I'm assuming Morgan did very well out of it?'

Hart nodded. 'You could say that. He made forty million in the space of a month.'

'Nice,' Frank said, 'but did you ever find out where the leak came from?'

Hart shook his head. 'No, we didn't. The FCA compliance team interviewed loads of people in the bank and swarmed all over our emails and phone records, but they didn't get anywhere. And of course Morgan denied there ever was a leak at all. He claimed it was pure coincidence, that he had been building up a position in HBB simply because he had been researching us and decided we were poorly managed and the shares had underperformed for years.'

Frank nodded. 'Plausible I suppose? Because I think I've already worked out that's how his company operates.'

'Oh yeah,' Hart replied, his tone sarcastic, 'highly plausible. Except I happen to know it's complete bollocks. You see, I've done my research too.'

'How do you mean?' Frank said, his eyes narrowing.

'Five companies in the last three years where Brasenose Trust just happened to have taken an interest just as something big was kicking off. Two take-overs, a big contract loss, and two management screw-ups to be exact. And each time, Morgan made a killing.'

'So what are you saying? That he does this thing as a matter of course?'

Hart nodded. 'He calls it activist investment. I call it industrial espionage because that's exactly what it is. I don't know how he does it, but it's not through bloody research, believe me.'

It wasn't Frank's area of expertise, but questionable though the practice might be from a moral standpoint, he wasn't sure if it was actually illegal. Although what you did with the information you found out, well that might be a different matter. But he wasn't here to pass judgement on Hugo Morgan's business practices.

'Getting back to Chardonnay, if we can for a moment. Can I ask, how much was the bank paying her? The reason I ask is that her dad thought she was getting seventy-five grand a year, which seems a lot to me.'

Hart looked perplexed. 'Paying her? She was an intern Inspector, so we weren't paying her anything. We paid a fee to the agency, but that was it.'

'The agency? That's that Oxbridge outfit isn't it? So would they have been paying her, do you think?'

'What, are you kidding?' Hart said, suppressing a laugh. 'The internship business is just one step away from slavery. We all go along with it of course but, no, they definitely wouldn't have been paying her, no way.'

'And yet she had money, didn't she? I've heard she had a very nice flat in Clapham for instance, and what sort of rent would that command? Fifteen hundred or maybe even two grand a month? That's a lot of money for an intern. For anybody when it comes to it.'

Hart shrugged. 'I just assumed her dad was paying for it all. He's a London plumber after all. You know what they charge. And anyway, I only went there once. You see, I never... we never slept together.'

Frank looked at him sharply. Years of experience in the job had given him a well-honed instinct for the truth, or more accurately, for sniffing out untruths, and his instinct said that Jeremy Hart was telling the truth about all of this. Although it did seem a bit surprising they weren't having sex given how much in love they had supposedly been.

'Why was that sir, if you don't mind me asking?'

He smiled uncertainly. 'Chardonnay said she wasn't quite ready for that side of our relationship. I was perfectly happy with that of course.' From the waver in his voice, Frank knew that *this* was a lie. He'd been rejected and he hadn't been happy about it at all. But then who would be when you were so tantalisingly close to having a woman like Chardonnay in your bed? Perhaps Hart had misread the whole thing, and that she saw their relationship in an entirely different light. Perhaps she had decided it had run its course and was trying to pluck up the courage to tell him.

'You said that something had changed in the relationship towards the end. About the time the Brasenose thing was happening.'

A cloud of sadness seemed suddenly to envelop him. 'Yes, I don't know what it was. Something was troubling her, but she wouldn't say what it was. I speculated of course. I thought perhaps her parents were pressuring her to break it off, you know, because she was so young and with the age gap and everything.'

Frank shook his head. 'Well, I spoke to her father not that long ago and he didn't say anything about that. On the contrary, I remember exactly what he said. *That Jeremy was all right.* So it wasn't that I'm pretty sure.'

Hart gave a faint smile. 'Yes, they're nice, her parents. Good solid folks.'

'I haven't met the mum,' Frank said, 'but aye, Terry Clarke's a good bloke. And he's totally convinced that his daughter wouldn't have taken her own life, and yet I'm getting the sense that you're not so sure. Why would that be Jeremy?'

For a moment he hesitated. 'I..it was just... well as I said, she seemed troubled. There was something on her mind, but of course at the time, it never entered my mind that she would kill herself. But afterwards... there was that suicide note on Facebook...'

'Which she never actually sent,' Frank said.

'No, she didn't. Look Inspector, I don't really understand what this is all about. Are you saying her death might have been... well, suspicious?'

He shrugged. 'I don't know if it will make you feel better or not, but aye, we've uncovered certain information that raises that possibility. It's early days, but you see we found another case with some quite disturbing similarities. A lad called Luke Brown who died in exactly the same way. He was one of these interns too. Assigned to some insurance company. Arixa or Avimto or something like that.'

'Alexia maybe? Maybe that's who you mean.'

Frank nodded. 'Aye, that was it. Alexia Life. You know something about them?'

'Two years ago Alexia were facing nearly half a billion in losses over that hurricane that hit the south-west of the US. Remember it? You see, they should have re-insured it out through Lloyds but they'd decided to keep most of the risk in house so that they could book the full premium value to their accounts. It was a huge mistake on their part.'

'I won't even pretend to understand any of that Jeremy,' Frank said. 'Just give me the edited highlights if you would.'

'There's not much more to say. It was a massive cock-up, but if you're looking for a connection back to Hugo Morgan then you're barking up the wrong tree I'm afraid.

'Why do you say that Mr Hart?'

He gave a condescending smile. 'Alexia are a mutual. They're owned by their members, not by shareholders.'

\*\*\*

Connections. That's what you were always on the look-out for in a case, and as Frank headed back to Atlee House, he gave a mental shrug of the shoulders. Two good-looking interns, two tube-station deaths, the Oxbridge Agency. Three connections, and in his mind, that was already too much to be just coincidence. Sure, it would have been all neat and tidy if Hugo Morgan had been involved with Alexia Life too, but he wasn't and that was something he would have to deal with. And anyway there would be something else, he just hadn't stumbled across it yet.

Now he needed to chase up the half-wit Ronnie French to see how he'd got on up in Oxford with Sophie Fitzwilliam, and then a bit more legwork, see what he could find out about that lad Luke Brown. He might do that himself or ask French to do it, and while he was at it, he could take wee Yvonne Sharp along with him.

Then it would be useful to speak to that brother of his, take him for a pint and see what they knew about Morgan. And if Maggie just happened to be there too, that would be nice. And awkward.

# Chapter 17

It was an anniversary that would never ever be forgotten, but not one to celebrate. Two years on from what she now called meltdown day, the day when every ounce of sense she had ever possessed had evaporated. The day when, maybe, she had tried to end her life and that of her beloved Ollie. Except that in her waking hours, she was unable to remember a single thing about it. It was inconceivable that it had been a deliberate act, that she had planned it and executed it so coldly, and that, as Camden Social Services had asserted at the time, she had been only too aware of the likely outcome. Inconceivable, but she could never be quite certain, which is why the terrible dream came back, again and again, night after night.

Perhaps it should have been expected that last night it should have been particularly vivid, given the significance of the date, but maybe the copious quantities of red wine she had consumed during the evening might also have had something to do with. The date with Robert had been lovely, an early visit to the cinema followed by a late supper, and this time she hadn't slept with him. He had been absolutely fine about that, and in fact expressed some surprise about the turn of events on their first date. He had seen her to a cab, kissed her gently on the cheek, and expressed a wish that they could do this again.

Three quarters of an hour later she was tucked up in bed, her cheeks still rosy red, partly through excitement but mainly because of the wine. She drifted off thinking pleasant thoughts of love and marriage, soon to be ruthlessly replaced by the replaying of that horrible scene that could not be erased. She awoke at 4am, shivering with sweat and with a pounding headache, and thereafter was unable to get back to sleep. She tossed and turned for an hour or so before giving up, and at five-thirty she was in the shower, the hot jets of water helpless against her growing hangover. At least the coffee helped a bit, the extra spoonful of finest Columbian thrown into the cafetiere producing a powerful caffeine hit that went some way towards dragging her into the day.

But today was auction day and likely to be an interesting one, and so gradually she found her spirits rising. More than that, it was looking pretty conclusive that Miss Lotti Brückner was one hundred percent authentic, meaning that matter could be brought to a conclusion and she could, if she chose reveal her true identity to Robert. Although that was going to be very risky, because she would have to tell him why she had posed as Magdalene Slattery. Firstly, there was every chance that he would be angered by her deception and want nothing more to do with her. Secondly, and this was the thing that worried her the most, he was bound to tell Lotti, and that could make it very awkward indeed with Hugo. But she wasn't going to worry about any of this today.

The bidding was scheduled to start at midday with the auction room open from 9am for viewing. The Casagemas was one of the star lots, heavily promoted on the auction-house's website and having pride of place on the front page of their catalogue. They had been undecided whether or not Jimmy should come along, and he was not keen, but she had managed to persuade him it was worth having a final check on Lotti's fidelity before they wrapped up the investigation.

The viewing gallery was packed to the rafters when she arrived at around eleven, hawk-eyed auction-house staff mingling with the crowd, focussed on separating the serious bidders from the more numerous window-shoppers. Glancing around the room, she saw that Jimmy was already there, catalogue in hand, staring vacantly at a large gilt-framed painting of an undistinguished hunting scene. Alongside him stood Lotti Brückner, looking as ridiculously beautiful as on the previous occasions they had met. And still looking annoyingly young for her age.

'Morning boss,' he said as Maggie joined them. 'Sorry, I mean darling Magdalene.' He leant over and kissed her on the cheek. If Lotti had noticed his little slip-up, she didn't say anything.

'Good morning Magdalene,' she said brightly. 'I was just saying to James, I think it's going to be an exciting day. We have a very big attendance and I recognise many regular collectors. We may see some very big bids.'

'And what about our Casagemas?' Maggie said, slightly nonplussed by her colleague being addressed by his undercover name. 'Is there a lot of interest?'

Lotti nodded. 'Yes, there is. It's a pity from our point of view that they have marketed it so heavily, because that will of course push up the price. But that does not matter so much with fine works of art since it only establishes the baseline value should you choose to sell it in the future. So it will still be a good investment if we managed to secure it, I'm sure of it.'

'Good to know,' Jimmy said, stroking his chin in the manner of an expert he had seen on the *Antiques Roadshow*. 'Good to know.'

They were approached by young man wearing a nametag that identified him as *Harry Radford-James, Valuer.* He pointed up at the painting.

'Good morning ladies, sir. It's an interesting piece isn't it? Very classical in subject matter but a good example of the genre.' Correctly surmising that Maggie was the buyer, he had directed his smiling gaze at her. 'The price will be modest I think, but it would be an excellent addition to anyone's collection.'

It seemed that Lotti knew him. Giving him an affectionate look she said, 'Yes very good Harry, but we both know that this is a *very* unremarkable work. I'm afraid you will have to find some other prey.'

He seemed unperturbed by her barb. 'But art is a very personal thing, isn't it Lotti? What about you sir, do you find it pleasing? I noticed you were studying it quite intently.'

'Nah,' Jimmy said. 'It's crap.'

Harry laughed. 'Well between you and me sir, I think you may be right. But please, don't tell my boss that I said that. Anyway, I hope you have a good auction and as Lotti suggested, I'll slip off now and see if I can find another victim.' He gave a half-wave and ambled away.

'Nice lad,' Jimmy said, 'although a bit posh for me.'

Lotti smiled. 'They are here to help the lots to sell. Even the poorer ones. He was only doing his job. But come, we must move through to the sale room to get a good position. Somewhere towards the rear of the room is normally best, but seated, not standing.'

Maggie was intrigued. 'Why is that Lotti?'

'It makes it easier to see who is bidding against you. For example, if it is someone you know is very rich, or has a big interest in a particular type of work, you know you will have to bid very high to win. And so maybe you decide it is not worth it. And I prefer to be seated so that it is difficult for them to see you.'

They made their way in, finding seats just one row from the back. The room was rapidly filling up and within a few minutes it was standing room only, with hopeful bidders packed three-deep along the rear and down the sides of the room. The auction-house's staff were already on the platform, the auctioneer flanked by half a dozen colleagues who would be taking the telephone bids from keen buyers from around the world. At twelve midday precisely, things got under way.

'Good afternoon, ladies and gentlemen, and I hope you're all well and ready to raise your arm when I catch your eye.' A ripple of laughter spread through the room. He was younger than she expected and with a rich northern accent, in stark contrast to the plummy received pronunciation that seemed to be *de rigour* in his trade. A Lancastrian, she decided, speculating that he might perhaps be from Oswaldtwistle or Ramsbottom or Rawtenstall or any other of these delightfully-named former mill towns.

'Eighty-seven lots we have today, each one a gem in its genre, and many with *no reserve*.' His comic emphasis on the last two words was greeted with a loud 'Ooh' and a crescendo of applause. Maggie smiled to herself. She hadn't expected a vaudeville act at such an august gathering but it was certainly entertaining.

The first few lots were unremarkable, quickly dispatched by the auctioneer and none achieving more than two thousand pounds under the hammer. The Casagemas had been allocated lot fifteen, relatively early in the running order, but its position had been chosen quite deliberately by the auction house. The catalogue was by any standards relatively run of the mill, but at the last minute they had managed to secure a minor but attractive early work by Hockney, which had been listed towards the end of the sale. As Lotti had explained to them in perfect colloquial English, you couldn't really expect an auction to be a success if there wasn't anything to keep the bums on seats through to the end of the programme. The hope was that collectors who missed out on the star attraction - in this case the lovely landscape by Picasso's pupil - would stick around for the Hockney so as not to go home disappointed.

The screen behind the platform was now filled by the arresting abstract of a white-washed Spanish town.

'Lot fifteen, a very pretty little landscape by Carlos Casagemas. This is authenticated by the leading authority on the artist's work in Barcelona, the city of his birth. A genuine work, and one of his last before his tragic death. And of course today, we are offering this remarkable work at no reserve.'

Maggie could feel her heart start to pound as the auctioneer got the bidding under way. 'Where do we want to start with this?' he said, beaming out at the audience. 'Do I see twenty pounds?' A huge gust of laughter reverberated around the sale room. At the end of the platform, a colleague raised an arm and mouthed something in his direction.

'We're underway,' he shouted. *'Twenty* thousand pounds, on the telephone, thank you. Do I see twenty-five? Twenty-five anywhere? In the room, yes thank you sir, down there on the left. Twenty-five has it. Looking for thirty now. *Thirty* thousand pounds.'

Maggie got to her feet and peered forward, hoping to catch a glimpse of this new bidder, but he was tucked away on the right hand side of the room and obscured by a pillar. Lotti tapped her on the arm and whispered. 'Don't worry about that. We don't need to bid right now but we will watch carefully before we make our move. But forty-five thousand, that is our maximum bid, isn't it?'

Maggie nodded uncertainly. 'Yes that's what we agreed I think.'

At the other end of the platform, a second colleague gave a discreet nod.

'*Thirty* thousand. On the telephone. A new bidder. Do I have thirty-five? *Thirty*-five. Thank you sir. We're in the room again. Forty thousand, anyone?'

Alongside her, Lotti gave an almost imperceptible nod. The auctioneer, catching her eye, smiled.

'*Forty* thousand, thank you madam. Forty-five. You sir? No? Forty-five I'm asking. A sublime work with an impeccable provenance. Forty-five thousand. Do I have it?'

'I think it was the right moment,' Lotti whispered. 'It will slow down from now I think.' She pointed to the stage, where one of the assistants manning a telephone was shaking her head.

'Do I have forty-five? I will take forty-two if that helps.'

For a moment it seemed as if the bidding had stalled. The auctioneer scanned the room anxiously, then looked along the row of his colleagues, who shook their heads in unison. He glanced at the screen on front of him, his face now wearing a frown, but no internet bidder came along to offer salvation.

'Fair warning,' he said, sounding rather deflated. 'I'm selling... make no mistake...I'm selling...to you madam at the back of the room...selling at *forty* thousand once... forty thousand twice...'

Maggie squeezed Lotti's arm and gave a smile. But then suddenly there was a collective gasp from the room as the auctioneer evidently caught the eye of the bidder at the front of the room.

'*Fifty* thousand pounds. Fifty thousand. I have it here in the room. Thank you sir.'

'What do you want to do?' Lotti whispered. 'I think we are now up against a bidder who really wants this picture.'

Maggie could feel heart pounding in her chest, which she realised was stupid. Magdalene Slattery, rooky art collector, wasn't real, and anyway she was spending Hugo Morgan's money, not her own. But somehow, crazily, she had caught a dose of auction fever.

'What do you think Lotti? Perhaps it's worth more than we thought.' Without waiting for her reply, she shot up her arm and shouted 'fifty-five.'

'Fifty-five thousand! Thank you madam. At the back of the room. Do I have sixty? This lovely work by young Carlos Casagemas. Solid provenance. Sure to grace any collection. Sixty thousand I'm looking for. Do I have it anywhere?' Now the excitement in the room was palpable, as they looked forward to two motivated buyers slugging it out over a piece which had already reached more than twice its perceived market value. And it seemed the mystery bidder was not yet ready to drop out.

'I have sixty thousand pounds. Thank you for your bid sir. Madam, are you in? Can I have sixty-five?'

Maggie looked first at Jimmy, who simply shrugged, then at Lotti, who was now wearing a serious expression.

'I think we are reaching the limit of value Magdalene,' she said. 'Perhaps just one more bid but I would not advise going much further.'

'Ok,' Maggie said, raising her hand.

The auctioneer gave a nod of acknowledgment. 'Sixty-five thousand. Thank you for your bid madam. Sir, do I have seventy?' It wasn't possible for Maggie to see directly how the mystery bidder responded, but it was clear from the reaction on the platform that he had indicated a 'no'.

'I'll take sixty-seven if it helps,' the auctioneer said, smiling in the bidder's direction. 'Sixty-seven I have. Do I have sixty-eight? Madam?'

'Go straight to seventy,' Lotti whispered. 'I think that will finish them off.'

Maggie nodded. She was enjoying this, playing with Hugo Morgan's Monopoly money, and a second later she was on her feet yelling. 'Seventy!' at the top of her voice. There was a burst of laughter around the room and a beaming smile from the auctioneer.

'Thank you madam, thank *you*.' It seemed the mystery bidder had already signalled his intention to go no further, as the hammer was raised in anticipation.

'I'm selling at seventy thousand pounds... in the room...make no mistake...fair warning...once...twice...' and then with a theatrical flourish, he slammed the hammer down on the wooden lectern.

She wasn't sure if she saw him first, or it was he who spotted her. Whatever the order of events, there was no getting away from the fact that it was an awkward situation, for when the hammer had come down, Jimmy, overacting furiously, had taken her in his arms and kissed her full on the lips. Taken by surprise, she had involuntarily succumbed and returned both the embrace and the kiss, which between them lasted several long, and much to her surprise, blissful seconds. It must have been during this interlude that the mystery bidder appeared from behind the pillar. Robert Trelawney, with a strikingly attractive forty-something redhead clinging to his arm in a manner that suggested they were more than just friends. The parties made their way to the aisle to greet one another. And it was awkward, there could be no doubt of that.

'Robert...'

'Magdalene...'

'Congratulations on your purchase. An interesting auction, don't you think?' he said. 'And this is?'

Jimmy held out his hand. 'I'm Jimmy, eh...James. James McDuff. Magdalene's boyfriend I suppose.'

'Robert Trelawney.' He gave Maggie a quizzical look. For a moment she thought he was going to add something, something that might add exponentially to her discomfort, but he fell into silence. An awkward silence, due in no small part to the obvious doe-eyed devotion of this woman on his arm.

'Felicity Morgan,' she said, shooting them a beaming smile. 'But of course you'll remember me from the Hilton. I'm Robert's girlfriend I suppose.'

***

There were formalities to be attended to, and seeing the auction-house's invoice for eighty-four thousand pounds was the first time Maggie realised just how much it charged for its services. Fourteen grand commission was a tidy amount, and on top of that she, or more accurately, Hugo Morgan, would also have to find a five-figure sum to pay the Polperro Gallery's consultancy fee. She wondered what Morgan would say when he found he'd just shelled out nearly a hundred grand for a picture that had been expected to achieve no more than twenty-five. At least she could say truthfully that she had followed Lotti's advice, and of course he could easily afford it.

She tucked the receipt into her purse, then looked around to find Jimmy, spotting him standing just to one side of the doorway, chatting and laughing with Lotti. It was good to see he was taking the job seriously, especially since she appreciated how difficult it was for him. Three years since the split from his adored wife Flora, a split cause by a moment of madness or more accurately, by the ruthless machinations of the beautiful Astrid Sorenson. A woman that few men could resist, and to his shame, he had fallen for her hook, line and sinker, only to be discarded when she was finished with him, like the new toy of a spoiled child. Flirting with women evidently brought back bad memories and he wasn't anxious to go there again, but whatever he felt inside, it didn't show on the outside.

He raised a hand in greeting as Maggie came into view. As he wandered over to him, she saw him shake hands with Lotti before the beautiful young art dealer glided out of the room.

'That seemed to be going well,' Maggie said.

Jimmy laughed. 'Yeah, I hope you don't mind, but I said that I was beginning to think that you were a bit old for me and if she was ever on the market, I would be first in line.'

'Bloody cheek. So what did she say to that?'

'She let me down gently, that's the best way to put it. Said I'd definitely be somewhere on her list, but since she didn't expect to be on the market anytime soon it was all academic.'

Maggie shrugged. 'So that's it I guess. Our young Lotti gets a one-hundred percent clean bill of health. Hugo will be pleased.'

'I guess so. But changing the subject, don't you think we might have been the victims of a wee scam here? I mean, isn't it interesting that it ends up with just your Robert and our Lotti bidding against each other, and the price going up and up? And then suddenly, your Robert decides to drop out leaving you...'

She gave him an angry look. 'Look, he's not my Robert, will you stop calling him that.'

'Aye, sorry. But the thing is, you were left holding a seventy-grand painting that had an expectation of no more than twenty-five or so. Nice work if you can get it, that's what I say. And I'm assuming the Polperro is on commission, right?'

Maggie nodded. 'They get a fee from the owner. Twenty percent of the hammer price, same as Sotheby's.'

'So another fourteen grand then by my calculation. As I said, nice work.'

She was still a little bit angry with him, but the problem was the more she thought about it, the more she realised he might be right.

*Had* it all been pre-arranged, a nice little scheme to relieve a gullible rich client of a substantial sum? Maybe the auction house had been in on it too, she wouldn't be the least surprised. But no, surely not, not a revered organisation like Sotheby's, and in any case, although it wasn't her area of expertise, she was pretty sure that was against the law. As for the Polperro Gallery, that was a different matter. After all, Lotti had been very insistent that they took their seats as near to the back as possible, and on the right hand side. From where, conveniently, Robert Trelawney and his *girlfriend* could not be seen.

Yes, the girlfriend. He'd kept that damn quiet, hadn't he, before and after he had enticed her into his bloody bed. Christ, she hadn't been back on the dating scene for five minutes before she had fallen for a two-timing toe-rag.

But then again, he was probably thinking the same thing about her.

# Chapter 18

For once Ronnie French had come up with the goods, although Frank still couldn't work out how he'd managed to make a half-hour assignment up in Oxford last a whole bloody day. He assumed the fat slob had sloped off down to Henley or somewhere like that after the meeting, had a few beers in a nice country pub then slept it off in a lay-by on the way home. As a result, the conversation earlier that morning had been a bit terse to say the least.

'I expected you back in the office yesterday afternoon Ronnie. What is it, fifty, sixty miles? Even at the speed you drive, it should only have taken a couple of hours each way.'

'Traffic was terrible guv.' His answer was ludicrously improbable, but a few months from retirement, Ronnie clearly didn't see any point in trying harder.

'Aye sure,' Frank said, giving him a sardonic look. 'So what did you find out. Nothing I expect.'

French wheezed. 'That's a low blow guv. But that Sophie bird, I'd really love to give her one. We got on really well as it happens. Fancied me I think.'

Frank smiled to himself. Poor Frenchie, deluded as well as thick. 'Aye, I'm sure you can expect a phone call any day soon. So, come on, spill it. What did you get from our Mrs Fitzwilliam? And hurry it up, I haven't got all bloody day.'

'Well, I asked her straight out about Chardonnay Clarke, the fact that her dad thought she was on seventy-five grand or something like it. I said we knew the company wasn't paying it, so it must have been her agency that was doing it, know what I mean?'

'And?'

'Well she just laughed, said I was barking up the wrong tree. All very smooth like. But guv, I could tell by her eyes that I'd struck a nerve. Behind the mask and all that she looked worried. You can always tell when they're lying guv, can't you?'

Frank nodded. This was a new sensation for him, Ronnie French in the role of the brilliantly instinctive copper. But he played along.

'Aye you're right Ronnie, you can always tell. So what did you do then?'

He smiled. 'Yeah, so I decides to put the frighteners on her. I told her that I could easily get a warrant this very day to look at their books and then we'd all know the truth.'

'How did she react to that?'

'Well that's the thing guv. She seemed to relax when I said that. *Go ahead*, she says, *you won't find nothing*.'

Frank doubted Mrs Fitzwilliam was being quoted verbatim, but he wasn't there to give French an English lesson.

'You won't find nothing?'

'Exactly guv. It was as if this was something she was expecting. And at the moment I thinks to myself, she definitely knows something.'

'So then what did you do?'

'Then? Nothing, guv. Not with her at least. Just said we'd be in touch if we needed anything else and left it at that.'

Frank did the calculation. He'd have been in there ten, fifteen minutes at tops. He really was a lazy turd.

'Great work Ronnie,' he said, but irony was wasted on his colleague. And in any case, French wasn't finished yet.

'So anyways guv, that gets me thinking. I mean, it's obvious that *someone* was paying that Chardonnay bird a wad, so I thinks, get someone to take a look at her bank account. It's obvious, isn't it'

Now that Frenchie had said it, it was indeed obvious, but Frank didn't like to admit to himself that he hadn't thought of it first.

'Aye, it is.'

'So yeah, I thinks, that would be useful to know, wouldn't it?'

'Aye it would. But it's not that easy to get the banks to release that sort of information. Confidentiality and all that. Takes a lot of paperwork.'

French gave a smug smile. 'Yeah, it is tricky, but not if you've got a mate in the anti-terrorist squad who owes you a favour or three. Jayden Henry, he's one smart fella, but he likes a beer or two, which, well you know how it is guv. These Rasta lads aren't supposed to drink, so he needs it kept quiet like.'

Frank gave a deep sigh. Ronnie bloody French, the living embodiment of institutional racism. And he wasn't going to change no matter how many unconscious bias courses the Met sent him on.

'For your sake Ronnie, I'll pretend I didn't hear that. So this mate of yours, what did he find out?'

'Well guv, you know these security fellas have access all areas. So after I'd had a bit of lunch, I pulls into a lay-by and gives him a buzz. I just gives him Chardonnay's details, her address and the like, and then click-click-click, he's in. Turns out she's got a Nat West account out of a branch in Romford. And guess what guv? Twenty-eighth of every month, she gets lobbed over six grand. That's being going on for nearly a year.'

'Since she started with the Oxbridge Agency.'

'Exactly guv, I thought that too. Must be more than a coincidence. So anyways, obviously we've found out who's paying the dosh into her account, or at least we have a name. Rosalind Holdings Ltd. Some outfit based in Guernsey, one of these shell companies, that's what Jayden said. That's all I've got at the moment guv, but Jayden's doing a bit of digging to see if he can find out who's behind it.'

Frank didn't like to admit it, but he was impressed. Maybe he'd been underestimating French all this time. 'This is nice work Ronnie, well done. So how many favours have you used up?'

French laughed. 'That was all of them I think. But don't worry guv, another mate told me that Jayden's got a bit on the side. Someone a bit close to him, he says. Once I finds out a bit more about that, then maybe he'll owe me another one. Them black lads...'

Frank looked at him with disgust. There were still too many guys like French in the force, ignorant bigots who went about trashing its good name without a second thought.

'Ronnie, if I hear anything like that from you again, I'll personally make sure you never get to lift your pension. Understand *mate*?'

'Yeah, but Jayden's my big mate. He don't mind all that stuff. Gives it as well as takes it.'

Frank sighed. He doubted if Ronnie's big mate would share that analysis, but it was too late to do anything about the dinosaur now, after thirty years of institutional conditioning, and there was little point in trying.

But he could do something about Rosalind Holdings, that would be his next focus. He'd wait twenty-four hours or so to see what Ronnie's mate came up with, but if he drew a blank, that wasn't a concern. He could play it straight, filling in the reams of complicated paperwork which would grant them some sort of warrant that would force full disclosure of who was behind the company.

But he really hoped that Ronnie's bad lad Jayden Henry would deliver, because he bloody hated paperwork, complicated or otherwise.

# Chapter 19

The commissionaire gave a double-take as they entered the atrium.

'Sorry folks, but I could have sworn I'd let the gentlemen in not half-an-hour ago. But now that I takes a proper look, you're a lot younger than he was. You don't have a brother sir, do you?'

Jimmy gave a wry nod. 'Aye I do. But he doesn't look anything like me mate, trust me.'

Maggie laughed. 'Actually he does. But surely, it couldn't have been, could it?'

But it was, a fact that became self-evident when they emerged from the lift into the reception area of Brasenose Investment Trust to find Frank leaning over the reception desk, remonstrating loudly with Harriet Ibbotson.

'Look I don't care if he's a busy man and something important's come up. I'm bloody busy too, and I had an appointment at quarter-to. So unless I'm in there pronto, I'll have you arrested for obstructing a police officer in the performance of their duties. Is that clear enough for you?'

She looked as if she was about to argue the point, then thought better of it.

'I'll go through and ask him when he will be available. Please wait here sir.'

'Aye, you do that.'

'Hello Frank,' Maggie said, smiling, 'We didn't expect you to be here too. Always nice to see you of course.'

As Harriet opened the door to Morgan's office, the sound of raised voices drifted through to the reception area. It appeared Morgan was arguing with a woman. A woman whose voice they instantly recognised. Asvina Rani.

'Look Hugo...'

'Never mind the *look Hugo*. I paid you bloody well to fix this and I expect it to stay fixed, understand?'

'We can't do anything if she's set on this course...'

'We can't do anything? That's not what I want to hear. So you need to do better than that, understand?'

A moment later they emerged from his office, she tight-lipped and unsmiling, he red-faced and clearly worked up. He surveyed the reception area, catching Frank's eye and giving an exasperated sigh.

'You must be the bloody policeman I suppose. You look like one.'

Frank smiled serenely. 'Won't take long sir. Just a few questions for you, that's all.'

Maggie had drawn Asvina to one side and was whispering to her. 'What the hell was that all about?'

'It's Felicity Morgan.'

'What about her?'

'Trouble, that's what. She's decided to contest the settlement.'

Maggie looked puzzled. 'What, can she do that? I thought that was all done and dusted.'

'It was, but she's claiming Hugo hid some material assets from the court. It's a tired old tactic, but there's not much we can do to stop it if she's got the money to pay the legal fees.'

'Which she has of course. Thirty million if I remember rightly. God, you'd think that would be enough for anybody.'

Asvina gave a wry smile. 'It's not about the money Maggie. Felicity's still consumed with hatred and she'll do anything to make him suffer. It's personal for her, believe me.'

Maggie nodded. 'That explains the scene Jimmy and I saw. I don't know if I told you, but she went off on one at one of his investment updates. She was a bit pissed and firing out all sorts of wild threats. So this is what it was all leading to? I bet Hugo isn't very happy.'

'No, he's not,' Asvina said, 'and now he's blaming me for not tying up all the loose ends, as he puts it. He seems to think I've got some sort of legal magic wand that can make it all just go away.'

'Well, at least I've got good news for him about the lovely Lotti. That might cool him down a bit.'

Asvina smiled. 'I hope so. Anyway, I think I might need your help on this Maggie. I'll give you a call later.' She gave Maggie a hug then glided over towards the lift.

The imminent departure of his divorce lawyer appeared to have calmed Morgan's mood. He smiled at Maggie and Jimmy. 'You guys ok to wait until Inspector Stewart's finished with me?'

'They're my pals,' Frank said. 'They can sit in if they want. As I said, I'll only be a few minutes.'

Jimmy gave a thumbs up. 'Fine by us. If you don't mind Hugo that is.'

He shrugged. 'Whatever. But let's get this done. I'm a busy man.'

'Aye, so I've heard,' Frank said. 'That's twice now.'

Morgan ignored the dig, leading them through to his office.

'Grab a chair,' he said, gesturing at the conference table. 'Anywhere you like.'

Jimmy had taken the seat next to Frank and for the first time, Morgan recognised the obvious likeness.

'Wait a minute. Are you two...'

'Aye, brothers,' Jimmy said. 'Just a coincidence, that's all. I'm the amateur, he's the professional, although you wouldn't know it to look at him.'

'Thanks pal,' Frank said, shooting him a wry smile. 'Anyroads Mr Morgan, I don't want to take any more of your time than necessary. The thing is, I'm investigating a couple of suspicious deaths, and it turns out one of them has a connection back to your company.'

'Well of course Inspector,' he said smoothly, 'I'll do everything I can to help you.'

'The firm in question is HBB Bank. I'm right that there's a connection there?'

'We invest in that company, that is true, but then we have positions in more than three hundred organisations across the globe.'

Frank nodded. 'Aye, but I think that one's a bit different. You didn't just have a position in that outfit, as you put it. As I understand, you were very actively involved.'

Morgan smiled. 'Naturally. It's what we do. Activist investors. But we're not involved in the day-to-day management of any of our companies. Our job is to ensure the leadership of firms we invest in is focussed on delivering value to shareholders, and when it isn't, we act. That was the case at HBB and yes, we took steps to effect change. But there's nothing unusual in that, I can assure you. As I said, it's what we do.'

'Aye, that might be the case, but you see, not everybody sees it in as straightforward terms as you do sir.'

Morgan's eyes narrowed. 'What do you mean?'

'I'm sure you're familiar with the concept of industrial espionage. At least, that's what the top financial guy at HBB was suggesting when I interviewed him. He thinks that's how you find out about all this internal stuff that's supposed to be confidential.'

He shook his head slowly and gave a sardonic laugh.

'Dear dear, not these tired old conspiracy theories again. I hate to disappoint you, but there's no magic Inspector. We just look harder at the numbers than others are prepared to do, that's all. Because believe me, it's all there in black and white if you know where to look.'

Frank smiled. 'Well I'll need to take your word for that sir. Now can I ask you, do you have any involvement with Alexia Life?'

He smiled. 'No, afraid not inspector. They're a mutual you see, *so* nineteenth century. They're run by a spectacularly useless management, but since they're owned by their policy holders, unless there's a mass revolt to kick out the moronic leadership team, I doubt much will change there. It hasn't for the last two hundred years, so I don't see why it will now.'

'I must say sir, you do seem to know a lot about them. For someone who's not involved I mean.'

Morgan shrugged. 'Business is my hobby Inspector. It's sad I know, but where other people waste their time reading trashy novels, I study the business pages. It's paid off handsomely, I think you'll agree.'

'Aye, if you say so,' Frank said. 'But coming back to the folks who died, Chardonnay Clarke at HBB and Luke Brown at Alexia. Did you know them?'

His voice took on a condescending tone. 'As I told you before, we're not involved in day-to-day management of our investments. I may have some interaction with the senior leadership, but even that is limited. I certainly wouldn't have any reason to know such junior staff.'

Frank was silent for a moment as if weighing up his next move. Maggie was studying him closely, fascinated to watch such a consummate professional at work. When she was just starting out as a lawyer, she often had to sit in on police interviews as a duty solicitor, so the situation wasn't new to her. But she'd seldom seen anything to match this, the tone of his questioning finely judged, gently probing but without risking an aggressive reaction which she knew would be counter-productive. However, to her surprise it seemed as if he was minded to draw the short interview to a close, as he nodded and said,

'No, I see now you wouldn't have known them sir. Well, it was just a loose strand of my enquiry that I had to follow up. Sorry to have troubled you.' He got to his feet and smiled at Jimmy and Maggie. 'Maybe catch up with you two in the pub later? Anyway, must dash. Got some bad guys to catch.'

\*\*\*

She waited until Frank had left the room before speaking. 'He always says that, the bit about bad guys I mean. And he's very good at it, apparently. Catching them.'

Jimmy laughed. 'Aye, so he says.'

'If that's the case,' Morgan said, half-serious, 'maybe I should ask him to look at the Justice for Greenway matter. Unless of course you've got something for me.'

Maggie smiled. 'Well as it happens, we've already asked him to help. Strictly in an unofficial capacity, but then again more or less everything he does starts off as unofficial.'

Morgan looked surprised. 'I didn't know you guys worked with the police.'

'Not the police per say,' she said. 'Just Frank.'

'And has he been able to help?'

'A little. Let's just say there's been some progress on the matter, but perhaps before Jimmy updates you on what we've found out, we can share some good news about Lotti.'

Morgan's eyes lit up. 'Good news? That sounds excellent.'

'Yes, I think it is,' Maggie said, then went on to tell him about how they had spoken to her mother who confirmed that her daughter Lotti was working in London, and that they also had confirmation from the University of Heidelberg that she had graduated from that prestigious institution as she had claimed. She didn't say anything about the fact she had doubted Lotti was as old as she had told her fiancé she was. That had been disproved by the facts, and so had to be dismissed as an issue.

Finally they addressed what could have been the trickiest matter, Lotti's fidelity or otherwise. Which in the end turned out to be the most straightforward of all, Jimmy explaining how he had sought to find out whether or not she was single, and had made it crystal clear he was interested in her whatever her answer. And how she had politely but firmly made it equally clear that she was not interested because she was blissfully happy in her existing relationship.

'So I think it's safe for you to make your arrangements for the big proposal,' Maggie said, smiling. 'Porto Banus, wasn't it?'

Morgan looked as if the emotion of the moment might overcome him. His face broke into a huge beaming smile, and Maggie saw him clenching and unclenching his fists. 'Brilliant news,' he said, 'that's brilliant news.'

She shrugged. 'Glad we could help. And she really is a lovely girl, you're very lucky.' But of course it had nothing to do with luck. This was the man who had quite coldly decided he wanted a new and younger wife and had simply discarded the old one when he was finished with her. Not for the first time she found herself hoping that the same fate would befall him when he was sixty and wrinkly and Lotti had decided there was more to life than just money. That would be a cracking moment of schadenfreude.

'So these Justice for Greenway people,' Morgan said, changing the subject. 'Tell me what you've got.'

Jimmy smiled. 'Will do. Right, so it made sense to start our investigation up in Cumbria. Seemed odds-on that it would be centred around there obviously, given where the mine is. By good fortune, we found a contact on the local paper, a nice lady called Liz Donahue. Smart too. Your mate Gary whats-it gave us her name.'

Morgan grimaced. 'That arse McGinley.'

'Funnily enough, that's what Liz called him too. Anyway, it turns out there's been a couple of incidents up there as well, directed mainly at Belinda Milner. The woman who drowned herself.'

'Yes, a terrible tragedy,' Morgan said, without emotion.

Jimmy nodded. 'Aye it was, a real tragedy. Anyway, they graffiti'd her house and her car, and I heard that they also tried to poison her dog. So kinda similar to the stuff you've experienced. But to cut to the chase, Liz Donahue pointed me to a local family. The Tompkins.'

Morgan gave him a sardonic look. 'Ah yes, the investment geniuses. Bet all their savings on Milner's lame horse then started bitching when it fell at the first.'

Jimmy looked at him sharply. 'Christ Hugo, William Tompkins killed himself because of the shame of it all. That's not something to joke about.'

He shrugged. 'I don't see it as my problem. So you think it may be them behind this?'

'We went to see them. Liz and I met two of the sons, Wayne and Karl. They're pretty sore about the whole thing and I'd put money on them being behind the Milner incidents. The one's down here in London, we're not too sure of at the moment, although Karl looks a nasty piece of work so I wouldn't put it past him. And he was a sapper in the Royal Engineers, so he'd have the wherewithal, there's no doubt about that.'

'That's where Frank - DI Stewart - comes in,' Maggie said. 'If either of them was involved, we think they would have driven down in his car or in his father's old van rather than taking the train. Frank is going to pull a few favours to get a couple of the traffic cameras on the M6 checked out, see if we can spot him en route.'

It was flimsy, she knew it was, but the good news about Lotti seemed to have had a positive effect on Morgan's mood. He shrugged, 'Well ok, let's wait and see where that takes us. Is that us done then?'

He half got up, seemingly anxious to bring the meeting to a close.

'There's just one more thing Hugo, if you don't mind,' Jimmy said quickly. 'It's kinda related to the injunction you took out against the Chronicle.' The one you conveniently omitted to mention, Maggie thought.

Morgan said nothing, but his expression had hardened as Jimmy continued.

'The wee local paper up there, the Westmoreland Gazette, they had a story that they tried to syndicate out to the Chronicle. I think that's the right term. But apparently McGinley had different ideas. Something about the South African guy, Mark De Bruin. McGinley thinks he's the one who told you about the screw-up with the cobalt content.'

'McGinley's a fool as well as an arse,' Morgan said. 'I raised that injunction just as a bit of fun. Now the idiots at the Chronicle are going to spend half a million to fight it, but what they don't know is I intend to drop the action five minutes before the judge announces his verdict. God, they're going to look so stupid.'

'So that's what it's all about?' Maggie said. 'Some sort of private vendetta against Gary McGinley?'

Morgan gave a smug smile. 'Exactly right. It's sport actually. His tiny little head is full of stupid conspiracy theories, but as I've said many times, there's no magic. And this one was all in the numbers, plain as the nose on your face.'

'What do you mean?' Jimmy asked, surprised.

'Eight weeks after Greenway were supposed to have been bringing all that lovely cobalt-rich ore to the surface, the revenue line in their monthly trading updates was still showing a big fat zilch. Nothing. Oh sure, our Belinda was spouting a load of shit about tidying up some fine print in their sales contracts, but I knew that was rubbish. If that ore was yielding like they said it would, they would have recognised the revenue there and then, contract or no contract. So you see, no magic. You just need to know where to look, and we do.'

The more Maggie thought about it, the more plausible his account seemed. She hated to admit it, but it seemed a lot more credible than the frankly wild suggestions of dark industrial espionage that Jimmy had uncovered up in Cumbria. But then again, she knew that even in the short time he had known the Westmoreland Gazette reporter, he had come to trust Liz Donahue implicitly. And if Jimmy Stewart trusted this woman whom she was yet to meet, then that was good enough for her.

'Jimmy's contact seems pretty sure there was more to it than that,' Maggie said, but then, anxious not to raise Morgan's hackles added, 'but from what you said about those monthly trading things, then maybe she's wrong.'

'Aye, and I didn't really get the full story anyway,' Jimmy said, tuning into where she was coming from, 'All Liz said was something about pillow talk, and to be honest, I haven't been able to make head or tail of it. But we'll find out soon enough, because I think her paper's planning on running her story at the weekend.'

Morgan sneered. 'Pillow talk did you say? Well, I'm sure it will be great entertainment for the locals. And no doubt your reporter friend, what was her name...?'

'Liz Donahue.'

'... yes, well no doubt your Miss Donahue will enjoy her fifteen minutes of fame.'

Morgan pushed back his chair and stood up, the smooth facade fully restored. 'I think we've made some progress, and once again, thank you both for putting my mind to rest about Lotti. It's a big weight off my shoulders, it really is.'

He ushered them towards the door. 'And if you and your pet policeman dig up anything more about those Justice morons, let me know immediately.'

Afterwards when she discussed the meeting with Jimmy, she couldn't help thinking that somewhere along the line they had missed something, and she said as much to him. He also agreed there was something, a vague something he couldn't quite put his finger on, but aye, definitely something. And then out of the blue, she realised what it was. Because when she replayed Frank's interview in her mind, she was certain he hadn't said anything about Charlotte and Luke being junior staff. So how the hell did Hugo Morgan know? Now she understood why Frank had been perfectly happy for the interview to be short and sweet. Because he had noticed too.

*\*\**

They normally met on a Thursday evening, but this time they had agreed on a supplementary lunchtime date earlier the same day. The Old King's Head was packed as usual, customers being attracted by what was in City terms a good-value menu. Charging twelve to fifteen quid for a main, it served pub staples like lasagne and steak and ale pie, nothing too fancy, but it was proper food, not the pre-prepared microwaved stodge favoured by the big chain places that she knew Frank despised. You couldn't reserve a table, so timing was everything if you wanted to bag a place. Either get there before twelve-fifteen, or wait until about half past one to be in the vanguard of the second wave. They had chosen the former option, turning up at a minute past the hour and had managed to grab a little table tucked away in the corner. It was barely big enough for three, but the quiet location meant it was just about possible to conduct a normal conversation. And they had a lot to talk about.

'He's quite an operator our boy Hugo, isn't he?' Frank said, as Jimmy brought the drinks back to the table. Maggie was glad that it hadn't taken long, because sitting there alone with Frank, even for just a couple of minutes had been, as she had expected, awkward. And confusing too, because she was a forty-two-year-old woman and she ought to by now be able to make sense of her feelings. Frank was nice, more than nice, but then, casting a huge shadow over everything, there was Robert. Already that relationship had become carnal, as lovely as it was unexpected, and everything had been going swimmingly until she had discovered that Mr Robert Trelawney hadn't been exactly honest with her. Somehow omitting to mention the presence of Felicity Morgan in his life. Not exactly a lie though, it had to be said. It was not as if he was pretending to be a completely different person entirely. Not like her. *Robert, I've got something to tell you. You see, I'm not actually Mrs Magdalene Slattery.* Now *that* would be a conversation.

'Yeah he certainly is,' Jimmy said, responding to his brother's observation. 'Food should only be five minutes by the way. Pie for me again.'

'Great, I'm starving,' Maggie said, pleased to be able to focus once again on the mundane. 'So Frank, getting back to Hugo Morgan, I'm thinking you noticed that thing about the interns?'

'Aye, I spotted it. How did he know they were junior staff when I never mentioned it once?'

'Exactly. Have you any ideas what it means?'

He shrugged. 'Well it means he knew of course, but why, that's a different matter. That's why I wanted to talk to you guys, see if you can help me shed some light on it. You see, I thought it would have been connected to his Brasenose Trust business, given that Chardonnay worked at HBB Bank, and we know he was knee -deep in that, with the German takeover and everything. But Luke Brown was assigned to Alexia Life, and the financial guy at HBB said exactly the same as Morgan, that it's a mutual so doesn't have any shareholders. Meaning there was nothing for Morgan to buy into or anything like that. No connection at all as far as I can see. A dead end.'

'Could it be something personal then?' Jimmy asked. 'We know he likes them young. Maybe he was having an affair with Chardonnay.'

Maggie gave a half-smile but she wasn't convinced. 'But not with Luke surely? No, I'm certain as I can be that his relationship with Lotti is important to him. He's not faking that, I mean why else would he employ Asvina to do the due diligence? I don't like the man, but he's not a sexual predator. You can always tell, and he's not.'

'Aye, you're probably right,' Frank said, sighing. 'I've got one of my team taking a look at Luke Brown's situation. We don't really know anything about him, except that he was another one of that agency's scholarship kids. Maybe that will turn up a missing piece in the jigsaw.'

'They both died in the same way didn't they?' she said. 'The suicides that weren't suicides.'

'Aye. The Aphrodite suicides, that's what I'm calling them now. Two good-looking kids. Special kids.'

'Except they were murders, not suicides.' Maggie said. 'You're sure of that now.'

'No question, but as to why they were killed, I'm still at base camp. I've got no motive and no suspects but apart from that it's going great.'

She laughed. 'Maybe you should subcontract to us. We've wrapped up the Lotti matter already, in double-quick time, and we're making some progress on Justice for Greenway too.' She hoped he would take it as a joke. Looking at him, she wasn't sure he had.

'Aye, maybe it will come to that,' he said, unsmiling. 'But I think you had a suicide too, am I right?'

Jimmy nodded. 'Yeah, but this one's not suspicious like yours. Belinda Milner, she was the boss of the mine. One morning she just put on her costume and took a swim in the lake. Left a husband and teenage daughter.'

An elderly waitress had arrived with their food, her expression broadcasting that she would rather be anywhere on earth but here.

'Who's the pie?' she snapped, staring vacantly into space.

'Aye, that's me,' Jimmy said, standing up. 'Here, let me help you with that.' He took the plate from her and smiled.

Maggie shot Frank a knowing look. *She'll melt*, it said, *they always do.*

And she did. 'Oh, thank you sir,' she said, beaming. 'It's always so busy in this place, run off my feet I am. People don't appreciate it.'

'Aye, tough job, I can see that. He's the lasagne and she's the fish and chips. Here, pass them over, save you stretching.'

He took the plates from her and laid them on the table.

'Right guys, tuck in. Thanks miss, we'll give you a shout when we want some more drinks, ok?'

The waitress nodded her appreciation and slipped away to collect her next order. For a few minutes they concentrated on their meal until Frank, through a mouthful of lasagne said,

'So this Milner woman. Do you two have any idea why she did it? I suppose *that* must be connected to Morgan in some way. Given all the Greenway Mining crap and that.'

'It's a bit of puzzle,' Jimmy said, 'because by all accounts the collapse of Greenway on her watch wouldn't have affected her one bit, certainly not enough to make her kill herself. She was one of these smooth Establishment types you see, the type that seem to flit from failure to failure with no apparent effect on their careers.'

'Yes, plenty of them about,' Maggie said. 'That's one of the things we're trying to find out. Because there must have been something else that drove her to that awful act.'

'And I think we're going to find out pretty soon. Liz Donahue's paper's running a story in the next few days.' Jimmy nodded in Frank's direction. 'It ties up with the stuff that you heard from the HBB financial guy, industrial espionage and all that. I think her story is going to spill the beans on how Morgan found out about that problem with the cobalt content.'

'And you think there's a connection between that and Milner's death?' Frank asked.

'Got to be,' Maggie said. 'Morgan spun us some line about it all being in the numbers or in the monthly trading statements, but it sounded like bullshit to us. Or to me at least.'

'Aye, well that would be great for you,' Frank said. 'But being selfish, I don't think it helps me with my murders.'

Maggie shrugged. 'No, I guess you're right there. But maybe it reinforces what we probably already know about him. That he's not above sharp practice to get what he wants.'

But she knew it and Frank knew it and Jimmy knew it, although none of them said it. *Billionaire indulges in sharp business practices.* It didn't pass the test. The *so what* test.

# Chapter 20

Frank swiped his debit card in the direction of Atlee House's new high-tech drinks dispenser and took grateful delivery of a *grande* double-shot Americano. Alongside, a sophisticated whirr from the equally hi-tech vending machine signified that a Mars Bar and a packet of cheese and onion crisps was about to join it, completing his lunch order. Scooping them up, he smiled to himself, reflecting on his earlier brief encounter with Hugo Morgan, and how excellent it was that he had caught him lying. An easy slip to make, not that he sympathised in any way, but now the connections were beginning to rack up and he loved it when that began to happen in a case. The Oxbridge Agency had supplied both Chardonnay Clarke and Luke Brown, and despite his denials, Morgan clearly knew of them both. And actually by an admittedly small margin, Luke was the more interesting of the two. Alexia Life was a mutual and therefore it was off limits as far as Brasenose's activist investor MO was concerned. So why would Morgan know of some insignificant intern in an organisation he had zero connection to?

Back at his desk, he pulled out an A4 pad from his drawer and began to doodle. He wasn't any sort of an artist, he knew that, but somehow these indecipherable sketches helped him organise his thoughts. *The connections.* Two identical murders made to look like suicides, the stand-out good looks of the victims, the Oxbridge Agency, the modest backgrounds, the billionaire Hugo Morgan. It all had to mean something, and he'd figure it out soon enough.

On a whim, he picked up his phone and called Ronnie French. It rang nearly a dozen times before he answered, Frank assuming that the fat turd was probably snoozing in a favourite lay-by somewhere off the beaten track. But he was wrong.

'Guv?'

'Where are you Frenchie? I need you to do something for me.'

'Me? I'm in Atlee. On the top floor with your pal Eleanor Campbell.'

'What, with Campbell?' This was a surprise to Frank, because he couldn't think what business Ronnie could possibly have with the young forensic officer.

'Yeah guv, there's been a bit of a development with my mate Jayden and your pal is helping me instead. With that Guernsey bank account. You know, Rosalind Holdings.'

'Right, stay there and I'll come and join you as soon as I've finished my lunch.'

Five minutes later, he was at her desk and pulling up a chair alongside them.

'You're keeping some dodgy company these days Miss Campbell.'

She shot him a sardonic smile. 'Yeah, like you for instance. But look at this,' she said pointing to the wide-screen laptop that seemed to cover half of her desk. 'It's running this Fraudbreaker app with sixty-four-bit decryption and eight-layer packet tracing straight out of the box. Ronnie got me it. It's like awesome.'

'I got it from Jayden,' Ronnie said in way of explanation. 'He doesn't need it at the moment due to him being sort of incapacitated. So I sort of borrowed it.'

'Along with all his passwords,' Eleanor said helpfully.

Frank grimaced. 'Christ Ronnie, I thought you said your Jayden Henry guy works for the anti-terrorist division.'

'Yeah, so? We're not doing nothing wrong, are we?'

Frank could think of a dozen things they were doing wrong, starting with theft of valuable government property, which got him pondering how Ronnie had managed to sneak it out of MI6's offices over on Albert Embankment in the first place. For the second time in a week, he wondered if he might be guilty of underestimating the corpulent slug.

'Anyway guv, what did you want me to do for you?'

Frank smiled. 'That can wait for a bit. I want to watch what's going on here first. It looks interesting.'

'You can watch, but you won't understand any of it,' Eleanor said, matter-of-factly.

'I won't,' he answered, smiling. 'That's why we pay you your pittance. But how come you got a hold of this piece of kit? Frenchie, tell us what happened to your mate Jayden.'

Ronnie shrugged. 'Our boy Jayden got caught with his trousers down. With his wife's sister. A bit of a doll so I've heard. Anyways, word got out in the community and he had the shit beaten out of him. You know what them black lads are like, all that disrespect stuff and all that.'

Frank gave him an angry look. 'Ronnie, I've told you once and I'll tell you again, if I hear any more of that bloody racist nonsense from you or anything like it, I'm going to haul you up in front of HR so fast that the skin will be scraped off your arse on the way. I won't bloody have it on my watch, you hear?'

He gave another shrug. 'Loud and clear boss.' In one ear and out the other more like, and it was too late to do anything about it now, no matter how many courses they forced the fat twat to sit through. But he meant what he said. One more strike from Frenchie and he was out.

'So you say he's incapacitated then?' Frank said, trying to calm himself.

'Yeah, and some. Stuck in the Royal Free and looks like he'll be in there for a week or two. But he gave me his pass and so I just wandered in to pick up his stuff.'

'What, you just waltzed into the headquarters of MI6, and then waltzed out again with a laptop the size of a wide-screen telly?'

French looked puzzled. 'I had a pass,' he said simply.

'God save us,' Frank muttered under his breath.

Frank noticed for the first time that Eleanor was holding something in her hand, a slim plastic device that looked a bit like an old-school iPod music player.

'What's that?' he asked.

'It's for two-factor authentication. I've told you about it before but you won't have remembered.'

'That was Jayden's too,' French said. 'You know when you're paying someone new on your banking app, or you're logging on from a different device it sends an authorisation code to your phone? Well this is a fancy gizmo that lets the spooks intercept the code. Some stonking software behind it and make no mistake.'

Frank gave him a look of astonishment. 'So you're an IT geek Frenchie? Who'd have thought it.'

French smiled. 'Not really guv. My lad's a programmer and I've picked up the lingo from him.'

'Are we like ready?' Eleanor said, not bothering to hide her impatience.

'Aye sure,' Frank said. 'Let's go.'

She hammered a few keys of the laptop, bringing up what looked like a bank statement.

'See, that's Chardonnay's and there's the six thousand you guys are interested in.' She moved her mouse so it hovered over the line in the statement. Immediately, a box popped up containing three rows of text. *Account Name, Sort Code, Account Number.*

'See, that's the account details of who paid it in. The Fraudbreaker software retrieves that from a high-security mega transaction database shared by the banks.'

'Don't tell me,' Frank said, stifling a laugh.

'What?' Eleanor said.

'It's awesome.'

'Well, like, it is,' she said, in a tone that questioned why anyone could possibly think otherwise.

Punching in a few more characters caused a dialogue box to pop up in the centre of the screen.

*Welcome to Internet banking.*
*Enter user code and password.*

'We don't need to worry about this.' A few seconds later, the device in her hand gave a gentle vibration. Immediately the lap top display changed.

*Enter one-time access code.*

She glanced at the device and carefully keyed in the six-digit number. 'We're in,' she said, pointing to the display, which was showing another statement, this time for Rosalind Holdings, an account held with Guernsey Bank.

'So does this work globally?' Frank said, vaguely aware that organisations and individuals often tried to hide their financial affairs behind a complex web of international accounts.

'Pretty much, according to the system docs.'

'Jayden gave us them too,' French said, with no hint of apology.

'Although not Russia or China,' Eleanor continued, 'defo not, but then, guys take their money out of these places, they don't put it in.'

'Sweet.' It was one of her favourite expressions and Frank liked to drop it into conversation just to annoy her. But this time she chose to ignore him, continuing to manipulate her mouse around her desk.

'So, this is like interesting. I've scrolled back a few months and look...' She clicked to highlight a line.

'RGBX. No idea who this is but they're paying forty thousand Euros a month into this account.' She clicked on the line and the same dialogue box as before popped up.

'Looks like a Santander account. That code's for their Spanish branches. The IBAN. So it's in Spain.'

'So this maybe explains where Rosalind gets some or all of their funding,' Frank said, surprising himself that for once he actually seemed to understand what she was talking about. 'Now you can use this mega database thing to get to RGBX's account, and then the Fraudbreaker stuff and that wee iPod gizmo gets you in. Or is it the other way around?'

Eleanor looked equally surprised. 'You're sharp this afternoon, aren't you? Yeah, like you're right, exactly. But maybe there'll be lots of layers in the web, so it might take a while to get back to the original source. And there will probably be a few false trails. Or maybe the trail will go cold. So it's not that simple.' Frank knew her well and was able to read between the lines. Stop looking over my shoulder and let me get on with my work in peace.

He gestured at French. 'Come on, Ronnie, she doesn't need an audience. Let's wander downstairs and chew the fat about the case whilst she's working on it.'

'Yeah, sure guv. Off you go and I'll catch up with you in a minute.'

Frank got up and headed towards the stairwell. Taking a glimpse back, he saw Ronnie scribble something on a piece of paper then give Eleanor a thumbs-up, which she returned with her normal disdainful look. Intrigued, he waited for him to catch up with him.

'What was all that about Frenchie?'

'What? Aw, nothing guv, just a thought I had. Eleanor's going to take a look but as I say it might be nothing.'

It seemed that he wasn't going to give anything more away, so they went back down to Frank's office where he updated Ronnie on his interesting interview with Hugo Morgan, conscious of a growing respect for his DC. Sure, Frenchie was the laziest man ever to be issued with a warrant card, but when it came to sniffing out a wrong 'un, as he might put it, it seemed his instincts were of the highest order. Frank wondered what he would make of Morgan, whether he would see through the effortlessly smooth facade, whether he would sniff out the lies that hid behind it. Because that's the job he had pencilled in for his colleague. Put the shambolic detective constable in front of Morgan and see if the billionaire, to his cost, underestimated him too.

Out of the blue, French said, 'So who do you think is behind this guv? These payments I mean.'

So Frank told him who he thought was responsible, and French, amiably disagreeing, gave him his contrary view, and then they agreed a modest wager on the outcome. Thirty-five minutes later, Eleanor Campbell appeared, laptop under her arm and a deep frown on her forehead, which Frank knew from experience meant that she had cracked it, and after a lengthy preamble describing the mountainous difficulties she had overcome, settled the bet. Forcing Frank to reach into his wallet and withdraw a crisp new ten-pound note.

* * *

'There's something else guv,' French said, after he'd tucked the tenner safely away in a trouser pocket. 'I asked her to look at the other one too, that Brown lad.'

Eleanor nodded. 'Fraudbreaker's got awesome search. You just like key in a name and it brings up every account they have. Luke Brown's only got one.'

'Don't tell me,' Frank said, excited. 'He was getting six grand a month too.'

'What?' Eleanor said, looking puzzled. 'Like, no way. He gets nineteen hundred a month from the Oxbridge Agency. That's like not much more than minimum wage.'

Eleanor was exaggerating of course, but this was nothing like the seventy-five grand that Chardonnay Clarke had been receiving. And then he remembered. *We also provide them with a nominal salary whilst they are on deployment.* That's what Sophie Fitzwilliam had told him, and nineteen hundred a month, or twenty-three grand a year, was certainly nominal. But there had to be something else. Because Luke Brown had been murdered in exactly the same way as Chardonnay Clarke. It was just a matter of finding it, that was all. He'd give it to Frenchie and wee Yvonne Sharp for forty-eight hours' max, and if that didn't work, he would have to dive in himself. Not a problem, that.

* * *

Fair play to Ronnie French, he hadn't tried to take the credit for it himself. That nudged him up a notch in Frank's estimation, although it didn't balance the fifty he'd gone down on account of him being a racist twat. But credit where credit's due, and it hadn't taken forty-eight hours, in fact it had barely taken forty-eight minutes.

'She spotted it right away guv,' he had said when he called Frank with the good news. 'On the bank statement. You see, Yvonne knows the threshold is twenty-one grand a year, so she says, why isn't this

Luke paying nothing back? So we gives them a call up in Glasgow, all official like, and they confirmed it, sweet as a nut. Paid off in full it was. Nearly forty grand. Nine months ago. Lucky sod, that's what Yvonne said, to have your student loan paid off just like that.'

Aye, lucky sod, apart from the fact Luke Brown was dead. But now he had something more solid to work with and that was good. He knew Chardonnay was pulling down seventy-five grand and now he'd found out that the dead boy had his student loan paid off. Now that they more or less knew who, that just left one big question to be answered. Why?

# Chapter 21

*Oh what a tangled web we weave, when first we practice to deceive.* Everybody knew the quotation, and everyone knew what it meant, although Maggie, with no little smugness, reflected that not everyone knew it was Sir Walter Scott and not William Shakespeare who had come up with it in the first place. *What a bloody mess you get yourself into when you pretend to be somebody else entirely.* That might be a better way of describing the situation she now found herself in, or to be more accurate, *they* found themselves in.

Felicity Morgan, the bitter ex-wife, had decided to challenge the settlement that everyone involved thought was long done and dusted, and was now asking for another seventy million on top of the thirty million she had already been awarded. On the basis that a journalist - the trouble-maker Gary McGinley -had seemingly discovered that her ex-husband had squirreled away a tidy fortune over in the Channel Islands, out of sight of the authorities. And now Asvina Rani, having failed in her technical bid to prevent the original deal being contested in court, and getting some serious grief from her client Hugo Morgan as a result, had to come up with a Plan B. Which was to find out how much the ex-wife really knew. Or rather, to get Bainbridge Associates to find out for her.

The only problem was, Maggie Bainbridge was now Magdalene Slattery and Jimmy Stewart was James McDuff. And the former Mrs Morgan had met them both, which left them with only one option if they were to win the trust of Mrs Morgan, enough to get her to share confidences. An option that Jimmy was probably not going to like. But to her surprise, he didn't object at all.

'I thought you were going to ask me to seduce her'.

Maggie laughed. 'Seduce her? How delightfully old-fashioned.'

'And I was going to say *no way*. The next Mrs Morgan, that was bad enough, but the old one, that would be a step too far. That sort of stuff's not in my employment contract you know.'

'Of course it isn't.' They both knew no such document existed, but that didn't stop him referring to it whenever she asked him to do something he didn't like. 'But you'll do it then?'

'Aye, no bother. But no seduction stuff, ok?'

'Of course not. All we want is to find out where's she coming from. See if she really has anything concrete about Hugo's finances so we can report back to Asvina.'

So he picked up his phone and called Felicity Morgan.

*'Felicity? This is James McDuff, we met at that auction a couple of days ago, do you remember? What it is, I think your man's cheating with my lady.'*

Two hours later, he was back in the entrance atrium of the Park Lane Hilton, just a few weeks after attending that eventful quarterly update of the Brasenose Investment Trust. Arriving ten minutes early, he found a seat tucked along a wall of the room and settled down to read that day's *Chronicle* which a previous occupant had left behind. Absorbed in a story about cuts to military budgets, he failed to notice that twenty minutes had passed and there was still no sign of Mrs Morgan. Glancing at his watch again, he was about to wander over to the reception when he caught her out the corner of his eye, dressed in the same skinny black jeans, leather blouson and stilettos as in their previous brief encounter. But unexpectedly, she wasn't alone.

Today, trailing a metre or so behind her and wearing an archetypal teenage scowl was a young woman who he assumed must be her daughter. Felicity Morgan marched up to the reception desk and, ignoring a Japanese couple who were in the middle of checking out, said loudly. 'I'm meeting someone. A Mr James McDuff.'

The young receptionist, obviously displeased by the interruption, gave her a cold look then nodded wordlessly towards where he sat.

'Thank you. Come on Rosie.'

She tottered over to him and sat down opposite.

'This is my daughter Rosie. We're booked in for lunch at one, so I haven't got long. Family time is so important, don't you think?'

Rosie Morgan was attractive, although it was difficult to tell under the layers of Goth-punk make-up. Her eyes were encircled in black mascara and her lips coated in a deep navy gloss. She wore purple Doc Martins, ripped fishnets and a skirt so short it barely covered her bottom. In a different way from her mother, she too looked amazing. But she wore a look suggesting she regarded the date as duty rather than pleasure. And then he remembered that the kids had chosen to live with their father rather than their mother. One day he would try to find out why they had made that choice, but today wasn't that day. Whatever the case, her presence was going to make the meeting a bit awkward. But he'd been on some tough missions in his time, and by comparison this would be a walk in the park. So he got straight on to it.

'Aye, I'm in a hurry too. So, I was checking my lady's phone. I always do that when she's not around. Doesn't even have a pin code, stupid bitch. That's when I saw them. Texts, loads of them. I thought you should know.'

She gave him an angry look. 'I don't believe it. Not my Robert.' *My Robert*. He'd heard *that* one before.

'Aye, that's exactly what I thought, not my Magdalene. But it's true. And I don't know about you, but I'm not going to stand for it.'

'But you're all the same you men. Use us for sex and then throw us away when you get bored. We had fantastic sex you know, the night before he dumped me. He never could have any cause for complaint in that department. I was a bloody fantastic shag all through our marriage. Anything he ever wanted, and I never had a headache, not like some women.'

Confused, Jimmy eventually cottoned on to the fact she was talking about her ex-husband. And now she was in full flow.

'He was a pig you know,' she said, taking no trouble to hide her bitterness. 'And Robert's a pig too. You're all pigs.' He was taken aback by the ferocity of this woman's anger. Her rejection had clearly opened a wound that didn't look as if it was going to heal anytime soon.

'And look at me. I'm still attractive and sexy, aren't I? James, do you find me sexy? You do, don't you?'

'Mum!' Her daughter's embarrassment was so acute you could almost taste it.

'Well, aye...,' Jimmy said, 'you're a very attractive woman Felicity.' And as mad as a box of frogs he thought, but he didn't say it.

'That's it mum, I'm going.' Rosie was on her feet, slinging her bag over her shoulder, her eyes burning with anger. 'Some other time, ok?'

'Rosie, please...' Felicity reached out a hand, trying to grab hold of the bag, but with a deft flick, her daughter swung it out of her reach, before hurrying off towards the door.

Now she was speaking so loudly that everyone in the atrium could hear her. Jimmy suspected that was her intention. 'You see, he's turned them against me. Her and Yazz. All of them. Fucking daddy is so wonderful and perfect, that's what he's got them believing. But if only they knew the truth, they would think differently, believe me.'

He gave her what he hoped was a sympathetic look. 'Kids eh? It must be awful for you, I can understand that, everything that's happened. But you know, you have to move on, there's not really any other option.'

God where had that come from? Jimmy Stewart, the relationship councillor.

'I don't want to get over it,' she said bluntly. 'I want him to suffer, the way I'm suffering. For the rest of his damn life. Fuck him. And fuck Robert Trelawney too.'

He looked up to see a smartly-suited man approaching them at speed. On his lapel, the badge read 'George Konstantinou, General Manager.' When he spoke, he was smiling but his tone was grave.

'I'm sorry madam, but we do not like to hear foul and abusive language in the hotel. I'd be very grateful if you could think of our other guests when you are speaking. Otherwise, and with the greatest reluctance I assure you, I will have to ask you to leave.' Talk about lighting the blue touch-paper. But just as Mrs Morgan was about to say something, and probably something both foul and abusive, Jimmy jumped in. He stood up and held out a hand, screwing up his eyes to read the badge. 'Mr Konstantinou, is that right? I'm James McDuff.' He spoke slowly, his gentle Scottish lilt apologetic and mollifying. 'Sorry, we were all getting a little bit excited back then but we're good now. Look, my companion and I are booked in for lunch, so maybe you could get someone to point us in the direction of the restaurant? It's under Morgan I believe. Table for two. And it would be good if you could find a nice private spot.' When next he saw Maggie, he'd make sure she knew that he had bloody taken one for the team.

It seemed to be enough to satisfy the manager, who was smiling again, this time with evident relief. He didn't want a scene, not here in his spectacular atrium in full view of his customers, and so he was grateful for this man's intervention. 'Certainly sir, madam. I'll take you there myself. Please, come this way.'

It also seemed to have had a temporarily calming effect on Felicity Morgan, who, standing up, had taken Jimmy by the arm and was already snuggling up against him, if not quite cheek-to-cheek, then not far off it.

'This will be so lovely, and so unexpected. And now I'll be able to tell you everything about me. And you can tell me about your bitch of a girlfriend. I want to know *all* about her.'

# Chapter 22

The eighteen-twelve from Euston to Glasgow Central doesn't call at Oxenholme-for-Windermere, so waiting customers are told to stand well back from the platform edge. Wise advice, because no-one would want to be blown off their feet by the shock-wave of a Pendolino roaring through the station at over a hundred miles an hour. Or fall onto the track as it approaches from the south. At nine o'clock on that dull November evening, there hadn't been many passengers around, with the last northbound stopping train, a local for Penrith and Carlisle, not due for at least another forty minutes. So as a result, witnesses to the tragic event were thin on the ground. That is to say, non-existent.

The driver hadn't seen or felt anything, hardly surprising when four hundred tonnes of solid steel runs over fifty kilos of flesh and bone at a three-figure speed, and his train was already pounding up to Beattock summit over the border in Scotland before the message was relayed through to him. It was left to the station manager, doing a final sweep of his domain in preparation for closing up for the night, to make the stomach-churning discovery. Twenty minutes later, an inspector from the British Transport Police turned up to take charge of the incident. A quick call to the ops centre in Preston established that the northbound service could be switched to the top end of the southbound platform, well away from the mangled body of Liz Donahue, allowing service to continue with minimum disruption. By two o'clock the next morning, the incident medics had all they needed and the body, or what was left of it, was carted away to the mortuary.

\*\*\*

Jimmy was surprised but pleased when he glanced at his phone to see who was calling him this early. It was barely six-thirty in the morning, but already he was up and dressed, and thinking back on his bizarre lunch with Felicity Morgan. There was a lot to report to Maggie when he got into the office. The bill for a start, thankfully taken care of by his dining companion, which had run to a ridiculous four hundred pounds, inflated by the bottle of Louis Roederer Cristal she had insisted they ordered to accompany their meal. Her husband had been a pig and now it seemed Robert Trelawney was a pig too, that had been the thrust of the dialogue, or rather monologue, because she had done all the talking. Luckily, the ordering of the champagne had allowed him briefly to steer the conversation onto money, and she confirmed what they half-knew already. She had been sought out by the journalist Gary McGinley, who asked her what she knew about Brasenose Trust's network of shady offshore companies, set up to avoid the scrutinising gaze of nosey tax authorities. When she told him she knew nothing about it, and found it hard to believe his allegations were true, he had given her his evidence. Which explained why she was now looking for another seventy million quid from her ex.

'Hi Liz,' he said breezily. 'Must be important if you're calling me at this god-forsaken hour.' But it wasn't Liz on the other end of the line.

*'Jimmy, it's Ruthie. Do you remember me? Liz's wife. Liz Donahue.'*

Remember her? She'd hardly been out of his thoughts in the last two weeks. But there was something in her voice that caused his heart to pound, and instinctively he knew he was about to get some terrible news.

'Of course I remember. What's happened Ruthie?'

*'She's dead Jimmy. She's dead.'* He could hear her muffled sobs and another female voice urging her to take a sip of her tea.

'Christ, I'm so sorry. What happened, can you tell me that?'

*'An accident, a terrible accident. At the station. Last night. They don't know exactly what happened, but she fell in front...in front of a train. The police are here now. Oh God Jimmy, I don't know what to do.'*

And then suddenly it struck him. This woman whom he had met only once, had chosen to call him no more than what was it, eight or ten hours after the tragic death of her wife. Why? Why of all people, had she called him?

He spoke as softly as he dared so that she could still hear him. 'Ruthie, what do you mean, you don't know what to do?'

*'She wasn't here. She wasn't here when I got back from work. And it was her turn to cook on Wednesdays and she never ever missed it. And it was cannelloni, her favourite. She wouldn't have gone out without telling me.'*

His mind was racing as he ran through a list of possibilities why Liz hadn't been at home to cook her wife dinner. She could have popped out to a convenience store in search of a missing ingredient. Or maybe, perhaps more likely, something had come up at work, a big local story that needed to be followed up right away. But in that case, there would have been a message. *Had to pop out. Big story. Back in an hour or so. All my love xxx.* Or something along those lines. But according to Ruthie, she had left no message, and in any case why did she end up at Oxenholme station? It wasn't inconceivable that something so big would come up that she needed to travel to London at short notice, but surely she wouldn't have done that without letting Ruthie know. No, there was only one logical conclusion. Liz Donahue had been abducted. And then murdered by person or persons unknown. Now there was urgency in his voice.

'Ruthie, what are the police saying? Have you told them that Liz wasn't there when you got home?'

She sounded confused, which he thought was hardly surprising given what had happened. *'What? Oh yes, there's a policewoman here at the moment. Should I tell her?'*

'Yes, tell her, definitely. And ask her to get her sergeant or an inspector involved. It's important, really important.'

*'Ok,'* she said, uncertainty in her voice, *'but why?'*

'Listen Ruthie, is there anyone you can stay with up there? Someone you can trust one hundred percent?'

*'I...I don't know. Maybe Helen at book club. Her husband's a farmer, perhaps I could go there for a few days. Or I could go back to mum and dad's in Leeds.'*

Jimmy thought for a moment. 'No, I don't want to alarm you Ruthie, but it's probably better not to stay with family right now. Helen sounds like a good bet.'

*'Ok Jimmy,'* she said, her voice wavering, *'and Jimmy, do you think this had got anything to do with the story she was working on? That's why I called you, I thought it might.'*

'I don't know. It's possible.' It was more than possible, it was a bloody certainty, but he didn't want to say that right at that moment. 'Look, just get in touch with your friend, but please, don't tell anyone else. I'm going to get up to see you as soon as I can. I should be able to get there this afternoon. Tell me, how much do you know? I mean about Liz's big story.'

*'She didn't tell me everything I don't think, but I know quite a lot.'*

Suddenly, there was another voice on the end of the phone, the tone prim and abrupt. *'Sir, this is police constable Fairburn. I don't think the young woman is in any fit state to continue with this, and in any case this is now a police matter. Thank you.'* And that was it. End of conversation. The policewoman was right, of course, it was a police matter now.

But then, with a sinking feeling, he remembered that case Frank was working on. Two kids who died in the same way. Two kids who minutes before their deaths, and posted suicide notes on their

Facebook timelines. He wasn't much into social media, but he did, reluctantly, follow a few friends and acquaintances. With trepidation, he touched the icon to open the app. There it was in his timeline. Just six hours ago, a posting from Liz Donahue.

*I'm sorry, I just can't go on.*

Maybe it *was* a police matter, but Jimmy was certain of one thing. He needed to be on the next train to Oxenholme.

# Chapter 23

Ruthie had arranged that her farmer's-wife friend would meet him at the station, and he would stay with them at their remote farm near Cartmel Fell for the duration of his visit. The train was just a few minutes late into Oxenholme, and as he stepped off onto the platform, he saw a woman wave then hurry along to him wearing a wide smile. In appearance, she was exactly as he expected, around forty and quite tall and broad-shouldered, dressed in faded jeans and a navy sweatshirt, with a mass of curly reddish hair held back by a mottled headband. She was attractive but he couldn't help thinking her husband would have first and foremost saw her as good breeding stock.

'You must be Jimmy Stewart,' she said, smiling. 'At least I hope so. You certainly fit the description.'

He held out a hand. 'Guilty as charged. And you must be Helen.'

'Yes, that's me. I'm just parked outside, follow me.'

She led him down the exit stairs and along a short underpass which led out to the road down to Kendal. A battered Subaru occupied the first drop-off space.

'This is us,' she said, blipping the remote locking. 'Sorry it's a bit messy inside. Combination of kids and sheep.'

'How many do you have?' he asked, tossing his bag into the back and settling into the passenger seat.

She laughed. 'Sheep, about eight hundred, kids about five at the last count. Four girls and a boy. The girls came first and Bill insisted we kept going until we got a boy. The men are a bit old-fashioned up here in that regard.'

Keeping going wouldn't have been any hardship for Bill with a wife like you, he thought, but he didn't voice it.

'It must be quite tough, farming up here I mean.'

'I suppose it is, but we get by. We're mainly Herdwicks and they're a hardy old breed. We've also got a dairy herd on the lower pastures near the lake and they do ok. It's hard work all right, but it's all we know. And the truth is we love it, even if we're always moaning.'

Once they were clear of Kendal, the journey took about thirty minutes, the narrow road winding up from the Lyth Valley into the remote fells where every now and again they caught a distant glimpse of majestic Windermere, sparkling in the afternoon sunshine. The farm was at the end of an unsurfaced lane about a half a mile from the road, with a traditional stone-built farmhouse and a clutch of modern corrugated iron sheds arranged round the muddy farmyard. Everything looked neat and tidy and well cared for. Ruthie evidently had heard their approach, emerging from the front door with her arms wrapped tightly around her. Even from thirty yards away he could make out the dark-ringed eyes and ashen complexion. It was just forty-eight hours since she had received the terrible news and God knows how she was coping with it. Not well, if first impressions meant anything.

She forced a half-smile as he approached her. 'Hello Jimmy. Thank you so much for coming.'

'Come on, let's go back inside and have some tea,' Helen said. 'It's getting chilly.'

They sat around an old oak table in the cosy farm kitchen, heated by a cast-iron range that looked old but that Jimmy suspected was a modern reproduction.

'So how have you been Ruthie?' He knew what the answer would be but he had to ask.

She shrugged. 'Shell-shocked I suppose. I still can't believe it's real. I keep looking at my phone, expecting her to call. We must have called each other a hundred times a day normally.'

Helen brought over mugs of tea and placed them in front of them. 'I'll leave you two for a while if you don't mind,' she said soothingly. 'It'll be time to pick up the kids soon.' She gave a half-smile then slipped out of the room.

'So what are the police saying?' he asked.

'Not very much,' she said. 'They've made enquiries at the station but nobody saw anything.'

'What, even on the CCTV?'

'It wasn't working. It hadn't been for a few days but they hadn't got round to fixing it.'

That didn't surprise him, not up here, where nothing ever happened. They'd probably never had to use it in anger since it was installed, so it wouldn't have been a priority.

'I guess they know about her post?' He hoped he could have approached the subject more delicately, but it had to come out.

She stared at the floor. 'Yes. I don't believe it. She would never have killed herself. And you saw how she was, didn't you?'

Was he misreading the situation, or was there an element of doubt in her voice?

'I did, and no, I don't believe she would have. No way.'

'We'd had words you see. That morning. And we never argued, never.'

He wondered whether he should ask her what the argument was about, but decided to leave it to her to decide. Instead he said. 'But the police are still investigating, aren't they?' he said. 'Taking it seriously I mean?'

'I don't know. They sent an inspector around, but she just kept asking me if Liz had been depressed. I had to tell her about the argument, although it was nothing.'

He guessed that they would be grateful for the easy way out, no doubt about it, because it was going to look much better for the clear-up statistics if you didn't open the case in the first place. Besides, people were stepping in front of trains every day, and often their loved ones hadn't had a clue that anything was wrong. Whereas people being murdered by being pushed in front of trains, he guessed that was a whole lot rarer. Except that right now, Frank was working on two.

'Look Ruthie, my brother's a DI in the Metropolitan Police, and he's on a case right now where two young kids died... well, in exactly the same way as Liz. And those were definitely suspicious.'

And at least one of them had a connection to Hugo Morgan and his Brasenose Trust. It seemed unlikely in the extreme, but now he began to wonder.

'I'm going to get Frank to call your inspector, I think it might help. I didn't know Liz very well, but there's no way she killed herself.'

Ruthie gave him a sad look, and again he wondered whether she was having doubts. After all, they said you never really knew the person you were married to.

'Ruthie, can we talk about the story? You know, the big one that Liz was working on. How much did she tell you about it?'

'Quite a lot but not everything. Actually, I'm not sure she knew everything. She said a few times she was just waiting for a couple of things to fall into place.'

Jimmy nodded. 'Aye, I know she was very secretive about it. All she said to me was *pillow talk*. Do you have any idea what she meant by that?'

'It was to do with Belinda Milner. Liz had found out that she had been having an affair, and she thinks that's maybe how the news about the mine's problems leaked out.'

'Pillow talk? Aye, now that makes sense. And this affair, how much did she know about it? Did she know who Belinda was having an affair with?'

She shook her head. 'That was the last thing she was working on. She guessed that her husband must have found out and maybe that's why she had killed herself. She'd arranged a meeting with him and I think that's what she meant when she said she was just waiting for a few things to fall into place.'

'Do you know where they live? The Milner family I mean.'

'Yes, over near Wastwater. I know where it is, but I don't have a phone number or email or anything.'

'Of course, it's on the lake isn't it? Where she drowned. Liz told me about it.'

Ruthie nodded. 'Yes it is. Wasdale House. It's up for sale. It must be terrible for them, looking out and remembering what happened.'

He glanced at his watch. Just past three o clock. He knew vaguely where it was, over on the western side of the National Park, sitting in the shadow of mighty Scafell Pike. Quite a trek from where they were, an hour and a half's drive at least. And Ruthie was in no fit state to drive him. But if he knew one thing, it was that Belinda Milner was the reason Liz Donahue was murdered. So he had get in front of her husband, and there was no time to lose. He ran out into the yard where he found Helen loading bags of feed into the back of an all-terrain pick-up. He gestured towards the Subaru.

'I know it's a lot to ask Helen, but can I borrow your car?'

***

Wasdale House was notable enough to get itself named on the Ordinance Survey map. According to his copy, it was tucked away between the narrow road and the lakeside, on a little peninsular that jutted out just where the Nether Beck tumbled into the lake. The journey had taken nearly two hours, the distance clocking up at fifty-three miles. He knew you couldn't get anywhere fast in this neck of the woods, but even still it had been a slow and tedious drive, the unforecast rain conspiring to negate the beauty of the landscape through which he'd passed.

It was now pitch black, and he was lucky that his headlights picked out the *For Sale* sign as he rounded a narrow bend. And then a red board that had been pinned below it. *Sold*. He hoped the family hadn't already upped and gone. Finding the entrance gates open, he swung the Subaru into the driveway, crunching over the gravel and pulling up at the front of the house, alongside a gunmetal Range Rover. Promising. His entrance triggered a trio of bright security lights, and he could see that the place was stunning, constructed in a honey sandstone under a red pantile roof with decorative leaded-glass windows. He was no student of architecture, but he guessed it was late Victorian or early twentieth century, probably built by some industrialist from the North-West who had made his money in the cotton trade or in shipping. He got out the car and wandered across to the entrance. The solid oak front door, sheltered beneath an arched porch, was equipped with a sturdy brass knocker. He gave it two sharp raps then waited. Nothing. After a minute or so, he tried again, but still there was no response.

'Mr Milner?' He thrust his hands in his pockets and walked to the side of the house, where he had spotted a gate in the white picket fence, presumably leading into the garden. He released the latch and went through, closing it behind him.

'Mr Milner?'

The garden sloped away to the lakeside, about a hundred and fifty feet away, barely visible under a watery moon. It was here just a few weeks earlier where Belinda Milner had decided to end it all and as he surveyed the scene, he found himself wondering how any human being could take that ultimate step. How deep did the depth of despair have to be and what if anything could drive you to it? In the darkness, he could just about pick out the shadowy outline of a man standing by the lakeside. The man who might be able to explain it.

'Mr Milner?'

The man spun round but didn't move, as if he was unsure how to react to this unexpected visitor. And then he made up his mind.

'Who the hell are you?' he shouted, with unmasked aggression. 'Get off my property or I'll call the police.' It wasn't an unreasonable reaction but Jimmy hadn't come all this way to be disappointed.

'I'm not here to cause any trouble, Mr Milner.' As he got closer, Jimmy recognised the pain and loss etched on his face, the same pain and loss as he had seen on Ruthie only two hours earlier. 'I think you'll find we're on the same side. But it's your call, naturally. A minute, that's all I need to explain what I need from you, and if you can't help, or don't want to, then that's ok, and of course I'll leave you in peace.' He realised he'd not actually answered Milner's question and it wasn't an easy one to answer. *Just who the hell was he, and why was he here?* Nominally, he was working for Hugo Morgan, but the matter had gone way beyond that. Now he was looking for justice for Liz Donahue, and by extension, maybe for Belinda Milner too. He decided that honesty was the best policy.

'My friend Liz Donahue died under the wheels of a train two days ago. I think she was murdered and I think the reason was connected in some way to your wife. And to Greenway Mining.'

'What are you, a policeman?'

'No, I'm not the police. I'm a private investigator, but I'm working in a personal capacity. As I said, Liz was a friend and I'm anxious to find out what happened to her.'

The man held out his hand, his aggression disappearing as quickly as it had arrived. 'I'm Rod. Rod Milner.'

Jimmy shook it warmly. 'Jimmy. Jimmy Stewart. Good to meet you Rod.'

'Come inside,' Milner said. 'I could do with a drink, what about you?'

Jimmy shot him a smile. 'Sure, I don't like to see a man drink on his own.'

'I've done a lot of that in the last few weeks believe me. It's only April that's stopped me following my wife into the lake to be honest. She's my daughter. Off with her grandparents at the moment whilst I sort out the house.'

They went into the house through a back door which led to a small room that Jimmy imagined was called a boot room or something similar, then onwards to the kitchen. It had the same farmhouse feel as Helen's, but a lot grander, as if it had stepped out of the pages of an upmarket homes and gardens magazine. Which it probably had.

'Malt?' Milner asked. 'I seem to keep a bottle in every room these days. This one's hiding in the wine rack.' He slipped it out of its receptacle and placed it on the large oak kitchen table.

'Brilliant,' Jimmy said. 'Can't ever go wrong with a nice single malt can you?'

Gesturing towards the table, Milner said. 'Please, take a seat.' He took a couple of glasses from a cupboard and poured a generous measure into each. Jimmy took his and lifted it in silent toast.

'Cheers Rod. So just for some background, I work for a wee investigations firm and we were originally engaged by Hugo Morgan to find out who was behind the Justice for Greenway stuff. He was getting some harassment from them and I know Belinda was a target too.'

He nodded. 'Yes, it was quite disturbing and of course it upset Belinda a lot. They vandalised our Range Rover and there were some nasty threatening letters posted through our door. Your friend Donahue wrote all about it in that paper she worked for.'

'I'm sorry to ask,' Jimmy said, 'but do you think it contributed to Belinda... to her taking her own life?'

He dropped his head, staring at the table, saying nothing. For a moment Jimmy wondered if he had heard him, until Milner, his voice barely a whisper, said, 'It wasn't that.'

'Sorry?'

'I said it wasn't that.' Jimmy saw that his hand was shaking as he drained his glass and reached over to refill it.

'I can understand how hard this must be for you Rod. You know, I can come back another time if it's any easier.' That was the last thing he wanted to do, but he knew from his army days that when you were dealing with someone who had suffered a great trauma, you were walking on eggshells.

'I guess it must have been hard for her,' he said. 'All the problems with the mine and everything.'

Milner gave a bitter laugh. 'You think? She didn't give a shit about that actually. *Teflon Milner,* that's what the Financial Times called her. Nothing ever stuck on her.' For the first time, Jimmy wondered about the state of the Milner marriage. He wasn't faking his distress over her death, of that he was sure, but there was something else going on between them, definitely. And then out of the blue, he told him what it was.

'She was having an affair.'

*Pillow talk.* Now it was all beginning to make sense.

Milner threw back his whisky and for the third time reached across for the bottle. Jimmy adopted what he thought was a sympathetic look, but said nothing, content for the story to unfurl at its own speed.

'She had a string of the bloody things of course. Non-executive directorships I mean. It always made me laugh, because she knew bugger all about any of them. That never stopped her of course. You see, it helped these big companies tick the box for gender diversity on their boards. She was a very attractive woman and she always looked good in the annual report.'

Jimmy nodded. 'Aye, I understand what you're saying.'

'Of course, the job up here with Greenway should have been enough for anyone, and god knows it needed a CEO who could give it their full attention. But they needed someone with a City reputation to raise the finance so they were prepared to accept that she knew two thirds of shit-all about mining.'

Again Jimmy nodded, but said nothing.

'But she started being away almost every week, getting an afternoon train down to London and not coming back to late the following evening. At first, I thought nothing of it, until one evening we were sitting at home when she got a message alert on her phone, which was lying on the coffee table. Absent-mindedly I stretched over to pick it up but she got there before me and snatched it away. That's what made me suspicious.'

Jimmy knew what that felt like. Except it had been him who had been the cheater, and he'd regretted it every day since. But now wasn't the time to dredge all that back up again. Instead he gave what he hoped was an understanding smile.

'So I followed her one day,' Milner said. 'Pathetic really. I got on the same train, then followed her out of Euston, down Southampton Row. When I saw the route she was taking, I knew exactly where she was going of course. I saw her go into their offices, and then hung around for over two hours, just waiting. As I said, pathetic.'

'It's not pathetic,' Jimmy said. 'I'd have done exactly the same thing in your situation.'

'And then I saw them come out. They weren't holding hands or anything like that but I knew. You can tell can't you, just looking at a couple. The body language just gives it away. It made me sick to see it, even although I already knew in my gut she was cheating on me. You see, when I saw them together, I knew then this wasn't some cheap affair, it was so much more than that. I knew at that point that my marriage was over.'

Jimmy gave him a puzzled look. 'Why do you say that? What was so special about this man?'

'Special?' Milner said bitterly. 'He was half her age. That was what was so bloody special about him.'

***

And then it all came out, and with each revelation, another piece in the jigsaw fell into place. The affair had started at one of these organisations where Belinda was a non-executive director. *Alexia Life*. A place that Jimmy remembered Frank mentioning in connection with his Aphrodite investigation. The other man was young with stand-out good looks, causing his wife to quite lose her head. They'd tried to keep it a secret but someone had been watching and saw the signs. Then reported it to the trustees whom, after a cursory investigation, had asked the other man to leave. Two days later, he threw himself under the wheels of an underground train. Not long after Belinda Milner, consumed with guilt and heartache, took her last swim, following her lover to the grave.

*Pillow talk.* It was odds on that Milner would have shared the troubles of the Greenway Mine with her young lover, as certain as it was that *he* would have shared that secret with those that were employing him for just that purpose.

The same secret that Liz Donahue had uncovered, and that led to her death. The question was, who knew, and who cared enough to have her killed?

# Chapter 24

Frank had been down the canteen grabbing a bacon roll when his brother had called with news that had caused him to pump his fists and shout *Yes* at the top of his voice. Because now that he knew all about Belinda Milner and Luke Brown, everything was falling nicely into place. The only problem was, he didn't have a shred of credible evidence. That didn't mean that there wouldn't *be* any evidence, it was just that with the death of the two interns having been officially classified as suicides, nobody had been looking very hard.

Now, he *nearly* had the ammunition to change that. Just one more wee task to complete and then he'd be able to get in front of DCI Jill Smart, and it wouldn't take more than five minutes to persuade her to open a murder enquiry. Instead of just him and Frenchie, there'd be a team of fifty or more, with boots on the ground, and profilers and forensics and analysts, the lot. Soon they'd be swarming all over the CCTV and interviewing everybody who knew them and eventually something would come out. But first, a wee trip up to Oxford.

*** 

It had been Frenchie's idea to go in hard, giving it the full works as he called it, with the objective of scaring the living shit out of her, and so maximising the chances of a confession if one was to be had. Frank, though harbouring reservations that centred mainly around the amount of paperwork that would be needed to authorise the operation, had decided to go along with it. Aided and abetted by the fact that Ronnie had a mate in the Thames Valley armed response squad who told him they hadn't mounted a raid for over fifteen months and accordingly were itching for some action. But what had clinched it was that the Thames Valley lads had agreed to fill out the paperwork themselves. *Result.*

The commander of the squad, an over-promoted fast-track graduate on his first live op, was nervously talking into his walkie-talkie. '*Red squad in place, red squad in place. Confirm please. Over.*'

Having evidently received satisfactory acknowledgement, he strode over to Frank, who was leaning against his car, chewing gum and appearing totally relaxed.

'So you're sure there's not going to be any shooting then Inspector?' the commander asked.

'No,' Frank said, shaking his head. 'It's not the bloody mafia, they're only a wee employment agency. That's why it said no guns on the form. We're just here because we don't want anyone trying to destroy evidence and folks always take it more seriously when we come dressed for the part.'

It was quarter to eight in the morning, and the staff of the Oxbridge Agency were now arriving in dribs and drabs for their day's work. Frank had stationed his small raiding party round a corner and out of sight, eight brawny coppers in full riot gear squeezed into the back of an unmarked white Transit. Ronnie French had been assigned to loiter in the car park at the front of the building and give the signal when Sophie Fitzwilliam arrived.

She had recognised him immediately as she swept her Range Rover into her designated parking space a few yards from the front door, giving him a puzzled look that was mixed with haughty disgust. He shot her a lewd smile then drawled a few words into his radio.

Around the corner, the commander roared his response, simultaneously banging on the side of the van, then rushed round to the back to open the doors. 'Right guys, go!' The raiding party poured out into the street and followed him through the car park at pace. Altogether more languidly, Frank spat out his chewing gum and strolled around to join them. Fitzwilliam had reached her office's reception area when the squad flooded in.

'Right, nobody move,' the commander barked. 'Spread out guys and make sure everyone knows not to touch anything. Anybody goes near a keyboard, you grab them, got it?' A few seconds later Frank wandered in, smiling.

'Morning Mrs Fitzwilliam,' he said amicably, 'Maybe we can have a wee word in your office please?' It wasn't hard to tell she was angry, her eyes burning and an almost demented expression on her face. But behind it all, Frank detected fear.

'What the hell is this?' she screamed, 'You'll pay for this, believe me you will.'

'Now now, let's just calm down shall we? Your office please.' He took her arm and with some force, led her through, glancing over his shoulder and indicating to French that he should join them.

'You remember my colleague Detective Constable French I'm guessing. He interviewed you a few days ago about Chardonnay Clarke. When you denied that your firm had any involvement in the large salary she was being paid. I'm guessing you remember that conversation, don't you?'

She wore a defiant expression, but then they all did that when they'd been found out. Now it would be interesting to see if she tried to deny it. Generally they all did that as well, a natural reaction but practical too, because maybe the police might just be bluffing, or might not have any hard evidence.

'I remember,' she said, her composure beginning to return. 'A ludicrous accusation, and I'm sure you don't have a shred of proof.'

Frank smiled to himself. That was always the dead giveaway. First deny it, then ask to see the evidence. Hedge your bets. But before he could answer, the commander stuck his head round the door.

'Place is all secure now Inspector. And we've found a bank of filing cabinets in the basement. That's all secure too.'

'Good boy,' Frank said, smiling when he saw French stifling a laugh. 'Now Mrs Fitzwilliam, I have a warrant here that allows me to take away and examine all your financial records, but I'm hoping we won't have to go to all that trouble. You see, we know all about Semaphore Trust, your subsidiary company.'

She looked at him sharply. Admit it or deny it, he could see she was weighing up which path to take. So he decided to help her with her dilemma. He took a sheet of paper from an inside pocket, unfolded it and began to read aloud.

'Semaphore Trust - a subsidiary company of the Oxbridge Agency, according to Companies House -was paying nearly thirty thousand pounds per month into a Swiss franc account held with Zurich Landesbanken. Then the money was transferred to a Santander branch in Madrid, from where it ended up with Rosalind Holdings, a company registered in Guernsey.'

'What of it,' she said, her tone defiant. 'We're not doing anything illegal. It's tax-efficient, that's all.'

Frank smiled to himself. *Got her.* 'Perhaps it is, but I do find it interesting why there was the need for such a complicated arrangement just to pay a wee girl her salary. Oh aye, and there was something else too. DC French, maybe you can update Mrs Fitzwilliam on what our fine wee colleague Eleanor Campbell discovered yesterday?'

He nodded. 'Yeah sure guv. So as well as paying six grand a month to Chardonnay Clarke, a sum of thirty-two thousand eight hundred and fifty pounds and sixteen pence was paid to the Student Loans company for the benefit of a Mr Luke Brown.'

'Really?' Frank said, feigning surprise. 'The lad who supposedly took his own life? The other lad placed by your agency Mrs Fitzwilliam. The other lad on your scholarship scheme. Interesting that.' Now his voice took on a serious tone. 'Frenchie, I think this would be a good time to read this lady her rights.'

French smiled. 'Sure guv, my pleasure. *Sophie Fitzwilliam, I am charging you with conspiracy to murder, you are not obliged...*' He shouldn't have done it, he knew that, and the CPS would throw a hissy fit if they found out, but right now he didn't give a shit about them.

'Wait, wait,' she said, her voice raised in blind panic. 'Christ inspector, I didn't know they would be killed.' *Result.*

'But you knew they *were* killed, didn't you?' Frank said. 'You knew all along they weren't suicides. Come on Sophie, you can tell me all about it. Best for everyone if you did. Especially you. Because it wouldn't be fair if you were to take the rap for something you didn't do.'

So she did tell them all about it. Of course, she continued to deny knowing anything about the murders, and chatting with Frenchie afterwards, they agreed that she was probably telling the truth as far as that aspect of the affair was concerned. But for a while she asserted that it had all been her idea, a misplaced display of loyalty that quickly crumbled when Frank pointed out that as sole conspirator she was facing at least thirty years in Holloway. So then she told them everything, including who was ultimately behind it all.

Which caused him to ask Ronnie French for his tenner back. Because he knew he'd been right all along.

# Chapter 25

Maggie hadn't recognised the voice on the end of the phone, but she'd instantly recognised the name.

*'Maggie, Maggie Bainbridge? The investigator? This is Rosie.'*

'Rosie Morgan? Hugo's daughter?'

*'That's right.'* Her voice sounded nervous, uncertain. *'I think I need to see you. It's about mum and Lotti and stuff.'*

They agreed to meet at a little cafe nestled alongside the Regents canal. Arriving early, Maggie found an outside table conveniently located next to a patio heater which bathed her in a welcome curtain of warm air. She remembered Hugo telling her his daughter was studying fashion at nearby Central Saint Martin's, which explained the choice of venue, but other than her vague explanation on the phone, Maggie had no idea what she wanted to talk about. Jimmy had told her about the scene at the Park Lane Hilton of course, and she wondered if it had anything to do with that. But to Rosie, Jimmy wasn't Jimmy, he was James McDuff, cuckolded lover of rich old Magdalene Slattery, so it couldn't have been that. *Curious.*

She spotted her from a hundred metres away as she made her way down the quayside. You won't be able to miss her, Jimmy had said, and he wasn't wrong. Dressed like that, it wasn't hard to see why Miss Morgan had chosen to make her career in the fashion industry. But as it turned out, Maggie didn't need Jimmy's vivid description, because she had someone with her. Someone she instantly recognised. Maggie stood up and waved to get her attention.

'Hi, it's Rosie isn't it?' she said. 'I'm Maggie, it's lovely to meet you.'

'This is Jasmine,' she said fondly. 'My little sister. We call her Yazz.'

'We've met,' Maggie said, beaming the younger girl a smile. 'Hello again Yazz.'

Yazz gave her a shy look. 'Hi.' She was dressed in school uniform, a grey pinafore with navy blazer and brimmed felt hat, with a leather satchel slung over her shoulder. 'Rosie's taking me to the dentist,' she said in way of explanation. 'To get my braces adjusted.'

Maggie smiled. 'Yes, I had them when I was your age. They're quite annoying for a while but you soon forget about them.' But when she had gone to have hers fitted, nearly thirty years earlier, it was her mum who had taken her. She didn't have older siblings, but she was quite certain if she had, her parents wouldn't have palmed her off on one of them.

'Dad was busy today,' Rosie said, as if reading her mind. 'And I don't have any classes this afternoon. It's only down in Harley Street.' Of course, it would be. The expensive private school, the pursuit of a career in the precarious fashion industry, the up-market private dentistry. Maggie wondered if they appreciated how lucky they were.

'By the way, I love your look,' she said to Rosie, 'It's amazing.'

'Thanks. It's retro.' She didn't smile, but Maggie guessed that was because of the effect it would have on her makeup rather than any coldness in her mood.

'Yes, but it's great, really great. That fashion scene was a little before my time first time around, but not by much I'm afraid. Anyway, it's nearly lunchtime, do you want to eat?'

'I don't,' Rosie said. 'Do lunch I mean. I'll just have a water please. Sparkling.' Maggie remembered the old Kate Moss maxim and smiled. *Nothing tastes as good as thin feels.* The supermodel had long since apologised for saying it, but the suspicion was it was still close to a religious tract as far as the fashion industry was concerned.

'Can I have a cheeseburger please,' Yazz asked. 'With cola and fries. Double fries please.'

With obvious reluctance, Rosie nodded her agreement. Maggie ordered and then said, 'So Rosie, how can I help you?'

'I saw that guy yesterday. Your guy. Meeting with mum. I know who he is.'

'Ah,' Maggie said slowly. 'It's quite a long story.'

'You and that guy, you're investigating Lotti. My dad told me. I saw your pictures on your website.' So she knew. That would make this a whole lot easier. 'And don't worry, Yazz knows too. Maggie smiled. 'Well, investigating makes it sound more serious than it really is.' Especially since to all intents and purposes the investigation was over, all cut and dried and neatly tidied away. But now at least there was the opportunity to ask the sixty-four-thousand-dollar question. And one day she would google it to find out where that ancient phrase came from.

'So what do you think about it Rosie? Your dad and Lotti I mean?'

She gave her an impassive look. 'I want him to be happy.'

'And do you think Lotti will make him happy?'

Rosie shrugged. 'Suppose. She's quite nice.'

'I like her too,' Yazz said, temporarily suspending the demolishment of her lunch. 'She's quite nice and I like the way she speaks.'

'Yes, she has got a nice accent, hasn't she?' Maggie said, smiling.

'Although Rosie, isn't it a little awkward for you? I'm meaning the age difference. Lotti's only thirty and your dad is what, fifty?'

'You think?'

Maggie felt her heart skip a beat. Lowering her voice she asked, 'What do you mean?'

'Like there's no way she's thirty. Twenty more like.'

'How do you know that Rosie?'

'I don't *know*, not for defo at least. I searched her handbag one day, hoping to find something to prove it, but I didn't. But whatever, I don't care, it's like nothing to do with me, is it?'

'And have you told your dad? About your suspicions, I mean?'

She shrugged again. 'There not *suspicions*, it's not like some sort of big conspiracy is it? And anyway why should I tell him? It doesn't bother me what age she is.' Maggie could tell by the way she said it that the exact opposite was true.

'So do you think he knows?'

'Maybe. I don't care.' She took a sip of water and turned her head, staring into the distance. Maggie wasn't sure, but she thought she saw the hint of a tear begin to form.

'You said on the phone you wanted to talk about her. About Lotti.'

Rosie nodded. 'Yeah, it's mum. I think she's found out about Lotti and dad. She's seeing that guy from the gallery you see, you know, the one where Lotti works. He must have found out and told her.' *That guy from the gallery.* Robert Trelawney, the guy whom in a moment of complete madness she had slept with.

'And she's mental. I'm worried she might do something crazy.'

'Mum's not mental,' Yazz said.

'Eat your lunch,' her sister said in a kindly tone, 'and stop listening in to what the grown- ups are saying.'

'Ok.' She took a noisy slurp on her straw then returned to the fast-disappearing cheeseburger.

'What do you mean Rosie,' Maggie said, 'something crazy?'

'I don't know. Just crazy. Harm Lotti in some way. She's a complete nightmare my mum. She always has been, ever since we were little.' So now it began to make a little sense, why she and her sister had chosen to stay with her dad. Although Maggie was conscious that she would only be hearing one side of the story.

'I'm a mum too and it can be the most difficult job in the world. But have you told your dad about this?'

Suddenly Rosie looked sad in a way only a child can. 'I don't want to. It would just make everything worse than ever between them.' With what she knew about the Morgan's shattered relationship, Maggie doubted it would make the slightest difference. But that was the thing with divorces, whether bitter or amicable. The kids always wanted the parents to get back together.

'So what is it you want me to do?' Maggie asked. 'Because I'm not sure if I can help you.'

'Your guy...'

'Jimmy.'

'Yeah Jimmy. I think my mum likes him. Even though she's got Robert now. I can always tell. She's pathetic.'

Maggie laughed, immediately regretting it. 'Yes, I really don't understand it at all. It's not as if he's terribly good-looking or anything.'

She seemed unimpressed. 'Yeah whatever. But maybe he could talk to her. Something like that. I don't know. It might help, that's all.' Maggie very much doubted that, given what she knew about Mrs Morgan's feelings towards her ex-husband. But she didn't mean to disappoint this vulnerable young woman.

'We'll try,' she said. 'That's a promise.'

'Thank you. And please don't tell my dad.'

'I won't. Promise.'

Rosie gave a half-smile. 'Thank you then. Come on Yazz, we need to go, or we'll miss your appointment.'

The schoolgirl stood up, stuffing the last of the fries into her mouth.

'Ok,' she said politely. 'That was nice. Thank you Maggie.'

'Yeah, thanks Maggie,' Rosie said. 'I'll hear from you then?'

Maggie nodded. 'We'll do what we can.'

Reflecting on it as she sipped her coffee, she was still not exactly sure what the meeting had been all about. Was Felicity Morgan really a threat to Lotti, and even if she was, could she and Jimmy really do anything about it? And just because she might have been right all along about Lotti's age, she realised that it didn't pass that crucial test that she had learned to apply to situations like this one - *the so what* test. So what if Lotti was lying about her age? Other than the fact it was a deception, it probably didn't mean anything at all. And if Hugo Morgan already knew, then it wasn't even that. Anyway her job was to find out the facts, not pass judgement. She'd let Hugo Morgan worry about what to do with it.

But then suddenly she noticed it. Hanging over the back of the vacated plastic chair was Yazz's satchel. *Bugger.* Tossing her unfinished coffee into the waste bin, she set off along the quayside in pursuit, fumbling in her bag for her Oyster card. She wasn't sure how billionaires' daughters travelled in London, but it had to be at least an each-way bet that they would be heading for the tube. Kings Cross St Pancras, the busiest station in the capital, where you could take your choice of the Northern, Victoria, District, Piccadilly, Metropolitan, Circle and Hammersmith lines. Harley Street, that's where she said she was heading. Where was that exactly? She wracked her brain and then remembered. Yes, somewhere between Marylebone Road and Oxford Street, she was pretty sure that's where it was. But which tube line would they take? The Piccadilly, or maybe the Circle or Metropolitan westbound to Great Portland Street. Either would do, but she had to decide. *Piccadilly, southbound.*

To her dismay she saw there was a queue building up behind the barriers, which was being caused by a bunch of foreign tourists trying to figure out what to do with their tickets. Ignoring a squawk of complaints, she forced herself to the front and snatched a ticket from a confused-looking elderly man, maybe Japanese or Chinese, she wasn't sure which. Shooting him a forced smile, she slotted his ticket into the machine and pushed him through the opening gates, squeezing through behind him and ignoring his profuse thank-you's. The down escalator was busy but she was able to take the left hand side like a stairway, pushing aside the few travellers who were not aware of the convention that that side should be kept clear for those in a rush. Then a one-hundred an eighty degree turn where she descended the second escalator in the same fashion. A few seconds later, she was on the platform, which was unexpectedly heaving. Businessmen, shop girls, students, tourists, school kids, tradesmen, the usual rich mix of London life, packed cheek to jowl and speaking every language under the sun. Then she vaguely remembered an item on that morning's radio travel news. *Industrial action by the RMT union meaning a reduced service on the Piccadilly and Victoria lines. Expect delays and some disruption throughout the day.* She scanned along the platform, figuring that even with the crowds, a purple-haired punk-goth wouldn't be hard to pick out, but all she could see was a sea of heads. Glancing up she saw the indicator board predicting the first arrival in one minute, the next not for another fifteen. If they were only running four trains an hour, it was odds-on the approaching one would be already jam-packed and only those brave enough to have staked a claim at the platform edge would have any chance of getting on. That made her realise she might get a better view up and down the platform if she herself was at the front. She started to push her way through, muttering perfunctory *excuse me's* under her breath.

She could feel the pattering of cool air on her face as the train approached, acting like a tightly-fitting piston in the confined tunnel. And then she was enveloped in a haze of confusion as in perfect slow-motion she saw Rosie Morgan standing at the far end of the platform. Then spinning round, watched in horror as the young woman tumbled off it in front of the arriving tube train. The girl was able to stumble to her knees before it smashed full into her, tossing her like a grotesque rag-doll against the far wall of the station, then striking her again as she fell, catapulting her already-limp body onto the platform. The echoey station was filled with a cacophony of devilish noise, the screech of steel wheel on steel rail as the driver slammed on the emergency brakes all but drowned out by the screams of the horrified onlookers. And then, as the train finally came to a stop, there was an eerie silence. A few metres back from Maggie, someone was shouting, 'I'm a doctor, let me through please,' but everybody knew it was already too late. The crowd on the platform stood motionless, stunned into inaction, not knowing quite how to react. Except for a hooded figure that Maggie just caught a glimpse of, pushing its way towards the exit. A figure who was leading Yazz Morgan by the hand.

Desperately, Maggie elbowed her way through the crowd of paralysed bystanders. 'Let me through, let me through. Yazz, Yazz!' She was screaming at the top of her voice but the sound dissipated inaudibly as the mass of humanity absorbed her cry. 'Yazz!' They were no more than twenty-five metres ahead of her and still some way from the up escalator, but new passengers were still arriving, packing the platform ever tighter. But then miraculously, a gap opened up. At the bottom of the down escalator, a young mother, clutching a tiny baby to her chest, was struggling to re-erect her push chair, causing a tail-back of irritated travellers. And blocking the entrance to the up escalator too. The hooded figure ran up to her, picked up the pushchair and threw it to one side, then pushed the young woman in the chest, causing her to fall over, still holding her baby tightly.

A shaven-headed man wearing a hi-viz vest tried to intervene. 'Oi mate, what the fuck are you doing?' but he was caught unawares by a punch that left him staggering and bleeding.

'Yazz!' Maggie had now reached them and was able to grab the schoolgirl's free arm. The girl looked round, her face wearing a dazed expression, but her other hand was still tightly in the grasp of her abductor. Who had now decided to turn his attentions to this new threat to his escape, and for the first time, Maggie was able to get a proper look at the figure. A man, definitely, squat but powerfully-built. He was wearing shades, a hat and dark scarf covering the lower half of his face which, as was no doubt his intention, would make identification impossible. And he was in no mood to give up his quarry. She saw it coming, but was in no position to avoid it, as a huge fist smashed into her face, sending her sprawling. Confused, she tried to get back on her feet but then an overwhelming nausea hit her and she collapsed onto the platform, dead to the world.

But just before the lights went out, it came to her. *There was someone else.* A face on that crowded platform that shouldn't have been there. A face she knew, but right at this moment, as she lost the fight for consciousness, could not quite place.

***

Hugo Morgan was stewing in an interview room at Paddington Green Police Station awaiting the arrival of his lawyer when a message pinged into the inbox of his phone. Had it not at that moment been lying in the small plastic tray into which he had been forced to empty the contents of his pockets, he would have been able to read the news that would shatter his gilded life forever.

*Didn't we tell you actions have consequences?*
*Justice for Greenway*

# Chapter 26

'It's all kicking off ma'am,' Frank said. 'Big time. The desk sergeant's just been in to say he's got two women screaming at one another, and both of them demanding to see Hugo Morgan. One says she's his ex-wife and one says she's his fiancé. And it looks as if there's no love lost between them, if the language they're using is anything to go by.'

It was four o'clock, just three hours after the incident at Kings Cross and they were gathered in Incident Room Four at Paddington Green, which Frank had been able to commandeer for his Aphrodite Murders case, granted official status the previous day by his boss Detective Superintendent Jill Smart. In the room were Frank, Pete Burnside, Jimmy, Maggie, Jill herself and a gaggle of detective constables, tapping away on their laptops. As a DI from back-of-beyond Department 12B, he wouldn't be running the case personally, but he was pleased that it had been put in the hands of his old mate Pete, recently promoted to Chief Inspector. And in any case, it was odds on that Pete would leave most of the grunt work to him, which suited him fine. All the job satisfaction without any of the responsibility.

'You don't need to tell me it's kicking off,' Jill said, grimacing. 'I've already had an AC calling me and asking why the hell we've got Morgan in for questioning when one daughter has just been murdered and his other one's been kidnapped.'

'Aye, he's obviously got his lawyers right onto it, which is no more than I expected,' Frank said, shrugging. 'The truth is, they just overlapped ma'am. I had reasonable suspicions that he was involved in two murders himself, so it was right and proper that we brought him in. But yeah, it's bloody bad timing right enough.'

'And how are you Maggie?' Jill asked. 'Nice black eye, if you don't mind me saying so.'

'Yes, it hurts, but I'm absolutely fine,' she said, giving a rueful smile. 'I'm just so sorry I couldn't stop it happening. The abduction I mean.'

'Who's going to run that case ma'am?' Frank asked. 'I guess it can't be Pete, given that Morgan's a suspect in the Aphrodite ones. Conflict of interest I suppose.'

'No, I've given it to DCI Ahmed. In fact, Rashid's already up at Kings Cross looking at the CCTV, and I think he's going to organise a TV appeal for witnesses on the local TV news tonight.'

'Aye, he's a good bloke,' Frank said. 'And I guess one of his guys will want to speak to you Maggie in the next half hour or so. You saw it all I suppose?'

'I didn't see the push, but I saw the aftermath. It was too ghastly for words. And her little sister saw it too. God knows what's going on in her mind. I can't bear to think about it.'

'Are you sure you're ok?' Frank said in a worried tone. 'I heard you passed out. I can easily get a WPC to take you home if you like. I'm sure the interview can wait.'

She shook her head and smiled. 'No way. This is all far too important for that. And I told you, I'm absolutely fine.' Although she didn't exactly feel it. She had a crashing headache and great difficulty in seeing through her rapidly-closing eye. But despite all of that, she wasn't going anywhere.

'So Frank,' Jill said, wearing a puzzled look, 'you said you *had* reasonable suspicions that Morgan was involved in the murder of these two kids. Has something changed?'

'Aye, it has ma'am, don't you see? The murder of his daughter kind of makes me think I might need to look a bit deeper at the whole thing.'

'Because the MO was the same?' Jill said. 'Identical to your two other ones I mean.'

'Not just three,' Jimmy said. 'Four of them. Chardonnay, Luke, Rosie and Liz Donahue. Don't forget Liz.'

'And all the same MO?'

'Aye ma'am,' Frank said. 'Pretty much identical. So we've got means and opportunity, sure, But the problem is, where's the common motive? The two kids, I can see a link. Liz Donahue, we know there's a connection there, definitely. But Rosie Morgan? No way, not as far as I can see.'

They were interrupted by the desk sergeant sticking his head round the door.

'Sorry to disturb ma'am. Guv, what do you want me to do with these two woman I've got? I'm worried the older one's going to have a stroke or a heart attack or something.'

'Well, it's not exactly surprising given the news she's had, is it?' Burnside said, his irritation obvious. 'She's lost her bloody daughter for God's sake. Find a family liaison officer and put her somewhere comfortable. And get her a cup of tea.'

'Yes sir. And what should I do with the other one?'

'How should I bloody know?' he said, raising his eyes to the ceiling. 'Go and see Morgan and ask if he wants to see either of them. Or none of them. You're ok with that Frank?'

'Aye sure Pete, given the circs. And we should get a family liaison for him too I suppose. Don't want to appear heartless, do we?'

*　*　*

As Jill Smart had predicted, DCI Rashid Ahmed had rounded up the local early-evening news programmes to broadcast an appeal for the return, unharmed, of eleven-year-old Jasmine Morgan, abducted four hours earlier from Kings Cross St Pancras tube station. Given the prominence of her father, the media room at Paddington Green was packed out, attracting a full house of the dailies and national broadcast media. Maggie, Jimmy and Frank were lucky to find a spot, squeezed tight up against the back wall. Scanning the room, she noted Lotti Brückner was nowhere to be seen.

Hugo and Felicity Morgan were seated behind a desk on the low podium and holding hands, their grief evidently effecting a temporary halt in hostilities. Their eyes were blood-shot from crying and Mrs Morgan had made no attempt to re-apply her make-up, dark eyeliner tracing the path where the tears had run down her cheeks. She looked completely broken.

DCI Ahmed stared directly at the TV news camera, and although his manner was calm and commanding, he was reading from a small ring-bound notebook. 'Good evening, ladies and gentlemen and thanks for coming. As you know, there was a very serious incident earlier today at Kings Cross St Pancras tube station. Tragically Miss Rosalind Morgan lost her life and I can confirm we are treating her death as murder. At the same time, her younger sister Jasmine was abducted by a man who at this moment we have failed to identify. I appeal for eye witnesses to either incident to contact us by calling the number displayed across the bottom of your screen. Your call will of course be treated in confidence.' He paused for a moment and then flipped over a page. 'And now, I'd like to ask the Morgans to say a few words, and please, no flash photography until they've finished.'

It was Hugo Morgan who addressed the camera, his voice subdued and wavering, his message brief but poignant. 'We don't know who did this and we have no idea why. All we ask is that *please, please*, you return our lovely daughter to us unharmed.'

'Yes, *please, please*, bring her back to us. *Please*.' Felicity spoke almost inaudibly, then buried her head in her hands, motionless and numbed with pain. Immediately her ex-husband put an arm around her and gently drew a strand of hair back from her face.

'No questions please folks,' Ahmed said briskly, as the room was illuminated with the flashes from a dozen cameras now let off the leash. 'Suffice to say that we are pursuing a number of promising lines of enquiry and we will update you as and when. Finally, I should mention that the family are offering a reward for any information leading to the safe return of their daughter. Thank you for your attendance.'

The assembled press hacks waited until the Morgans had left the platform before asking the obvious question, leaving it to ITN's distinguished Home Affairs correspondent to put it into words. *How much?*

***

'Half a million?' Maggie said. 'It's a lot of money isn't it? But do you think it will have any effect?'

DCI Ahmed shrugged. 'You would think so, but this Justice for Greenway business would appear to be about exacting revenge on Hugo Morgan rather than money. So I don't know. I have my doubts, quite honestly.'

They were in a small airless interview room, the DCI accompanied by a colleague, a detective sergeant whose name Maggie hadn't quite caught and who thus far had not uttered a word. He seemed somewhat in awe of his boss, who was emanating the same aura of effortless authority that she had witnessed during the press conference. 'So tell us all about today please, if you don't mind. Take your time. And then maybe we can talk about Justice for Greenway too. Because I think you and your colleague were looking into that, am I correct?'

So she told him, about her lunch with Rosie and Yazz, how she had pursued them to the tube station. And how she had witnessed Rosie Morgan's terrible killing, and about her failed effort to prevent the abduction.

'Do you think you could identify the man if you saw him again?' Ahmed asked.

She gave him a doubtful look. 'His face was covered. His physique, maybe, but that wouldn't be good enough, would it?'

'No, probably not, but we've now got some CCTV from the scene. DS Johnston, can you show Miss Bainbridge the images please.' Johnston removed some large prints from a folder and laid them on the table facing Maggie. Dark and grainy, nonetheless they had picked out the abductor leading Yazz along the platform.

'Yes, that's him,' she said. And then she remembered. 'I thought there might be someone else.'

'What, you mean an accomplice?'

'I suppose so. I didn't really see clearly, it was just more of a feeling. Someone who I thought shouldn't be there. But I'm sorry, I can't put a face or a name to it.'

He shrugged. 'Well, these pictures will be in all the newspapers tomorrow, so maybe somebody out there might recognise him. Or your stranger. But what struck us was that she didn't seem to be struggling. Because of the shock we expect. Pity. It made it all too easy for him.'

'Yes, I'm sorry,' Maggie said. 'I could have done better too.'

'Not at all,' Ahmed said. 'You were very brave.'

He nodded at Johnson, who took out another photograph from the folder.

'Do you know who this woman is? We found this in Rosie's handbag.'

She took it from him and examined it.

'No idea, I've never seen her before.'

'And so you have no idea why Rosie would be carrying this picture?'

'No, I said I didn't know her.'

'Well if it's any help, there's a name scribbled on the back.'

'What?'

'A name. I can't quite make it out. Take a look yourself.'

She turned the photograph over and looked. The handwriting was poor, but she had no trouble in reading what it said.

*Lotti Brückner.*

'Miss Bainbridge?'

'Oh...yes, sorry. It's says Lotti Brückner. That's the name of Hugo Morgan's fiancé. Although he hasn't actually proposed to her yet. But Rosie told me that Felicity had found out about Lotti and her ex-husband. She was worried she might do something crazy.'

'What did she mean by that?' Ahmed asked.

'I don't know. But that was what she said. But this isn't Lotti. As I said, I've no idea who this woman is.'

'Ok,' Johnson said. 'And there was this too.' He rummaged in his folder for a moment then extracted what looked like a glossy sales brochure.

'*The Oxbridge Agency Scholarship Scheme*. And the same question as before. Would you have any idea why she would be carrying this around with her?'

***

'Give you a tough time did he?' Frank said, laughing. 'Hard man, is our DCI Ahmed.'

Maggie had just got back to the Incident Room following her interview, and her brow was furrowed as she tried to make sense of what had just been revealed to her.

'What? No, he's nice,' she said distractedly. 'On the ball too.'

'Folks, listen up, we've got some progress on the Cumbrian connection at least,' Burnside said. 'So yesterday when I saw what Frank had turned up on the Belinda Milner suicide, I got straight onto the local force, spoke to a DCI Bragg.'

'Not Melvyn?' Frank said. 'He's a Cumbrian, isn't he?'

'Melissa actually. Smart lady by the sound of things. So anyroads, they've now decided that there's grounds for suspicion around Liz Donahue's death and they've opened up a murder enquiry with Bragg in charge. Thing is, they're only a small force and a case like this can overwhelm them but I've agreed to second a couple of DCs for a fortnight or so, just to help them out, try to accelerate things a bit.'

'Hallelujah,' Jimmy said, 'and a nice gig by the way.'

'Yeah it is,' Burnside agreed. 'And as I said, there's already some news. It seems someone remembers seeing Donahue's car being parked up outside the station on the evening in question. And it turns out she wasn't alone.'

'Got a description?' Frank asked.

He nodded. 'The guy with her was hooded and wearing shades so nothing too definite. But he was described as fairly short but powerfully-built. Like a body-builder, the witness said.'

'What, just like the guy who punched me?' Maggie said, involuntarily tracing the outline of her shiner.

'Seems that way, yeah.'

'And what, she was just strolling into the station with him, nice as you like?' Jimmy said.

'Not heard of guns bruv?' Frank said, shaking his head. 'It's odds-on he was armed. And exactly the same today up at Kings Cross, that's what I'm guessing. A pistol in your ribs and you're going to do exactly what you're told.'

And then Jimmy remembered. Those Tompkins brothers. Specifically Karl, the ex-squaddie who was built like the proverbial brick shithouse. He fitted the description perfectly.

'Karl Tompkins. He's the guy that Liz and I went to see, him and his brother. He runs a business customising cars and knocks around in a blinged-up Fiesta, and this guy looks as if he pushes some weights, believe me. They didn't exactly admit being behind Justice for Greenway, but they didn't exactly deny it either.'

'Yes, but why would they want to kill Liz?' Maggie said. 'If anything, she was on their side, wasn't she? After what she had found out about Milner?'

Jimmy frowned. 'Maybe they thought Liz was going to run a story accusing them of being behind the campaign.'

'But her story had nothing to do with that,' Maggie said.

'We know that, but they didn't. So maybe they killed her to shut her up.'

A young detective constable looked up from her laptop. 'Jimmy, that customised Fiesta. Was it anything like this?'

She swung her screen round to face them. 'This was from the CCTV on the next street to Morgan's. On the night he reported the graffiti on his wall. I remembered the car because it was so unusual.'

Jimmy peered at it over her shoulder. 'That's it, I'm pretty sure of it. I recognise the alloys and the spoiler. But wait a minute...no, this is on a 59 plate and his was definitely a 57. I remember stuff like that.'

'False plates probably,' Burnside said, turning to the young detective. 'Emma, get on to the DVLA site and do a search, see what you can dig up. He'll have cloned it, I'm pretty sure. And then check with the Northamptonshire and West Midlands boys, see if these plates have been caught on ANPR cameras on the M6 or the M1 anytime over the last month. And today or yesterday, obviously.'

'Yes sir,' she said, scribbling furiously on her pad.

'And I'll nip back to my desk and get on to Melvyn, see if she can bring this Tompkins guy in for questioning.'

'Melvyn?' Maggie said, smiling.

'DCI Bragg,' Burnside said, a hint of embarrassment in his tone. 'The guys are already calling her Melvyn, I just hope it doesn't slip out anytime she's in earshot.'

\*\*\*

'So come on Frank,' Jill said after Burnside had departed, 'let's hear all about the Morgan angle and your Aphrodite case.'

Maggie watched him shuffle uncomfortably in his seat. She knew how he hated being in this situation, where to him the critical facts of a case were as clear as the light of day, but where the evidence was non-existent.

'I'm not sure you're going to like this ma'am,' he said.

'Try me.'

'Ok. Well this is a conspiracy so unbelievable and implausible that I'm afraid we're never going to get a conviction unless we get confessions by the principle actors. And I don't see how that's ever going to happen. So unless Burnside's investigation comes up with some miracle, we're stuffed. There's barely enough to question anyone, never mind getting the CPS to sanction a prosecution. It's bloody depressing, I don't mind telling you.'

'And that's the same for both of your murders,' Jill said. 'No evidence?'

'None. To be honest, I'm kind of clinging to the hope that DCI Bragg's investigation might uncover something,' he said nodding in Jimmy's direction, 'because we now believe the motive for the murder of Liz Donahue was a cover-up. To cover up the motive behind the killings of Chardonnay Clarke and Luke Brown. To stop her publishing her story.'

'Come on then,' she said for the second time, 'tell me all.'

'I suppose it was talking to Chardonnay's boyfriend or lover, whatever you want to call him, that sort of crystallized the whole thing in my mind. Hugo Morgan's always spouting this activist investor shtick to anyone who'll listen, as if he's got some magic way of predicting the future just by scrutinising accounts and trading statements and stuff like that. But this Jeremy guy, he said that was all bollocks, and that the real reason was that Morgan was actually heavily engaged in industrial espionage.'

'Which was what that journalist McGinley was saying too,' Maggie said.

'Aye, exactly. So I'm sure Morgan was involved in all sorts of subterfuge besides, but this particular one was an old classic, known since the dawn of time. Namely, a honey-trap.'

'Yeah, I get it,' Maggie said. 'The interns. That's why they were being paid these enormous sums. To do his bidding.'

'Correct,' Frank said. 'Sophie Fitzwilliam was an old university pal of his, at Brasenose college. He obviously knew that she ran this top-end agency and saw the opportunity for a bit of collaboration.'

'So she was roped in to do the recruitment I guess,' Maggie said. 'And the brief was pretty precise.'

'Aye,' Jimmy said. 'Get them beautiful and poor.'

'But it couldn't have been that easy to fill though,' Jill said. 'Are there lots of poor students at Oxford and Cambridge? I wouldn't have thought so.'

'More than you would think ma'am,' Frank said. 'Remember they've been making a big push in the last few years to get away from their privileged public school reputation. And this Oxbridge Agency is very well regarded amongst the students so they've got no shortage of applicants. You see, these days there's so many kids with degrees now that it's not easy to get a start. But they get you a foot in the door, even if it costs the parents a packet.'

'And of course they had the scholarship scheme,' Jimmy said.

'Aye, clever that,' Frank said, 'because it wouldn't have worked if poorer kids were put off applying because of the cost. Actually Pete Burnside's got a smart wee lassie on his team at the moment called Yvonne Sharp who's got direct experience of it. She applied to them but didn't get taken on. Lovely girl, and pretty in her own way.'

'But not a stand-out in the looks department I'm guessing,' Jill said.

'No ma'am, and all the better for it in my opinion. But Chardonnay Clarke was a real beauty, and that's why she got the scholarship. Except there were strings attached.'

'I can really sympathise,' Jimmy said, giving Maggie a hard look, 'being used as a sex object and all that.'

Maggie laughed. 'Says Captain James Stewart in all modesty. But when I think about it, they probably weren't overtly told to have affairs or anything like that. My guess is they were just instructed to do what they needed to do to get information out of the clients they were placed with. And then of course, being so incredibly attractive, well it was inevitable that something might happen.'

'Aye, I sort of agree,' Frank said, 'but maybe there was a bit more in the Luke Brown case. Remember, Belinda Milner was just a non-executive director there, so she wouldn't have been around at Alexia Life on a day to day basis.'

'Yes, that's easily explained,' Maggie said. 'It was Greenway Mining that Morgan was interested in, not Alexia. So Luke would have been specifically instructed to get close to Belinda.'

'But no one bargained on anyone falling in love,' Frank said. 'That's what happened with Chardonnay and Jeremy Hart. He was their top financial guy, and so he was right at the heart of HBB's takeover deal with the German bank. And it was that information that Morgan was desperate to get a hold of. The trouble was, Hart turned out be a decent guy and he was single too. Although he wasn't exactly Brad Pitt in the looks department he was kind and clever and she fell for him. And he fell for her too. So of course she was conflicted.'

'I can imagine what happened next,' Maggie said. 'She begins to get uncomfortable about what she's doing and decides that enough is enough. She tells Morgan's team that there's not going to be any more info coming their way.'

Frank nodded. 'It was worse than that I think. When she saw all the stress Jeremy was under after Morgan made his move, I believe she decided to blow the whistle on the whole thing, go public with it, and she told them that was what she was going to do.'

'Right,' Jill said, 'so Morgan decided she had to be silenced. Just to protect his damn reputation I suppose.'

'Aye, exactly ma'am. Wouldn't do if the big investment genius turns out to be a cheap con-artist, would it? But of course, he didn't do the killings himself, that goes without saying. That bit would have been subcontracted to person or persons unknown.'

'And what about the other one. Luke, wasn't it?'

'We don't know as much about that one ma'am. I think Belinda Milner was besotted with Luke, but I don't know if it was reciprocated. What we do know is that someone at Alexia found out about the affair and so Luke was quietly shovelled out the door. My guess is that Morgan then panicked and decided he'd better be shut up too, just in case he decided to blab.'

'And you say there's no evidence linking the murders back to Morgan?' Jill asked.

'I said that. Not unless Pete can catch up with the folks who shoved them in front of these trains and they're prepared to admit to being in his employ.'

'And what about that woman who runs the agency? Fitzwilliam isn't it?'

'Aye, well I'm ninety-nine percent certain that she wasn't involved in the killings, because you should have seen how she absolutely wet herself when we said she was looking at twenty-five years for conspiracy to murder. She knew that Morgan was using these kids, but that was as far as it went.'

Maggie nodded. 'If you ignore the murders, it wasn't actually a crime what they were doing. Obviously it's going to trash Morgan's reputation if it all comes out, but he'll still have his billion quid in the bank.'

'Morgan will deny knowing anything about it,' Frank said. 'I can tell you that right now.'

'So why did you bring him in?' Jill asked.

And then Maggie remembered the meeting, just two weeks ago, at the Brasenose offices.

'Because he's not infallible Jill,' she said. 'Without realising it, he let it slip he knew about Chardonnay and Luke. I guess you thought he might make another mistake. Is that right Frank?'

'Aye. Not exactly inspired detective work, is it?'

But there was something else about that meeting, and it came to her and Jimmy at the same time. He got it out first.

'It was us,' he said, looking at her in dismay. 'Do you remember, when we were bringing him up to speed on how we we're doing on the Justice for Greenway investigation?'

'I know, I know.' She felt her heart crashing as the consequences of what they had done hit her properly for the first time. *We told him about Liz and her big story*. We told him she was going to reveal how he managed to find out about the problem with the cobalt ore.'

'Aye,' Jimmy said ruefully, 'Morgan got it from Luke. And he got it from Belinda. That's what Liz meant by pillow talk.'

Suddenly Jill Smart leapt to her feet, clenching her fists. 'Right, that's it,' she barked. 'Three murders with the same MO and Morgan's got a clear motive for all of them. I don't care what's happened to his bloody family. Bring him in.'

'Pete's job,' Frank said, smiling broadly. 'I'll go and find him right now ma'am.' He swept out of the room, slamming the door behind him.

* * *

Now the incident room fell into silence, a mood of quiet satisfaction pervading in anticipation of *Aphrodite* beginning to pick up pace. But for Maggie, a dense fog was beginning to clear and through the shimmering mist, she could see the road ahead. Four murders executed in an identical way, the killers placing their trust in a *modus operandi* that had proved its efficacy and reliability. And the murder of Rosie Morgan the exception that proved the rule. This time, there had been no attempt to dress the murder up as suicide. The people behind this one had a clear objective. *Justice for Greenway*, that justice being delivered by making Hugo Morgan suffer for the rest of his life. So was it with cruel deliberation they had chosen the same method as he himself had used to prevent three people tell their damning story, a chilling copy-cat killing designed to maximise his pain? But who knew about his connection to these killings? The case, if it could be called that, hadn't made the papers, so almost nobody knew that Morgan was suspected, apart from her, Jimmy and Frank. Except of course, for one other group of people. *The killers.*

That just left one big unanswered question, a question that was currently conflicting with the crazy theory that was half-forming in her head. That picture of the girl Rosie was carrying in her handbag and that brochure. Where they hell did they fit?

In her pocket, she felt the gentle vibration of her phone, set to silent. A message. From Robert Trelawney.

*I hear you've had a tough day. Dinner? Pick you up at eight xx.*

It was the last thing she wanted after the day she'd had, but Robert had some questions to answer, and she wanted to hear him answer them. It all depended on whether she could find a babysitter at such short notice.

Luckily she had someone in mind. Two someones in fact.

# Chapter 27

It was ridiculous behaviour from a grown man of forty-two years of age, he knew it was, skulking around like some stupid love-struck teenager. Pathetic. The Protection of Freedoms Act 2012 had a lot to say about it too and he should know, he'd been on the course. Officially, they didn't call it stalking but it amounted to the same thing. *Following a person, watching or spying on them or forcing contact with the victim through any means, including social media.* He didn't do social media but he could pretty much tick off the rest of the list. No bother at all.

He had parked his car across the street from her house, about fifty metres further along so he couldn't be seen from any of her windows. This was the fourth or fifth occasion in the last month that he done it, and if that didn't qualify as stalking, he didn't know what did, but what he was trying to achieve, he wasn't entirely sure. He was pretty sure she was still seeing that gallery owner, but he had no idea how serious it was. He'd seen him just once, about three weeks ago, when he called for her in his convertible Mercedes. She'd invited him in, but it was no more than five minutes later when they emerged, and that made Frank feel a bit better, because in his nightmares, he'd imagined her showering him in kisses then ripping off his shirt and dragging him upstairs to her bedroom. But you couldn't do all of that in five minutes, thank God.

He'd already been parked up for three-quarters of an hour, inactive, but somewhere in an obscure recess of his confused mind he did have a plan. Tonight he was just going to get out of the car, walk up to her door, ring the bell, and when she opened it, he was simply going to tell her how he felt about her. How hard could that be? Hard enough to mean he hadn't been able to execute his master-plan on the previous four occasions he'd been sat there.

It was a quiet street, a few cars passing from time to time, a couple of these on-line grocery delivery vans, and the odd person out walking their dogs, wrapped up to repel the early-evening drizzle. Sleepy suburbia, where nothing much happened. He glanced in his mirror and noticed a small van making its way down the street, slowing to a crawl every few yards before setting off again. Frank assumed the driver was checking house numbers to find the one he was looking for. As it passed him, he clocked the elaborate graphics stencilled on the side. *Blooming Beautiful. Flowers for every occasion.* Fifty yards on the other side of the road it pulled up, right outside her front door. A man got out, squat and broad, wearing a dark leather bomber jacket with a beanie hat pulled down tight on his head. He made his way to the back of the vehicle, opened the double doors and emerged with a large bouquet which from a distance looked almost as tall as he was. From that bloody gallery fella no doubt. He was obviously a smooth operator, worst luck. Women loved flowers, he knew that, and of course, if he was with her, he would buy her them every week. *Some chance.*

The delivery guy scrutinised the label then, evidently satisfied, closed the doors, blipped the central locking and walked the few yards along the pavement to her gate, from where it was only three or four steps up to Maggie's front door. Frank watched as he rung the front bell and waited for her to respond. And then, with unfortunate timing, another van crept past his car, this time tall enough to obscure his view of the door. And when it was once again clear, the man was not there. A bit strange he thought, but then maybe she'd asked him to bring them through to the kitchen whilst she looked for a vase big enough to hold them. He should be back out in a couple of minutes, no worries.

But he wasn't. Five, six, seven minutes and still he hadn't emerged. Something was wrong, he was sure of that. He jumped out of the car and sprinted across the road, through the gate and then up to her door, taking the steps two at a time. He pushed the bell and waited. And listened. Nothing.

He looked in through the adjacent bay window but the room was in darkness and there was nothing to be seen. He hadn't been in Maggie's house, more's the pity, but he knew the typical layout of these upmarket Victorian terraces. Full height extensions out the back, built on top of luxury open plan kitchen-diners, with bi-folds or double doors opening into the garden. Her house was in the middle of a row of eight or so properties, with no way to get round the back except over the neighbours' fences. Awkwardly, he clambered over the low brick wall that divided her path from the nearest neighbour. No bell as far as he could see, but there was a flimsy-looking knocker. He wrapped on it firmly, four or five times, then banged the door with his fist. He waited a few seconds but there was no response. No surprise really because although it was nearly eight o'clock, it wasn't just the cops who worked stupid hours in the capital. Giving up, he jumped down the steps onto the pavement then ran the few yards to the neighbour on the other side. This time there was a bell, and he jabbed at it impatiently, muttering *come on, come on* under his breath.

The door was opened by an elderly man of South Asian appearance who gave him a curious look then asked politely, 'Good evening, can I help you?'

Frank flashed his ID. 'Sir, I'm a police Inspector, can I come in please?'

'Of course.' The man ushered him through the tiny entrance porch into his front room. 'Would you like a cup of tea?'

He shook his head. 'I need to get into your garden sir. This is an emergency. Can you show me the way please?'

The man led him through another sitting room into his kitchen, which contrary to Frank's expectations was small and had clearly seen better days. 'There it is,' he said, pointing to a green-painted panel door that looked as if it could have been there since the place was built. 'I'll get the key.'

'Quickly sir, if you don't mind,' Frank said, trying to mask his impatience.

The man walked over to a dresser, opened a drawer and began to rummage in it.

'I'm quite certain this is where I put it,' he said unconvincingly, 'or was it in the unit over there? I can't quite remember. I don't go out there all that often you see.'

Frank just managed to strangle an explicative at birth. 'Sir, I need that key. Shall I look in the other drawer?' Without waiting for an answer he yanked it open, pulling it clean off its runners, then emptied the contents onto a worktop. Which included a key.

'Ah there it is,' the man said, smiling. 'I remember putting it there now. Here, let me open the door for you. There's a bit of a knack to it I'm afraid. It can be rather stiff sometimes.'

He picked up the key and ambled over to the door, then attempted to slip the rusty key into the keyhole. After a few exploratory prods, it finally went in. Frank expected there would be more precious seconds of cocking about, but this time his fears were unfounded, as with a loud click, the lock yielded to a twist of the key.

'Right sir,' Frank barked as he swung open the door, 'I have to tell you that a serious police incident is currently ongoing and as a member of the public, I need you to stay inside for your own safety, do you understand?' He hated the cringe-worthy jargon but somehow it seemed to lend authority to the message. Fortunately in this case, the member of the public didn't need telling twice. Frank watched as he scurried indoors and closed the door. And locked it behind him.

It was a dark evening and the garden did not seem to benefit from any artificial lighting. As he had surmised, Maggie's house had been extended outwards, her wall forming the first four or five meters of their mutual boundary. As his eyes adjusted to the light, he could just about make out the fencing that bordered the unkempt garden. On the left, tidy and well maintained. On the right, the one bordering on to her garden, ramshackle and scruffy. No prices for guessing which boundary Frank's householder was responsible for.

He saw that the fourth panel along had separated from its concrete post, and was lying at an oblique angle, held precariously in place by the other fencepost. It was an eyesore, no arguing with that, but it left plenty of room for someone to squeeze through, even someone of his generous proportions.

Edging his frame into the gap, he cautiously stuck his head out, peering down the garden towards the house. As was the fashion, the kitchen extended the full width of the plot, its features illuminated by a blaze of light streaming through its windows. Although he guessed it was a relatively new addition, it had been constructed in traditional style, with a pair of glaze-panelled French doors framed on either side by decorative latticed windows above a brick base. He slipped through into the garden then tentatively crept towards the house, being careful to keep his back to the fence where the light did not directly reach. Now he was close enough to see into the kitchen. The lattice framework served to partially obscure the view but it didn't prevent him seeing all too clearly what was playing out in front of him. *Shit*.

The flower delivery guy had his back to him, but he was now close enough to make out the badge on the side of his hat. The staff-bearing lion rampant of Chelsea Football Club. In the room, facing him, were Maggie and her son Ollie, who was clinging onto his mother, his face set but betraying fear. Next to them, a young woman wearing a defiant expression, whom he vaguely recognised as the feisty girl who worked in her office, Polish or Latvian or something like that. And next to her, to his astonishment, stood his brother. Looking serious. A glint from something metallic caused Frank to involuntarily screw up his eyes, at the same time explaining the look on his brother's face. Chelsea man had a gun. *Double shit*.

Desperately, he tried to weigh up his options. Really, he should call in the specialists, trained and armed to deal with hostage situations like this. But maybe this wasn't a hostage situation and the gunman simply meant to shoot them all and be done with it. A gunman who neatly met the description of the Kings Cross abductor. And if it was he, then this was a guy who already killed once that day. *A professional.*

So that was it. *Decided.* He was on his own and the only weapon he had was the element of surprise. Doubtless, the killer would have weighed up the risks of his mission, but had he considered the chances of anything coming at him from his rear flank, such was the inaccessibility of these back gardens? Frank hoped not.

The problem was, not only did he have no clue what to do, he'd also no idea how long he had before the shooting started. Not long, was his gut feel. Calmly, he tried to put himself inside the gunman's head. This guy was a professional, so he would want to get out of the situation as quickly and cleanly as possible, but that wasn't easy when you had four victims to take care of. Shoot one and there was every chance that one of the others might make a grab for you, reasoning that there was nothing to lose, and it could go rapidly downhill from there. And then suddenly, it came to him. This was a hit that had gone belly-up. None of this had been meant to happen and now the gunman was in uncharted territory, just like he was. Frank played it through in his mind. God knows why, but it appears that Maggie is his original target. The job's straightforward, all he has to do is ring the bell, shoot her, then slip away. Mission accomplished. But to his surprise it isn't Maggie who opens the door but some unknown guy, a massive guy, and now he has to think on his feet. He jabs the gun into the guy's ribs and pushes him along the hallway, somewhere along the line bumping into Maggie, the kid and another woman whom he wasn't expecting to be there either. He ushers them at gunpoint into the kitchen which is where he is now, trying to figure out what the hell to do next.

That sounded a reasonable assessment of what had happened, but it didn't really help Frank work out what *he* should do. Somehow, the gunman had to be overpowered before he could fire his weapon, but how? That could only happen if someone in that room was prepared to act. The risk would be enormous, but perhaps he could cause a distraction that would at least give them half a chance.

But first, he had to make them aware of his presence, and that itself carried some risk. He couldn't simply knock on a window pane, obviously. Somehow he had to signal to one or more of them, catch their eye if he could, and pray that they didn't inadvertently give him away by their surprise. Right away he ruled out Maggie. From where he was, her line of sight to him was obscured by the gunman, and in any case, it would be nigh impossible for her to make any move without putting her son in danger. Jimmy would be his favoured choice, because he knew that already his brother would be working up an escape plan in his mind. He'd been in far worse situations than this during his time in the army and he wasn't going to let some second-rate football hooligan get the better of him. The problem was, he was now standing side-on to the window, his eyes seemingly focussed on Maggie and Ollie. Which only left the girl. *Elsa*, that was her name. Czech, he remembered now.

He dropped onto his stomach and began to crawl towards the kitchen. The ground was cold and muddy, the grassed area reaching right up to the doors. A couple of seconds later he was lying under the right-hand window, tight to the wall. After taking a moment to compose himself, he made his first move. As slowly as he could, he pulled himself up, edging his head above the window sill so that he could once again see into the room. *Excellent*. He had a clear sight of her, still wearing her defiant expression. Now, slowly, he raised an arm and then almost imperceptibly began a wave, his hand moving no more than two or three centimetres in either direction, and at a snail's pace. He watched her carefully for a sign that she had noticed, but there was nothing. So he tried again, moving his hand a bit further and a bit faster, his heart racing, his mind overflowing with the terrible consequences should it all go wrong.

And then he saw it. The slight change to her expression as she caught his eye. But not enough to give anything away. *Good girl*. Now it was in her hands and all he could do was wait and be ready. For what seemed an age, nothing happened. He guessed like Jimmy she was working out her options. Or maybe, out of fear, she had decided to do nothing. But then suddenly she started to scream at the top of her voice, loud enough for Frank to make out every word through the thick double-glazed panes.

'I don't want to die, I don't want to die. I want husband and baby and home. You can kill these but not me.'

'Shut the fuck up,' the gunman shouted, gesticulating with the pistol. 'Shut the fuck up bitch, or I'll blow your fucking head off.'

She took a step towards him. 'I will do anything you want. I good in bed, make all fantasies come true. Please don't kill me.' *Now*. Frank leapt up then steadying himself, smashed a foot against the gap between the doors, just below the handle, giving it everything he had. With a crack, they burst open, his momentum propelling him into the room and sending him barging into the gunman. Momentarily disorientated, he was taken out by Jimmy's huge fist slamming into his face, jerking his head back and sending him crashing to the floor onto his back, the gun spinning harmlessly across the floor.

'Nice work bruv,' Frank said, raising his hand to proffer a high-five. 'And Elsa, what a performance. Brought tears to my eyes it did.' Kneeling, he took out a pair of handcuffs and slipped them onto the prone figure.

It seemed as if the disturbing events had had no detrimental effect on Ollie, although he was careful not to let go of his mother's hand. 'Did you see that, mummy?' he said, his eyes sparkling. 'Uncle Jimmy biffed that man, and he fell over, and he dropped his gun, and then we were all safe.'

'Yes, well done Uncle Jimmy,' Maggie said, the relief tangible in her voice. 'But do you see who it is?'

'Aye, I do.'

Elsa had flung his arms around him and was nestling her head on his chest. Without thinking, he kissed her gently on the forehead, causing her to snuggle up even tighter. 'It's Morgan's security guy. I remember him from that do at the Hilton. He was the guy who chucked McGinley out, wasn't he?'

Maggie nodded. 'I met him later at that fast food place, with Morgan and Jasmine. His name's Vinny.'

'Well, we're not going to be seeing much more of Vinny when we've finished throwing the book at him,' Frank said, grinning. 'He'll be looking at twenty years just for this alone. Anyway, just give me a minute to summon reinforcements. I want this guy locked up in a nice comfy cell before he can do any more damage.'

'Just a minute,' Maggie said. She bent over the gunman and pulled open the bomber jacket. 'Yeah, here it is.' She took his phone and began to scroll. Then, under her breath, she let out an explicative, which Frank just managed to catch. *Swine.* He watched as she tapped something into it and then threw it across the room.

'Could you make us some tea Elsa please?' she asked, composing herself with a visible effort, 'and squash for Ollie.' With obvious reluctance, the girl released Jimmy from her embrace and forced a smile. 'Yeah, sure. I put kettle on now. Come Ollie, come over here and help me.'

Maggie turned to Jimmy and Frank. 'Let me show you something.' Lying on her kitchen table was a glossy sales brochure, opened at the centre spread. Looking for all the world like a school photograph, thirty or so young men and women lined up on the front steps of The Oxbridge Agency.

'DCI Ahmed let me take this away. D'you see? Last year's cohort, I think that's what you would call it.' She pointed to a figure standing in the front row.

'Recognise her?'

'Whoa,' Jimmy said. 'That's Lotti.'

'Except it isn't,' she said. 'According to the caption, this is Griselda Hauptmann, aged twenty-three years old. BA, History of Art, St Catherine's College Oxford.'

Frank was peering at Maggie through narrowed eyes. There was something in her expression which told him, even before she said another word. Something about that phone message and that brochure. *She's worked it out. Maggie Bainbridge's worked out everything.*

# Chapter 28

Frank barked the instruction into his radio handset whilst, barely in control, he steered with the other hand. 'We need an armed response team mobile pronto. Forty-seven Bedford Gardens, Kensington. Over and out.' Short and sweet, as he raced the Mondeo along another rat run, siren wailing and the flashing blue lights clearing the way.

'So come on Maggie, what's this all about?' A black cab emerging from a parking space was signalling but not looking, causing him to jam on the brakes. 'These cabbies think they own the bloody roads,' he shouted, banging on the horn.

'Calm down mate,' Jimmy said, grimacing. 'Don't want you having a heart attack before we get there. It's only five minutes or so from here.'

'We can't wait for the response team,' Maggie said, urgency in her voice. 'They're going to kill Yazz, if they've not already done it. I think that would have been Vinny's next job, after he'd killed me.'

'Who's they?' Jimmy said. 'Who are they? And why did they want to kill you?'

Before she could answer, a shrill ring filled the cabin, the car's infotainment panel displaying the name of the caller. *DCI Jill Smart.*

'Crap! She must have just heard the news,' Frank said. 'This'll be the call that tells me not to do anything stupid and to wait for the armed boys to turn up.' It continued to ring as Frank swung the car into a sharp left turn, the tyres squealing in protest.

'Aren't you going to answer it?' Jimmy asked.

'Stuff that.'

He let it go through to voicemail. *'Frank, it's Jill. Please listen to what...'*

'Aye, whatever,' he said, prodding the *end call* icon. 'You can tell me later.'

'So come on Maggie,' Jimmy said, 'Why did someone want to kill you? Was it something to do with Lotti?'

'Griselda you mean. No, I don't think so, not directly. Actually I'm not a hundred percent sure about any of it, in fact I might be one hundred percent wrong. But we'll find out one way or the other in a few minutes.'

'Hang on guys, this might get a wee bit hairy.' Frank gave another blast of the siren as he hammered off Sussex Gardens and into Lancaster Terrace.

'One way street mate,' Jimmy shouted, alarmed, 'and in case you haven't noticed, you're going the wrong bloody way.'

Frank shrugged. 'No worries. Police emergency. They'll get out the way. Almost certainly.' The engine roared as he dropped a gear and floored it. 'Best get it done as quickly as we can, eh?' Jimmy glanced over at the speedometer. Touching seventy, in a thirty mile an hour limit and going the wrong way. That must be worth twelve points on the licence at least. Fortunately though the late evening traffic was light and somehow they made it on to the Bayswater Road without incident. Less than a minute later, they had arrived.

'It's that one,' Maggie said, pointing as they leapt out of the car. 'With the red door.'

'You've been here before then?' Jimmy said.

She didn't answer.

'Right,' Frank said. 'I'll ring the bell, give it a minute, and if no-one comes to the door then we break it down. Ok with that bruv?'

'They'll answer it,' Maggie said. 'They're expecting Vinny back. I texted a thumbs up from his phone. And let me lead the way, because as far as they know, I'm now dead.'

He pushed the bell and waited, each of them silent. And then the door opened and without being invited, Maggie stepped into the hallway.

'Hello Griselda.'

'But you're...you're...' The young woman stammered over her words, the shock of this unexpected development severing communication between brain and mouth.

'Dead? I'm afraid I'm very much alive.' She grabbed Griselda Hauptmann by the wrist and twisted her arm behind her back, causing her to let out a yelp of pain. And then twisted it again.

'Where is she? Where's Yazz? Tell me.'

'She's... she's in the basement.' She nodded her head in the direction of a door.

Maggie pushed the girl up against the wall. 'Frank, we need to make this one secure. She's up to her neck in it. She was there. At Kings Cross.'

'Aye, nae bother,' he said reaching for a pocket. 'I always carry a couple of pairs with me. Goes back to my old days in Glasgow. Never know when they might come in handy.' He took out the handcuffs and slapped them on one wrist.

'Ok let's go, he said, giving the girl a shove in the back, 'and don't even think about shouting a warning, or I'll break your arm, got it?'

'I didn't know,' Griselda said, looking as if she was about to cry, 'that it would go this way I mean. This isn't what I signed up for.'

'Yeah sure,' Maggie said briskly. 'Let's leave the hand-wringing for later, shall we?'

'I'm going to lock her in the car,' Frank said, 'and don't do anything until I come back, ok?'

'Sure, but maybe I should go in first anyway,' Jimmy said. 'I'm trained for this sort of thing, remember?'

'Aye, but back then you were wearing full body armour and holding an assault rifle,' Frank said. 'You can go first if you want to, but just wait for me, ok?'

'They won't be armed,' Maggie said. 'That was Vinny's department.'

Frank returned a minute later and they made their way through the doorway and down the steep steps, Jimmy leading the way, the two brothers unsure of what awaited them. But Maggie knew. She knew who would be there and she knew precisely what had been planned. She just hoped they were not already too late. Too late to save the lives of Yazz Morgan and Robert Trelawney.

But she was not expecting this. Two tall barstools had been placed in the middle of the room. Yazz and Trelawney had been blindfolded and gagged, and were each now balanced precariously on top of a stool, their hands tied behind them. Suspended from an exposed beam in the ceiling hung the nooses that had been placed around their necks. Between them stood Felicity Morgan. And contrary to expectations, she had a gun.

'Miss Bainbridge,' she snarled, looking up, 'this is an unexpected pleasure. Oh yes, I know who you really are, do you think I'm a fool?'

'It's over Felicity, come on,' Maggie said, her voice calm. 'You don't really want to kill her, do you? Your own daughter for Christ's sake. How can you do that? Look at her, she's an innocent child.' Frantically processing the situation in her mind, it wasn't long before she reached a conclusion. It wasn't looking good.

'Over? But that's where you're quite wrong,' Felicity said, her eyes blazing with menace. 'Not yet. Not until I've decided which of these two to kill first.' She gripped a leg of Trelawney's stool and began to shake it. He gave a low moan as he struggled to keep his balance.

'You see, men are such pigs, aren't they? *You* should know that Miss Bainbridge, after everything *you've* been through. Oh yes, I know all about *that*. Just like you, my husband thought he could just throw me away like yesterday's newspaper, but now he's beginning to understand that actions have consequences.'

'You're off your bloody head,' Jimmy said. 'You won't get away with it you know.'

'Ah Miss Bainbridge's trained monkey. You are a cute little thing aren't you? Well, maybe I am crazy. So what?'

'There's going to be a response team here any minute,' Frank said. 'I'd hand myself over now, if I was you, because they'll shoot first and ask questions later.'

'It'll be all over by then,' she said. 'In fact, let's get the party started, shall we?'

Now she was shrieking like a demented witch, jabbing a finger in Maggie's direction. 'Don't think I don't know about your sordid little tryst with my *darling* Robert, you little *cow*. I've been having you watched you see. Both of you. It's just a shame that Vinny wasn't able to take care of you earlier, but well, you're here now, aren't you? But first, it's *his* turn. Goodbye my darling Robert.'

Viciously, she kicked out, causing the stool to spin across the room. There was a crack as the beam took his full weight, his body plummeting towards the floor then being arrested as the noose tightened, breaking his neck. Leaving him spinning like a sack of grain.

'Christ!' Maggie yelled, involuntarily turning her head away, the shock robbing her of breath,

Instinctively, Jimmy took a step forward but was stopped in his tracks as Felicity raised the pistol and pointed at him.

'Let me help him,' he said quietly, even although he knew it was already too late. 'Please. You don't want this Felicity.'

'That's where you're wrong, this is exactly what I want,' she sneered, her eyes burning with hatred. 'Actions have consequences. Everybody has to learn that.'

Maggie turned to face her, struggling to choke back her disgust and horror. She didn't know how, but somehow she had to get her talking, to buy some time until the response team arrived. Although god knows what they would be able to do when they got here.

'You've already succeeded Felicity, you must know that. Hugo will never have another happy day in his life, you've made sure of that. He's paid a huge price for what he did to you. That's what you wanted isn't it? His reputation is in ruins and his beloved Rosie is dead. Killing Yazz won't make it any worse for him.'

'But it will make *me* feel better,' she snarled. 'He turned them against me. My own children. They had the choice and they chose to live with *him*. Have you any idea what that feels like?'

'But they loved you. Rosie told me. Both of them loved you. They loved you very much. And Yazz is just a little girl. She doesn't deserve this. She's so lovely. You know she is.'

'But she loved *him*. She loved *him* more than she loved me. It wasn't *fair*, after what he did to me. It wasn't *fair*.' For a moment Felicity was distracted, wallowing in self-pity. And Maggie saw her chance. Shooting a glance at Jimmy and Frank, she began to creep towards her, speaking softly.

'It'll be alright Felicity. It'll be alright. Let's put an end to this now, shall we? Please, give me the gun.' The other woman stared straight at her, her expression a confusion of sadness and pain. Then with an almost imperceptible shake of her head, she let the gun drop to the floor.

But then as Maggie stooped to pick it up, Morgan gave a spine-chilling scream and lunged blindly at Yazz's stool. As if in slow motion, she saw Jimmy leap forward and thrust his strong hands under the little girl's armpits, holding her aloft to support her weight just as the stool collapsed from under her. At the same time, Frank yanked Felicity's arms behind her and pushed her on to the floor, face down, his knee in her back.

'Maggie, you need to get up on the stool,' Jimmy shouted. 'Get the noose off. I don't know how long I can hold her. Quickly.'

'It'll be easier if you climb on my shoulders,' Frank said. He grabbed a handful of Morgan's hair and yanked her head up. 'And don't you *dare* make a move, got that?' He pushed her away from her, causing her face to smash into the cold flagstones of the floor.

Now he was alongside his brother and down on one knee, allowing Maggie to swing her legs around his shoulders. 'Up we go now. Hold tight.' Slowly he pushed himself up until he was fully standing, squeezing her legs tightly against his chest.

'I think I've got it,' Maggie shouted, struggling to balance as she reached out to grab hold of the noose. 'Yazz, you'll be ok darling. Let's get this thing off you, shall we?'

'Hurry up, for God's sake,' Jimmy yelled. 'This wee thing's bloody heavy.'

'It's tight. It's tight. I need to try and loosen it first.'

Frantically she pushed her fingers into the tiny gap between the looped rope and the knot that was holding it in place.

'Come on, come on,' Jimmy shouted.

'It's budging... nearly... yeah, I can feel it.' With her free hand she grabbed the knot and pulled with all the strength she could muster. And then suddenly it gave, causing her to lose her balance. But before she collapsed on top of Frank, she just managed to flip the loop over Yazz's head. 'Got it!'

Instantly, Jimmy took Yazz's full weight and gently lowered the little girl to the ground.

'Here, sit down and we'll get you untied.' Beside him, Frank and Maggie were untangling themselves. Thankfully they seemed none the worse for their fall.

'Here, let me help you Jimmy,' Maggie said. 'And Frank, take her mother out of our sight. I don't think Yazz will have anything to say to her, do you?'

'Aye, I'll do that. I'll stick her in the car and chain her to the German woman. I can see them spending plenty of time together in the future.'

* * *

It was all under control by the time the response team arrived. Jimmy had managed to cut down Robert Trelawney's body and had laid him on the floor, untying his hands but leaving the blindfold in place for reasons he could not explain. Maggie had taken Yazz up to the kitchen and was helping her sip from a mug of hot chocolate, holding her hand whilst offering occasional but useless words of comfort. She knew from her own experience that kids could bounce back from even the most appalling experiences, but this was different. In the last twelve hours Jasmine Morgan had witnessed the murder of her beloved sister, and now she had found out that it was her own mother who had been responsible for the killing. No-one was going to come to terms with that, not ever. With a heavy heart, she realised that Felicity Morgan, driven to madness by bitterness and jealousy, had succeeded in her warped mission. Actions have consequences and the murderer Hugo Morgan was never going to forget it.

# Chapter 29

It was Friday night, and they were meeting in one of their favourite watering holes, the *Ship* over in Shoreditch. A bit of a fancy gastropub, it had gravitated to becoming their special occasion place, their patronage infrequent mainly on account of the steep prices. Maggie knew that Frank in particular found them objectionable, not because he was tight with money, because he wasn't. It was just he felt the place, or rather its regular clientele, was a bit pretentious, and he didn't like pretentious and he didn't like having to pay seven quid for a pint either.

They were six-strong, Jimmy, Frank, Elsa, Asvina Rani, Jill Smart and Maggie, gathered together for what was part-celebration, part-explanation. Because there was a lot to be explained.

Food had been ordered and they were now propping up the bar, waiting for their table to be prepared. Already the group had attracted inquisitive looks from their fellow diners. *What was it these two guys had, they were asking, to be able to pull four beautiful women like them? It must be a works do, couldn't be anything else, surely? Or maybe they had money, that would figure. Because the smaller guy wasn't exactly Brad Pitt, although to be fair the tall guy was amazingly good-looking.* Had they been able to look inside the head of one of the women, they would have been surprised to find it swimming with inadequacy. *Asvina Rani, Jill Smart, Elsa Berger.* Slim, beautiful, assured, sexy, each and every one of them. *Maggie Bainbridge.* None of the above. With an effort, she banished the negative thoughts to the back of her mind and tried to concentrate on the positive. An amazing night lay ahead, with amazing friends. What more could a girl ask for? Except, perhaps, for an amazing man to share it with. She had entertained high hopes for Robert Trelawney, but now that plan lay in ruins. But it hadn't worked out too well for him either.

'The Sunday Times Insight team are running a big story on it this weekend,' Frank said, propelling their drinks along the bar. 'They've dug up a couple more of these Oxbridge scholarship kids and apparently they're going to spill the beans on the whole operation.'

'Cheers bruv,' Jimmy said, raising his glass. 'So that's Morgan well and truly finished as far as his reputation goes, isn't it? Good, that's what I say.'

'That's right,' Asvina said. 'Although he's had our law firm talk to the paper and warned them against even the slightest insinuation that he was involved in the deaths of Chardonnay Clarke and Luke Brown.'

'So is he going to get away with it then?' Maggie asked, 'because that would be depressing and a complete denial of justice.'

Jill Smart gave a resigned look. 'We had him in a Paddington Green interview room for two days but we didn't get a thing out of him. Just sat beside his lawyer and gave us the no comment treatment. And Vinny Hadley is denying any involvement in these killings, even although it's odds-on he was responsible. So unless we turn up some other compelling evidence in the meantime, then yes, he's going to get away with it, I'm sad to say.'

'And the CPS are not that bothered,' Frank said. 'They've got our boy Vinny one hundred percent for Rosie Morgan's killing. Her mother's admitted that she paid him to do it. And of course he was caught in the act trying to kill all of you guys. So he's going down for thirty years just for those two alone.'

'But it's not right, is it?' Jimmy said angrily. 'Surely there needs to be closure for these kids' families, and for Liz Donahue too.'

'You're right,' Jill said, 'and I'm as angry about it as anyone. Rest assured the cases won't be closed until we've exhausted every angle.'

'And then they'll get quietly shelved and chucked over the wall into Frank's department,' Jimmy said, with some bitterness.

'Could do worse than that mate,' Frank said, 'And being serious, we'll happily take on these three cases if we have to. And then I'll nail that bastard if it's the last thing I do. Believe me, I bloody will.' Maggie wasn't quite sure whom this show of bravado was aimed at, but she shot a smile in his direction and was amused to see him redden.

'And what about Felicity Morgan?' Asvina asked. 'What's going to happen to her?'

'Going down for conspiracy to murder,' Frank said, 'although her lawyers are already trying to argue diminished responsibility on the grounds of her mental condition. I feel sorry for her in some ways.'

'She was completely crazy, wasn't she?' Jill said. 'And I guess her husband dumping her just pushed her over the edge.'

'I think she always was nuts, even before then,' Jimmy said. 'But aye, this was off the scale.'

'So come on,' Asvina said, 'who's going to take me through this thing from start to finish?'

Maggie smiled. 'I'll have a go, shall I? Although it's rather a long story.'

'We're in no hurry,' Frank said, downing his pint. 'But maybe wait until the food turns up. But hey, it looks like our table's ready now. Let's wander over, shall we?'

They picked up their drinks and made their way across the busy bar, Maggie watching with amusement as Elsa manoeuvred herself alongside Jimmy to make sure she was seated beside him. Which left her sitting next to Frank. Entirely fine by her.

'So, first, Felicity Morgan,' she began. 'Yes, when Hugo dumped her, she completely flipped, and her whole existence became dedicated to making him suffer. Actions have consequences, that was her mantra, and of course she had the money to make it happen.'

'So can you explain how she came to get Griselda Hauptmann involved?' Asvina asked. 'I've never really understood that.'

'Well, I think her original plan was simply to watch Hugo fall in love with another woman and then have her dump him, so he got to experience the same pain that she had. She had begun a relationship with Robert Trelawney and knew he was looking for an intern, and of course she knew of her husband's tie-up with the Oxbridge Agency. So she put Trelawney in touch with Sophie Fitzwilliam, who just happened to have the perfect candidate on her books.'

'A graduate in the History of Art,' Asvina said.

'Yes,' Maggie said, 'to Felicity, it was as if it was destined.'

'So she was paying them both for their part in this crazy scheme?' Jill asked.

'Yes. A lot. Tens of thousands of pounds, I think in Griselda's case. But the only fly in the ointment was that Griselda was too young. She was worried that Hugo would think twice about having a relationship with a woman so close in age to his daughter.'

'So Griselda became Lotti,' Jimmy said.

'Exactly. Robert knew of the Brückner family through his contacts in the art world. He'd met the real Lotti Brückner several times and as a consequence knew quite a lot about her.'

'Like her Heidelberg degree,' Elsa said. 'I spoke to University there. Lotti was real person.'

'Yes Elsa, that's right, she was. So Robert helped Griselda put together a convincing back story, and then all it needed was for Hugo to take the bait when she dangled it in front of him.'

'And he couldn't resist,' Jimmy said. 'I mean, what man could?'

'No indeed,' Maggie said, giving him a wry smile. 'Men are *so* shallow. But the problem was, Felicity in her blind anger, found that this wasn't enough for her.'

'And that's when she decided to murder her own children,' Jill said. 'God, the thought of it sends a cold chill through me, it's just too awful. Of course we do get cases like that occasionally but it's always the men taking revenge on the mother. I've never known it the other way.'

'Yes,' Maggie said. 'I think when Rosie and Jasmine decided to live with their father, that's what pushed her completely over the edge, and she decided to take the ultimate revenge.'

'So what about Justice for Greenway?' Jill asked. 'What was that all about?'

'Aye, well that was her half-arsed attempt to cover her tracks,' Frank said. 'It was Karl Tompkins who was responsible for the first couple of incidents, we're pretty sure of that. His was just the early low-level stuff, you know, the graffiti and the threatening letters. But when Felicity got to know about it, she saw the opportunity. So she stepped in, took over their identity and upped the ante. Or at least Vinny and Griselda did on her behalf. What they did to his Bentley, that really caused him some pain. Forty grand's worth of damage and Morgan got to see it all on video. And that's when we first saw the threats against the Morgan children.'

'So how did she get Vinny Hadley to switch sides and work for her?' Asvina said.

'That wasn't difficult,' Frank said. 'Hadley is a cold bastard, a professional hood who's happy to work for anyone who can afford him. He'd worked for her husband for years so she knew exactly what he was like. It was just a matter of agreeing a price, and when you have thirty million quid in the bank that wasn't going to be an obstacle.'

'And Griselda?' Asvina asked. 'Was she involved in that too?'

'Yes, she was,' Maggie said. 'She helped him with the harassment campaign, and worse than that. You see, she was there, on the platform. When Rosie was killed. I saw her. I didn't realise at the time who it was, but it came to me in the end.'

'There's no evidence at the moment to charge her other than Maggie's testimony,' Frank said. 'But we're hoping that we may be able to get a statement from wee Jasmine when she's feeling better. Because Griselda was involved in all of it, you can count on that.'

'And Robert Trelawney?' Jill said. 'What about him?'

'He didn't know Felicity's real plans, we're pretty sure of that,' Frank said, shooting Maggie a sympathetic smile. 'As we said, he was in on the Lotti cover-up, but in some ways he was as much a victim as a perpetrator.'

'And he paid a terrible price,' Jimmy said. 'I'm really sorry Maggie.'

She shrugged. 'It's Magdalene Slattery who's hurting, not me.'

Of course, it wasn't true. But as she scanned the table, she felt herself bathed in a fuzzy warmth that she knew she could never put into words. *An amazing night with amazing friends.* And a million miles from where she had been just two years earlier, despite still having no amazing man to share her life with. She looked at Elsa, bursting with life and quite certain she had already found her amazing man, although Maggie knew that she was to be disappointed, for Jimmy she had long known to be irreconcilably in love with his estranged wife. And then there was Jill Smart. An enigma. Improbably slim and elegant, attracting admiring and lustful looks wherever she went, but cool and inscrutable, revealing nothing of her true feelings to the world. And finally her dearest and truest friend, the friend who had rescued her from despair when her life had reached rock bottom. Asvina Rani, the super model beauty with the perfect life. The stellar career, her two boys, the adored husband, and so lovely in spirit that Maggie didn't bear an ounce of jealousy towards her.

And there was Jimmy. *Dear Jimmy.* Several pints into the evening, he was in sparkling form and presently speaking.

'Frank my boy,' he said, with the faintest of slurs and a wicked smile on his face. 'Frank my dear brother, there's just one think that I'm still puzzled about. Really puzzled. So tell us, how it was you just happened to be outside Maggie's house when Mr Vincent Hadley tried to kill us all?'

The table fell quite silent and five pairs of eyes stared at him.

Expectantly.

Printed in Great Britain
by Amazon

35821200R00116